BLOOD, FLESH, AND TEARS

ROBERT WEBER

Published by Crimson Web
Omaha, NE

www.crimsonweb.co

Edited by Tim Marquitz.
Cover design by MoorBooks Design.
Mask design by Scott Smith
Photography by Andrew Torkelson
Creative Direction by Robert Weber
Formatting by Polgarus Studio

Print ISBN 978-1-7354166-1-8
Ebook ISBN 978-1-7354166-0-1
Hardcover ISBN 978-1-7354166-2-5

First Edition October 2020

www.robertweber.me

For Penny, David, Whitney, Laura
&
Feyd

Chapter 1

Daemos throws open the flesh curtain entrance to the weapon shop and collapses onto the counter, dripping blood. "The Black Fangs!" he demands, gasping for air. He slams a bloody eyeball and ear on the payment scale. The few fingernails he has left are chiseled into talons. "Now!"

"That's not enough," the large flesh peddler says. Holding a bloody scythe, he crosses his burly arms. Daemos knows the posture and stance the peddler is taking. Feeble attempts at bartering are pointless. The peddler's ready to cleave him in two without a second's hesitation.

"I'm no tourist."

"Then you wouldn't be buying a weapon. Viscrucians *acquire* their own."

Daemos eyes the Black Fangs across the wooden counter. The dual-bladed weapon is forged of black iron. Its two black hooks resembling fangs precede two spoons, guaranteed to scoop out whatever the teeth rip through.

"Death is knocking," the peddler adds.

Coughing blood, Daemos grabs the Fangs. The

peddler tightens his grip on the scythe.

Daemos slices off his two end fingers with one of the teeth. Grimacing in pain, he pushes them over to the peddler. "Consider it a down payment. More's coming, I promise."

Esim, an immense man, throws open the flesh curtain to the shop. Blood runs down the side of his face from his missing eye and ear. The brute is riddled with scars. A stump lies where his right hand once did. His left raises a stubby ax, eagerly awaiting Daemos's flesh. "I'll feast like a king selling your flesh, ghoul!"

The ax races toward its victim. Daemos spins away and puts his new weapon to work. The Black Fangs tear through Esim's testicles, scooping them out along the way. The brute's breath escapes him as he plummets to the ground. Daemos steps over him. He rams his razor-like fingernails underneath the base of Esim's skull in the back of his neck.

Daemos pulls his head back toward him and slams the Black Fangs into his eyes. Esim wails. Using the top of his skull as leverage, Daemos snaps the Fangs back, cracking open the top of Esim's head.

Daemos breathes deeply. He steps back to the counter and presents the additional payment. "Here, one brain, and a set of nuts." Both squish as he places the matter on the scale.

The flesh peddler stands there unimpressed. "That's more than enough."

"Good, because I want my fingers back."

The peddler chuckles. "What for?"

Blood and sweat run down Daemos's face. He stares into the peddler's eyes. "What'd you say to me?"

The peddler leans in, staring right back. "What do you want them for, bleeder? You're gonna drop dead any moment, and soon I'll be selling you for parts."

Daemos stands up straight.

The weapons dealer tilts his head black and looks up at Daemos. He is a gargantuan brute with a shaved head. Blood pulses out from his mutilated body. Flies buzz, following the trail of death.

Daemos slides his hand to his severed fingers. Blood spurts onto them, and the tissue slowly reconnects. The peddler's eyes widen with disbelief. The blood seeps back into his fingers as if rewound in time. Not even a scar remains. Perfect.

"That's impossible. How did you do that? I've never seen anything like it," the peddler musters.

Daemos raises his hand and wiggles all his fingers. Before the peddler can say another word, Daemos rips the peddler's throat out with the Black Fangs. "Don't ever question me."

Daemos grabs a jar from the counter and sets it in front of him. The man collapses. His gaping neck lands on the jar and fills it with crimson.

Daemos walks outside. He scrawls the word "Closed" with his bloody hand across the curtain entrance. Limping back in, he slams the wooden door shut behind it.

Chapter 2

Back to the past.

A sword sharpens against a whetstone. Vultures caw flying above while another picks at a carcass in a sandy corner of the street. A few citizens banter amongst themselves. These familiar sounds signify a typical morning in Viscrucia. The usual violence is still to come.

Daemos prowls the streets paved from skull and bone. He hunches down in his blood-stained flesh cloak to conceal his actual size and identity. A scarred local walking in his path recognizes Daemos's lean and moves aside. The man smiles and nods, appreciating the hunt. The façade tempts the inexperienced, not his Viscrucian peers.

Even stooping over, Daemos sticks out among the masses. He stands well over two meters high and weighs more than one-hundred-fifty kilograms of scarred muscle, bulging beneath his tunic. However, size matters little here. Experience, and more often than naught, creativity, are the keys. Daemos knows this better than most.

He scratches the two-day-old stubble along his prominent jawline. The cloak's hood blocks the warm sun from his brown hair he shaved weeks ago. Scanning around, many Viscrucian men don a similar look. Short hair prevents their enemies from grabbing it and slitting their throats. A few scars mark his face, but his brown eyes remain unscathed.

A bone flute whistles through the streets. The Carving Ground is close by. It has been a while since he gazed upon the city's cultured side. Its unique sights always intrigue him. Sand crunches between his boots and the bone streets as he nears the Carving Ground. Daemos enjoys the music more than others.

"Quit playing that flute!" a disheveled man orders, emerging from the alley. He pulls out a club and raises his arm to block the sun from his eyes. Undaunted, the musician continues playing. Spewing profanities, the man stumbles with each encroaching step. He coughs and hacks up phlegm. From his disheveled look, it was a rough night. "Now, you're going to die, flute boy!"

Finding the right note, he turns toward the haggard man and blows. A dart fires and strikes the man in the chest. He stops, looks down and pulls out the dart. The musician keeps playing. The man sways to the music and drops to the ground.

Daemos smiles. He walks by the flutist and flips him a blood vial. "Good playing. I like that note," Daemos remarks.

"Gratitude, patron. I will use this blood to paint my instrument," the musician responds. The day's killing has begun.

Down the road, a fool falls for Daemos's ploy. Ever-vigilant, Daemos pushes a blade down on the back of his arm three inches past his elbow. The ignorant thug slides a rusty dagger between Daemos' legs and sweeps him into the nearest alley. The Viscrucian alleys are created for just this purpose. Witnesses of the attack continue with their day. Any sign of empathy reveals tourist status, followed by a swift reprieve.

"Get your fuckin' hands in the air!" the thug barks. "What type of money do you have on you?"

Pathetic, Daemos thinks, another tourist. Cut first and never bother with questions is his motto. Real killers make new currency, hacking it off his prey. If one steals, it certainly isn't for money. The amateur opens Daemos's coat.

"Kes!"

Daemos has plenty of money: vials of blood, tongues, and ears strung together, and a small pouch filled with fingers. But the thug doesn't notice. The vast array of fine weapons congesting Daemos's coat steals his attention: garret wire, chord, and enough blades to make any butcher salivate.

The distraction is all Daemos needs. He swings down hard with his elbow. The concealed blade cuts through his coat and into his attacker's left eye, causing him to drop his dagger. Daemos grabs the man's arm with one hand and a meat cleaver from his coat with the other. He lops off the thug's arm in one stroke. The fool's screams pierce the city streets while its passing citizens smile at the fresh catch of the day. Others' lips moisten from the thought. It is breakfast time, after all.

Daemos pushes his attacker back into the street. The mob doesn't fail. They pounce, ripping and hacking the cash-cow limb from limb. Swift and ever-efficient; the crowd parts in less than ten seconds. Each carries a souvenir and an early day's bounty.

A teenage boy speeds off joyously with the man's head, a profitable catch. A gaunt man gets his morning meal. With his only hand, his three remaining fingers feverishly rip the sandal from the foot of the leg he severed. He wastes no time and dives into the ripe flesh, devouring it as fast as he can. He looks up and nods to Daemos before fleeing. It must have been days since he last ate. He is too weak to travel through the surrounding desert.

All that remains is a bloody stain on the sandy streets where the melee occurred. Many killings like this bruise the roads. The next rain will wash it clean.

Daemos enters the Carving Ground, the arts district of Viscrucia. Walking between the storefronts, marred artisans peddle their crafts. One man boasts about his fine blood paintings set against skin canvases. Another carver taps a blade against his bone works, which shine with an elegant polish, hoping they'll resonate with the wandering customer.

"Want to impress? You won't find sculptures like this anywhere else!" a burly proprietor shouts as sweat drips from his brow. "The body parts are drained, dried, and oiled past death! No withering, no smell! Guaranteed to last longer than anyone walking these streets today!"

Daemos wants to laugh, yet he conceals his emotion

and remains on guard. Patrons from lands beyond inquire about the diverse carvings. The savages relish the grisly art. Servants and soldiers discuss their kings' and barons' wishes with the carvers. A carver spits in a servant's face and pulls out a bone shank. The soldiers pull their man away before he gets stabbed.

"Go back to your kingdom!" the carver shouts. "Before I chop you up for my next carving! Fucking tourists!" He pulls out another knife and spins it in his hand.

Passing more shops, Daemos finds the talent he seeks. He moves silently behind him. "What's for sale, Petrid?"

"There's always something new at my shop, Daemos," Petrid says, not bothering to turn. "You know that. Just like I knew it was you creeping behind me."

"That's why I asked."

Petrid turns around and smiles down at his customer. Petrid is the only one tall enough to do so. He is smart and dangerous; both know this. His dark skin contrasts with Daemos's. Tall, muscular, and lean, he's like a black widow in human form. His hair stands four centimeters above a groomed beard. A long, deep scar runs up at the left corner of his mouth through his eye ending just over his brow. The wound left his eye clear, and his mouth with a devious curl to it. This works to his advantage most times, either disguising his true intentions or by people second-guessing themselves. Daemos admires this painful attribute.

Daemos and Petrid each move a hand to a concealed weapon. They nod, following the Viscrucian greeting.

"How are the carvings?" Daemos asks.

"Bloody as usual. Has anything caught your eye today?"

"I always like what I see but, so far, nothing special," he says with a shrug.

Petrid's eyebrow raises above his dead eye. Saliva accumulates at the corner of his scarred mouth. "Nothing special, you say. Have our streets of blood and bone hardened you to appetite alone? Has the wandering meat of our city spoiled the kill?"

Daemos takes a finger from one of his money bags beneath his coat and flips it to Petrid. "As long as blood runs in and from my flesh, theirs will never spoil," he says, avoiding Petrid's gaze.

"I hope so. It'd be a shame to kill you now. My carvings are worth a four seasons' journey just to see! This was commissioned at a price you wouldn't believe," he says, drawing Daemos's attention to the art. Bones of ten hands and forearms form a vertical circle. The hands open at its center. "I'm guessing the lord wants to place his enemy's head in the center of it. Maybe his queen's. Who cares?"

"How did you come by the materials?"

"That's the blood of the kill! A captain of ten soldiers came to me with the deal. Five in front, five in back. I told him the cost of such a piece. He nods to me and snaps his fingers. The soldiers behind put swords to the other's throats. The captain orders the five to raise their arms. The screams follow…and so do my materials. I doubt those poor bastards made it out of the city alive that day. Some kings are just cruel."

"Most kings are cruel," Daemos interjects. "Many

have no idea what it means to live and die by the blade. They know words and make demands. Pathetic rule. They couldn't survive without others doing their bidding."

"The outside lands and lords are what they are. They have their way," Petrid says and pulls out a large knife. "We have ours. Everywhere is different. Light and dark. We all have our escapes."

"What was your carving price?"

"My price is whatever I want. Meat, blood, or bone. Jewels or slaves. Depends on what I require. *I* set my price. You know that. My payment scale weighs heavy."

Daemos looks over to his scale, resting on a wooden table caked in blood. "That it does."

"Enough talk of payment and pathetic lords. I have something only a true Viscrucian like you can appreciate." Petrid raises his token of payment to his mouth and holds it with his teeth. He reaches into his shirt and pulls out part of a human jaw adorned to the beaded necklace he wears. "Follow me."

Petrid leads Daemos to the back of his shop. Petrid slides the jawbone into a wooden door's keyhole and turns it. A weakened wail follows the unlocking of the door. Petrid's dead eye beams back at Daemos as he pushes the door open. "Enjoy."

The men enter Petrid's abattoir. The wailing continues. "This is my latest masterpiece."

"Kill me...I beg you..." says the art. A masterpiece indeed, Daemos has never been privy to such a diabolical working of human meat. A balding fat man stretches across a large circular frame of bone. Skin and sinew are spread and tied around the frame. Each appendage and section of fat varies in its aesthetic construction. Even the skin from his ears is peeled and pulled back. The living art stands above a trough to collect sweat, blood, feces, and other bodily fluids the carving relinquishes.

"Please…God…" the man pleads, drooling on himself.

Petrid walks behind his masterpiece. The muscle and skin of the obese man are stretched so wide it completely conceals Petrid behind it. The art screams and contorts. Blood permeates multiple places like a fountain.

"What did I tell you about that word here? We citizens of pain have no God, you pathetic tourist! Pain is God here!" Petrid says.

Daemos can only imagine what contraptions and elixirs Petrid's applied to keep his masterpiece alive. "Why does he still have his tongue? Easier to cut it out."

"Easier, yes," Petrid answers, "but I don't think I'm finished with this one yet. I could sell it. His wailings may amuse the owner or entertain a crowd. There's ways to shut him up." Petrid pulls out a well-crafted knife. The man's eyes widened at the sight. "This leaves more room for carving should I choose," Petrid says as his scar curls up with a smile.

The once fat man passes out. The level of sewage rises in the trough. Petrid steps out from behind him. He rips off a piece of meat from his art's love handle, dips it into a saucer filled with a dark liquid called

Dona, and bites into it. He offers Daemos a piece while he chews. The meat has an odd taste to it. Daemos isn't sure what drug Petrid added to his victim.

"Good thing you have the Dona sauce, otherwise it'd taste like kes…but I must say, I haven't seen its equal."

"I know," Petrid says, lifting his chin high.

Daemos smiles as he walks out of the Carving Ground. He finds the stretched fat man to be magnificent. No one has captured life before in the blood arts while it still breathes, and it appears the victim has been in that state for a while.

Petrid had yet another trick up his sleeve for Daemos. The two have known each other for years, which is several lifetimes in Viscrucia. Petrid kept his arrival quiet, a smart move for his size. He would disappear for weeks sometimes to nurse his wounds. Now he has built up his tolerance for the Viscrucian grind.

As much as Daemos likes Petrid, he doesn't trust him. Anyone who could devise such a device that could simultaneously torture and prolong a pathetic soul's misery is not to be trusted. One false move and Daemos could wind up as Petrid's next exhibit.

The passing thought makes Daemos question why he hasn't cut him into currency already or turned the artist into art, like that of his own victims. Not yet, though. Petrid is more interesting alive than dead. His existence keeps Daemos on his eight remaining toes. The challenge and humbleness please him.

Chapter 3

The fleshy appetizer brews a hunger inside Daemos. He doesn't want to hunt in the wild, nor does he want to spend his own money or travel to one of his hideouts for food. No, a quick kill is in order. Daemos feels like doing more than merely defending himself today. His last kill was even charitable. Daemos is hungry. Hungry for a kill, someone worthy.

He walks into the streets, the ultimate preying ground. Victims and killers walk amongst each other. Before Daemos can even distinguish between the flock, a skirmish breaks out. An older scurvy man with a wooden leg slashes a teenager across his chest. The elder foolishly lunges at him and loses his balance.

As the two tumble to the ground, the kid shifts his weight to the top position. He head-butts the old man, shattering his nose, and dousing them both with blood. The youth bites off the thumb of his opponent's hand, which holds the blade. The kid grabs the knife and raises it for the kill as the man screams. But it's too late. The skirmish takes too long. They're pinned against the ground, allowing little movement and minimal peripheral vision.

Oglodor, a hairy beast of a man, stands up from his nearby table, still drooling over his meal. He hunches to two meters tall and weighs one-hundred-thirty-five kilograms. He grabs his heavy ax with his one remaining arm.

Just as the teen raises the elder's blade, Oglodor lops off both of their heads with one swing. But Oglodor knows better. It's not a coincidence he only has one arm and scars covering his obese body. After the dual decapitation, Oglodor instinctively swings his ax behind him. His caution prevails.

The ax hacks deep into a woman's stomach. The blow hunches her over. The spiked stick she held high drops into Oglodor's shoulder. No matter. His wound is insignificant. His victims' are fatal. The kill of his oncoming attacker not only saved him but served notice. The bloodshed subsides for the moment.

Oglodor kicks the two heads down the nearest alley and follows, dragging the three bodies. It's a nice payday considering the few seconds it took and the minimal damage he sustained.

Opportunity and death go hand in hand in Viscrucia. Now, Daemos looks for his. The aroma of sizzling meat from the vendors and the freshly spilled blood perpetuates Daemos's hunger. His eyes scan the crowd. Some hunters stand against the walls while on the prowl.

"Tourists," Daemos grumbles to himself.

Daemos peruses the walking scarred. He observes the cues: limps, weapons, missing appendages, state of health, and the unseen. Small spikes raise the sleeves of a short man walking past. Knife handles protrude from another man's coat at his waist. A woman leans against a grimy wall with sleeves much too wide. Her deliberate, yet awkward pose suggests she's concealing poison.

In time, Daemos finds his mark, a brawny man named Uglicerous. His amethyst necklace shines through the crowd. A femur handled machete adorned with jewels is secured to his leg. No one else challenges such a worthy adversary. Daemos grins at the fight to come, one on one and bloody. Uglicerous veers down an alley. He must sense that he is being followed. He leads him to a location suitable for one-on-one combat. Daemos moves in closer. His muscles tighten with excitement. Uglicerous turns and throws a knife. Daemos dodges to the side as it sails past and plunges into the earthen wall.

"I knew it was you. Finally grow the balls to challenge me?!" The men circle each other. Sweat runs over the scars on Uglicerous' face. "I've thought about this for a long time. Now, I get to send you to the Suffering myself. I'll stake your body in the Heart for all Viscrucia to see. Everyone will know, Uglicerous slayed the mighty Daemos." The men stop. Their eyes are locked. Uglicerous wields his machete. "Time to die, Daemos."

"I've always admired that blade, Uglicerous," Daemos says looking at the machete. "It will serve me well." He pulls out an ax.

Uglicerous roars. He marches forward and swings. Daemos backs up, allowing his opponent to close the distance. Uglicerous feints high, then swings for Daemos' stomach.

Daemos dodges and pounces, plunging a small hook in the side of Uglicerous' neck. Uglicerous counters but misses. He reaches up to check the barb in his throat and immediately jerks his head back, evading the ax swinging at his head. Daemos backs up and yanks his free hand away.

The space glimmers between them as the hook rips across Uglicerous' neck. He gasps for air, stumbling to his knees. Blood spurts across a nearly invisible thread of silk attached to the barb. Daemos opens the rest of the man's throat with his ax.

Uglicerous falls. The alley returns to silence. No one else comes to collect. No scavengers seek to profit. Daemos is glad. This is his kill, and his alone.

Daemos kneels, reaches out, and closes the fallen's eyes. "Season after season, year after year, you killed proudly. Many times, more than most. Entertained the citizens, educated the tourists. You gave us those gifts. I will remember you, Viscrucian." He pulls out a jar and places it under his victim's neck.

Uglicerous' blood dries as war paint on his killer's face. The amethyst necklace hangs from his neck. Uglicerous' jeweled machete hangs from Daemos's waist. Gold daggers glimmer in plain sight. Daemos delivers the body wrapped in a net behind the kitchen.

"Give me a full rack of boar, potatoes, and blood tear wine," he orders from the cook. He pulls out the blood jar and a much smaller jar filled with clear liquid. The cook smiles as he takes the ingredients.

"Do you want any of him?"

"No. I prefer animals."

Sitting at the tables overlooking the Death Pit, Daemos watches the butcher prepare his food and wine. He fills a bucket with wine, then mixes in the supplied liquids. Daemos isn't about to die a quick, whispering death on such a fine day. To die with no one knowing other than some cowardly poisoner would be a disgrace. It would be an insult to his recent prey. Daemos grins and takes a drink to the man who paid for it.

Daemos isn't without entertainment, either. He savors his wine while watching the fights below in the Pit. Like every other city, Viscrucia has its stage for gladiatorial combat. Pounds of bloody flesh slap onto the payment scales as savages wager on the fight. The bookmakers' aprons and gloves run slick with blood. One man has trouble picking up the wet payment. Among the crowd, a drunken brawl breaks out, amusing the spectators.

The Death Pit contestants vary: gladiators by choice, buffoons placing bets on themselves, slaves, captured outsiders, drunks tossed in by the crowd, pathetic tourists, beasts, and more. Each victor keeps the spoils of their felled opponent. The main concerns are if their foe is intact enough to be considered quality currency, and if they themselves are intact enough to walk out of the Pit to spend their winnings.

Daemos bets wisely, and his winnings pile high. Sitting in the corner with his back against the wall, he cheers on the contestants below. The fight is exciting and ends to the roar of the crowd. The champion raises his weapon in victory.

Daemos motions to the bookmaker. "Give him my winnings," he says and points down. Recognizing this, the victor nods and points his weapon.

Later on, a fight disappoints the crowd. Severed feet and other items are hurled at the sluggish combatants in disgust. Throwing money away is always worth it if it kills someone. The wet slap of a tongue splashes against a fighter's skin. Distracted, the fighter checks himself long enough for his opponent to move in and impale him with a spear. The crowd smiles.

Chapter 4

A fellow gambler by the name of Silmeir takes a drink as he scours the bar above the Death Pit. Viscrucians exchange flesh for drink. Silmeir shakes his head as he touches his own bag filled with currency to make sure it's still there. Feeling its contents he spits on the floor. "Savages."

Gazing further, he notices an extremely large man laugh and throw some of his own winnings at the combatants down in the Pit. He hurls even more with drunken amusement. The sight transfixes Silmeir. He peers closer. He sees a long curving scar behind the large man's right ear that trails down to his neck. He quickly pulls out a piece of cloth and unfolds it. He compares the drawing on the cloth to the scar. The similarity is unmistakable.

"At last, I've found him," he whispers. Silmeir bolts to the exit and nearly trips over the light pieces of armor concealed beneath his clothes.

Silmeir's holiday in Viscrucia has come to an end. He slithers out of the city without conflict. He has a knack for it. Testing his fate in Viscrucia doesn't thrill him like the others. He is more than glad his time is up.

He races across the desert to the east of Viscrucia. It's not long before the city's maniacal revelry fades in the distance. The cooling dusk air makes his trek easier. Tranquility. Silence. The world returns to normal outside of the bone streets. Not every city is a living hell. Much of the world is at peace…some of it…at least.

The thought soothes him. Silmeir knows it won't last, though. It's merely the calm before the coming sandstorm. Another brews on the horizon. Silmeir fears their rumored winds greatly. After a few days' ride, he may hear the faint cries from the castle. He welcomes those screams in comparison. Not *every* city.

After his serene journey, a growling storm greets him at the gates of Kilsan. Rain washes down his hooded cloak as he peers at the looming castle. Grime cakes its stone walls. The rain never manages to cleanse the tarnish. Silmeir shakes his head.

"Castle of kes," he grumbles and then spits into the rain. To him, it's a reflection of the castle's soul. He takes a deep breath, greets the two sentries, and enters the black gates.

The castle bailey is expansive and sparse. The villagers have retired for the night. Only the two guards stand duty at the keep. The ground is uneven dirt riddled with weeds. Even the soil is unclean. A few torches shed light through the night, but not nearly enough.

Silmeir walks to the keep. "I have important information for the lord."

The guards nod and go to work. The thick, wooden

doors to the keep are twice the height of a man. They struggle but force them open. The keep interior paints the same gloomy picture as the rest of the castle: dirty stone rooms cloaked in shadows. Silmeir makes his way to the back and ascends a spiral stairwell. Cobwebs and spiders inhabit the walls.

Soon, darkness prevails. Silmeir can't see his next step. He curses the guards. *How hard is it to keep the torches lit?* A scream bursts through the stairwell. Silmeir shudders. He hates thinking about what goes on behind the doors and, sometimes, what's out on display. He walks back down and grabs a torch. Another wail breaches the silence. *Let's get this over with.*

Silmeir reaches his lord's chamber. Two guards fitted with heavy armor seize him immediately.

"Wretched spy!" a guard named Tar spits. "What word do you bring?" Tar's beautiful face and piercing blue eyes mark a sharp contrast to the grim surroundings.

"I come bearing witness to the sign."

"Let him forth," a hoarse voice calls out from behind the chamber door.

The guards open the door and push Silmeir inside. A single torch burns in the center of the room, revealing nothing but leftover scraps of rare cooked food on its table. Silmeir hears the growing rainfall outside a single window. Something slurps behind the darkness, followed by the glint of a golden dagger.

"Thank you, my lord." Silmeir says, lurching forward.

"Your words must be true," the lord's hoarse voice continues. "Otherwise, only slow pleasing death get you." An eloquent man the lord, is not. Foul and disgusting, he lacks wit and manners because his title requires neither.

"It is the truth, Lord Villous. I swear it." Silmeir lifts his depiction of the scar. A guard takes it to the lord.

"So many years, the time be upon us." Lightning strikes outside. The flash reveals the obese lord, gulping down his goblet of wine. He is not whole. "Come forth. Deliver your obedience."

Silmeir drops his head and takes a deep breath. Trudging forward he rolls up his sleeve. Little scars run down his forearm, revealing he's no stranger to the ritual. A bead of sweat runs down his cheek. A sharp sound hits the ground, followed by a dragging footstep as the lord limps forward. The Toll of Obedience emerges from the shadows. Silmeir has no choice.

Tar grabs Silmeir's arm. Unnecessary overkill, Tar shakes with excitement, two of his trademarks. Not needing Tar's unwanted help, Silmeir pushes his hand into the Toll. The thorns of the salvia bush lining the inside bite into him like teeth. Silmeir grimaces more from what is to come than the pain. His polluted blood funnels down the plant leaf into the lord's awaiting wine goblet.

"Good. Your due paid."

Silmeir removes his bleeding arm from the Toll. He staggers back to a wall and collapses. The guards laugh. Tar rubs his hands with excitement. The reaction always amuses him.

Silmeir's eyes roll back in his head, and his body convulses. He tries to raise his arms, but his limbs sink like lead. The drug created by the salvia plant is much more potent when directly introduced into the bloodstream. Silmeir can't even wipe away the drool accumulating at the corner of his mouth.

The lord's eyes widen as he gawks at Silmeir. He takes a hefty swig from his goblet and walks back into the darkness. The lord smiles as his body trembles.

"Yes," the lord's mangled voice slurs. "Is time. Hear me, guards? What we've waited for!" The lord guzzles the remains of Silmeir's drug-laced blood, spilling without care. "Alert my captain of arms!"

The lord sways slightly. He looks down at his cup and grins at the sight of Silmeir's blood.

"Blood," the lord sputters. "Yes, more blood. Crave more! But soon, will be Daemos's blood that I drink!" The lord limps his mutilated body toward Silmeir. Metal strikes the ground, followed by a dragging footstep

Silmeir quivers against the wall. He rolls his heavy eyes to his tormentor. It matters little, however. Silmeir is on a different plane. His body feels as if it's sinking deeper than the pits of the Suffering itself. His filleting death could reach legendary agony, or simply numb away in his paralysis. Hopefully, the latter. Either way, fuck it. His life in this cursed place is kes. He knows it. Why not go out in a river of blood?

Chapter 5

The sun passes away. The fire in the cave keeps Daemos warm, but it's the fires in Viscrucia that entertain him. Some of the fires provide light, the others continue the spectacle. Their screams sing through the night sky.

Daemos admires it from the hills in the distance. Sleeping this far away from the city allows him better chances of a peaceful night. The screams soothe Daemos to sleep like a childhood lullaby. He has hideouts and places he sleeps in the city, but he usually doesn't utilize them. You never know when some drunk or drugged out thug might stumble upon your whereabouts and kill you, or the desperate, dying citizen who will kill you at your most vulnerable time to delay their own death.

The rising sun wakes Daemos. After the initial discomfort, he enjoys the morning grogginess. It reminds him that he's survived another night. He loosens the grip on his nighttime companion and cradles it back in its sheath. His fire has extinguished like those of Viscrucia.

Daemos takes a drink from his jug of water on the table. The narrow river Aquen runs just north of Viscrucia, on its outskirts. It's this river that supplies the city. The city used to run right along Aquen's edge, but the citizens destroyed the bordering buildings and commerce. The perpetual spilling of blood sullied their life source. To protect their water supply, the killing had to be moved. After his drink, Daemos is hungry. It's time to find some food.

It's a quiet day. Fewer citizens than usual roam the streets. The daily grind must have been a little harsher over the last few days than the others. This happens regularly. Every couple of weeks or months, the numbers of Viscrucia dwindle from all the killings. The injured retreat to safety where they can nurse their wounds. They usually come back, however. Like a drug, the city hooks them.

Daemos walks the skeletal streets of Viscrucia. The air is putrid. Daemos glances at the butchers; hacking and preparing their bloody cuisine. Seeing the cleaver fly through the air reminds him of…Mom.

Not too far off, a man screams. The sound is beautiful, pure, agonizing pain. Daemos marches forward. A tourist stands in his way, frozen from the immense sight approaching him. Daemos wastes no time. He raises his fist high in the air. The tourist reacts stupidly and looks at the feint. Then Daemos buries a bone pick in his temple with his other hand. Blood spurts out of the tourist's mouth as he bounces off Daemos' chest. Daemos grabs another weapon. The few citizens remaining in his way heed the warning and move.

Daemos turns the corner and walks into the alley. He's impressed. A man quivers on the ground. His body is cut in half. A whip coils between the gore. The weapon is composed of barbs and poison thorns amongst other sinewy materials. A gloved hand with long black nails retracts it.

She is a short, sultry minx of a killer. Her body is svelte but muscular. Her skin is a bronzed, olive tone. Jet-black hair stops at her chin. Daemos finds this very intriguing. Even in Viscrucia, most women keep their hair very short. She is an adversary not to be taken lightly. Daemos's mouth waters at the thought.

Her lavender eyes catch sight of Daemos. A smile emerges on her placid face as she slaps a hook into the torso of her victim.

"Daemos, I believe," states a voice behind him.

Daemos realizes the origin of the minx's smile. He spins and cleaves down with his weapon. A gaping crevice pours blood from where a guard's face used to be. He falls to the ground. The idiot doesn't even have a weapon in his hand. Tourist. Five of the six remaining guards ready themselves.

Before Daemos slashes his way through the rest of them, the center guard, Huemic, quickly speaks up. "I'm glad I didn't stand in front. We're not here to fight. We need a man with such," the guard looks at his fallen soldier, "talents. We have a job for you."

Daemos looks back. The girl is gone. Only a trail of blood remains in the sand. Daemos turns back to the guard and tightens his grip on his weapon. "Fine, let's talk. You're buying."

Daemos sits down to eat with the guards. He dives into his rare breakfast. One of the guards is hesitant about eating, to say the least. He's not sure what the meat is: animal or human. He might be paranoid, but it doesn't smell right to him. The Viscrucian air isn't appreciated by all.

"I'd eat up if I were you. You might make me nervous," Daemos says.

The guard looks at Daemos and gulps. Sweat drips from his helmet. He leans in closer to his food. It's not going anywhere. He shoots a glance at Huemic, his captain, but he offers no assurance. The guard picks up his knife and fork. He cuts a piece of his meat, but quickly covers his mouth with one hand as his cheeks puff out.

Daemos chops off the guard's pinky with his breakfast knife in disgust.

The guard bawls and proceeds to vomit.

A woman in the street laughs. She plucks the edge of her mace with her finger.

The guard quickly wraps his hand with his napkin. He pulls it tight with his teeth. Some of his blood trickles into his mouth. He coughs and tries to spit it out.

Aemeggur, the butcher walks from his shop. He dries his hands with a bloody rag. It's unclear what color his apron used to be. The flies sure don't mind. "There something wrong with your food, minion?" barks Aemeggur.

"I…" the guard says.

Minion, Daemos thinks. What a perfect insult.

Aemeggur's remaining eye peers intently. Dark scars cover his missing eye.

"Not at all, Aemeggur," Daemos says, smiling. "Bloody good!" Daemos bites off a hefty piece of meat. "Servant man here just found his appetite."

The guard chokes down a morsel of food.

Aemeggur takes the meat cleaver from his belt and spins it in his stubby hand. The guard abides, not wanting to lose anything else. While fighting the pain, a tear runs, down his cheek.

Daemos sees this and quickly raises his knife to the man's throat. "Don't move," Daemos commands. He pulls out a small vial with his other hand, pops the top off, and collects the guard's liquid suffering. "Good boy."

Aemeggur smiles. "That will make a good wine," he says

"Yes. Nothing tastes better."

A scream pierces the air. Daemos and Aemeggur look to an old stone tower standing above the rest of the stores, only a few streets down. Begging precedes another scream. A few towers and other taller buildings remain throughout Viscrucia. Rubble and sand stand where many have burned down.

"I won't be the only one enjoying Viscrucian wine. Make them weep." Daemos raises his glass.

Aemeggur walks back to his kitchen.

"Spit it out. What the fuck do you want?"

"My name is Huemic. I'm the captain of the guards

to Lord Villous of Kilsan. I'm sure you've heard of him."

Daemos shrugs and continues eating.

"He's a very powerful and wealthy lord."

"Not here. He wouldn't last a day."

Huemic clears his throat. "He can offer you anything you desire. Every Viscrucian wanders from the city now and then. Lord Villous can give those things to you. Wealth, women, a home, and even a title! How many Viscrucians have that?"

"Weapons and body parts are a Viscrucian's wealth, tourist! Carved from the kill. Taken from severed hand. Armor from the dead. Clear as an open vein if you open your eyes. Stories told. Songs sung. Honor. Death. Maybe I remove your eyelids so you see how I see."

Huemic looks around. Viscrucians nod, holding their weapons in plain sight. Many of them are handcrafted from bone. The weaponry is unlike anywhere else in the world.

He smiles. "It pleases me to see you react this way, Daemos. I told him you would. Why would a Viscrucian seek—"

"So why are you here? And make it quick before I lose my patience and make you my dessert."

"Because of the challenge that accompanies the task. No one has been up to it yet. I wonder if you are."

"Ha. And what challenge would that be, Huemic?"

"The Abyss."

Daemos grabs the table and flips it onto the soldiers in front of him. He seizes the bleeder next to him, reaches into his mouth, and rips off his jaw. He throws the dying man at Huemic. Daemos spins and blocks the weapon of an oncoming Viscrucian attacker looking to take advantage of the situation. He slams the soldier's jawbone into the side of the Viscrucian's head. Daemos turns back around ready for any other attackers. No one pushes forward.

"Pathetic attempt, Captain! I'm tired of your boring proposals. The Abyss doesn't scare me! What else do you have to offer? Perhaps the bounty of your lord's wench mother? At least that would make me laugh!"

Huemic breathes heavy. "The wraith! My lord wants its spine."

"If it's really a wraith, it doesn't have a spine, maggot!"

"There's only one way to find out, and you're the only one for the job. No one else we've sent has survived." Huemic tries to catch his breath.

"How many?"

"At least twenty. Soldiers. Mercenaries. We tried to contact you before, but it appears they died before they could deliver the message or make it back."

Whispers of the wraith and Daemos break through the crowd. Most understand the significance. A fair portion of the people have no clue what they're talking about because they're fucking tourists. Some look on simply because it's another fight.

"Think about it, Daemos. You kill the unkillable, the legendary wraith itself, and your legend will surpass it, even in Viscrucia. There's your unattainable prize. *You* can become a Viscrucian nightmare."

"If I do this, there might be something I want from your lord. Perhaps something fleshy."

"Easy, Daemos. My lord offers everything and more, I promise. Just bring your kill to our castle. Your name etched in Viscrucian sand for an eternity. Riches outside and beyond. My lord will make you a god."

Daemos spits to the sand beneath Huemic's feet. "There is no god here."

"Think it over. Legend awaits. Men! Let us take our leave. We've experienced enough Viscrucian hospitality."

Swords shake in the soldiers' hands. They circle around one another and back away. Onlookers close in on them, weapons ready.

"Huemic! If you betray me, I will drown you and your owner in blood. Get the fuck out of here before we Viscrucians tear you servants apart."

Chapter 6

It had been a rough day for the captain of the guards. By the time Huemic got to the edge of the city, he was another two guards short. The city burned through his patience like wildfire. He now understood his lord's hatred for this cursed place. It was something else.

"Captain!" one of his guards calls out. He points to the distance.

"Figures," Huemic says.

Upon arrival, Huemic paid a supposedly reputable shopkeeper to watch their horses. Thirty meters away, they see three scarred men feasting on one of their horses like lions in the plain. The others are nowhere in sight.

"You can't trust anybody in this fucking kes pool."

Wooden doors seal the shop closed.

"What should we do?" asks one of the guards.

"Are you joking?" Huemic then yells out to the scavengers gorging on the horse. Heads pop up from the heart, blood dripping from their mouths. "Still hungry, you ugly fucks?"

The horse eaters grab their weapons and charge. Huemic draws two elegant swords as his men nervously ready their bows. Huemic slices through the scavengers with ease. His men are awestruck, having never witnessed his adept swordsmanship firsthand.

"That's what we do!" Another horse eater makes a run for it. Huemic throws a sword through the man's back. "Burn it down!"

Huemic's soldiers obey. They ignite their arrows and fire them into the shop until the entire structure is in flames. The shop owner limps out on his only leg as fire consumes his clothes. A soldier readies another arrow.

"Leave it. He deserves to burn."

Daemos stomps along the bone streets. Holds a skinning knife in one hand and spins a dagger in the other, he hits the blades against each other. He makes it clear for people to stay the fuck out of his way. How dare some tourists come into his town and challenge Daemos. Now word may be spreading. Had he thought about facing the wraith before? Sure, but the risk wasn't worth the reward. If he dies, no one would know. He'd simply disappear.

"Daemos."

He stops and turns. Petrid stands in the shadows of an alley.

"What?"

"Follow me." Petrid creeps back into the alley.

Daemos checks his surroundings. He tightens his grip on the blades and proceeds with caution. Perhaps this is it. Maybe this is his final battle, and he'll never face the wraith. After a few steps in he stops.

"Got something to say, Petrid? It's been an interesting day, but I didn't expect you'd call me out, as well. If you want to die today, so be it."

Petrid moves a hand to an unseen weapon, giving Daemos the Viscrucian greeting. Daemos sees it but still doesn't trust it. Why did Petrid bring him to this alley? He remains ready.

"Don't trust me, Daemos?"

"Never have."

"Good. You haven't lost your edge then."

"What the fuck do you want, Petrid?"

"Easy, Daemos. I heard about your offer."

"And?"

"Are you thinking of challenging the wraith?"

"What's it to you, carver?"

"If you go and return with the wraith, I shall very much like to see it."

"I bet you would…if I live."

"As a token, I will mark your place here. I will create a mural or a sculpture in the Heart of Viscrucia. Everyone shall see. Citizen and tourist alike will know."

Daemos ponders this for a moment. "My mural…in my home," Daemos mutters.

"Yes, the place you call home."

"Watch your tongue, Petrid! I was *born* here. This *is* my home!"

"Kes. No one is born here, Daemos. Most people last days, sometimes less—" Before he can finish, Daemos swings for his throat.

Petrid pulls out his knife and blocks the attack just in time. Daemos's eyes burn as Petrid holds him back. "*I* was born here! My parents raised me here. They died here. I've killed here for years before you dared step foot on the bone streets!" Daemos pushes Petrid back.

Petrid's expression changes. "Is that true? It must be. I've never seen you...angry before."

"Lying is a waste of my breath." Daemos checks behind him. "Did Huemic put you up to this! Is this another set up?"

"I should cut your tongue out for such an offense! No outsider has influence over me."

"Why then? Why this offer?"

"I told you, I want to see it! No one has truly seen the wraith and lived to tell about it. There are only myths and legends. Dark shadows flying through the night sky. If you do, then you'll be worthy of my carving, worthy of your own legend. Then my work in the Heart of the City will become legend, too. We'll both reap the rewards."

Daemos smirks. He now understands Petrid's angle. It's an easy way for him to make his own mark while risking nothing. Bastard. Daemos backs up to exit the alley.

"Good luck, Daemos, son of Viscrucia. That makes you the only one then. *Only you* would have a chance to kill it."

"If I do it, you may not want me to make it back." He leaves.

Daemos makes his way out of Viscrucia as prying

eyes follow. He needs space. He needs time to think. Meddlesome people can bring out the worst in Daemos.

The offer is tempting, but extremely dangerous. Petrid and that piece of kes, Huemic, do have a point, however. People die in Viscrucia every day. It's only a matter of time before Daemos dies, too. Far off lands and other cities have legends, songs, and tales. Viscrucia does, sure, but not about individuals, not of the warriors who make this city great.

If he survives, perhaps this will be a way for him to live beyond. *This* could be his legacy. Anyone can kill a man. He could be the one to slay the monster even Viscrucians fear, the terror of the night.

After a couple days outside of the city, his head clears. Daemos walks to a cliff that overlooks the Abyss. Drizzling rain wets his face. Below the ledge lies the canopy, a faint haze separating it from the land above. It serves as a warning, although the Abyss is still far away. It lies deep down in the valley below. Most people who have even made it this far have never considered venturing further. The ones crazy enough are gone.

Daemos hears something behind him and spins around.

"Boils" Bogilocus greets the pondering Viscrucian with his hand over his weapon. "I see you're considering the offer," he says with a wheezing voice.

Daemos returns the gesture, not fearing any deceit from Boils. Perhaps the company wouldn't be so bad, at a distance.

"Any new scars since last time?" Daemos asks.

"None worth mentioning." His boil-covered skin looks like vomit. Its smell churns rancid meat. A snot-like leakage is common. He has lived ages compared to most stalking the streets. His hide would supply no reward, only insult from the stench. And yet as foul as can be, the fat man is somehow charming. "I heard you killed Uglicerous."

"Yes."

"Why is that? Did he challenge you? Wrong you?"

"No."

"Always the talker, Daemos. We joke that your tongue was cut out and you replaced it with a blade."

"Doesn't sound so bad." The men laugh. "I needed it. I tire of tourists playing. Uglicerous was a strong Viscrucian."

"Seems the flesh parts for the blade." Daemos studies Boils. "You seek new death. New death is death itself. The wraith."

Daemos looks away, contemplating.

"You have a plan, I'm guessing. It'd be a shame for you to die from a simple proposition."

"I didn't know you cared." Daemos kicks the foliage in front of him. "I'm working on it, whether or not to go through with it or simply kill them all."

"I know a few secrets to this place."

"So do I."

"Be smart, Daemos. Considering the challenge you're up against, it's not the time for a killing contest."

"I know. So, tell me, what do you know that I don't?"

"Look around. What do you notice about this place?"

Daemos looks to the black sky. Ominous clouds cover every inch. "It's black, like death. It's a land of shadow. Always this dark. Maybe that's why the plants are poisonous."

"Exactly. There's no light here, only death and darkness. It feeds this land. But if that were changed…"

"Yeah." He wasn't sure Boils knew of the plants' fatal effects. He may have some useful information after all.

The demon only snatches victims at night in the outskirts of the land away from its shadowed domain. It's never been seen during the day. Daemos might be able to use this.

Chapter 7

Silmeir opens his eyes. The blood brought to light from the Toll of Obedience has dried on his arm. Its teeth marks have bruised. Arms still heavy, he manages to wipe the drool from his chin and sit up. Feeling somewhat numb still, he looks over himself for any permanent damage. Luckily, only a few stitches will suffice. Silmeir is an expert at this point.

The guards threw him down into the dungeons in an open cell. The acrid smell reveals his location without looking. The prisoners laugh in their cells behind Silmeir. He lays a few feet away, but close enough for the deviants to piss on him.

Silmeir reaches into his pocket but stumbles down in front of the cell cage.

"Little guard boy can't even stand!" says one of the captives as he walks over. He leans his hands on the cage opening to rest his weight.

Silmeir grabs dirt from the floor and heaves it into the man's eyes. He seizes the man's hands and scratches them with the shell from his pocket. The man recoils. "I'll tear your..." He wipes his eyes and yells. "What have you done to me?"

"Enjoy," Silmeir says and walks away. The cragguss shell he scratched him with doesn't kill. It inflames the area, leaving a contagious rash. Often, the most diabolical trait is when the infected touches his genitals to relieve himself. Depending on his prisoner brethren, however, he might not make it that long. Silmeir doesn't care. He exacted his justice.

Silmeir looks at both exits. One leads to the castle above, while the other leads to the caves below, where the *creatures* dwell. Their faint movement cannot be heard from the levels above, nor can any screams. Their victims slowly turn and *become*.

Silmeir shudders at the thought. No use thinking about that horrid fairy tale. He doesn't want to think about much of his recent life. Time to get paid and wash off the filth.

Silmeir makes his way out of the bowels of the castle. Every floor he ascends is increasingly better, though still very hostile. The air is not as pungent. The screams dwindle. The walls are cleaner, and there are more servants near the surface. From there, the farther someone ascends the towers of the castle is the same as if going below. All female servants work as close to the main floor and exits as possible, if they have a choice.

Two floors below the fresh air, Silmeir finds Noilurtiss at the only treasury known to all the lord's workers. Noilurtiss is the most jovial of anyone in the castle, besides the sadists. Everyone who comes to see him is happy. If they aren't, it's not his fault, and he has ways around it. He knows everybody and their vices.

He is short, quick-witted, and handsome. His skin is smooth. His dark, short hair is always coiffed to perfection.

"Silmeir, the survivor! Back from the Suffering, I see."

"Noils," Silmeir says with a raspy voice. The two men touch the outside of their forearms together, forming an X, the customary greeting of Kilsan, Lord Villous's domain.

"From the smell of it, not too soon, either."

"Walk with the dead, you cock. How's the safe life?"

"Happy and healthy. Wemms has a new flower that could help with the smell. She also has other benefits."

"Thanks. Seeing how this last trip went, I might have to take her up on that. So, let's have it. My payment for my trip to that kes hole."

Noilurtiss grabs coins and gems and slides them to Silmeir.

"Noils, don't do this, pay hound. This is short."

"Apologies, Sils. The lord told me himself."

Silmeir hangs his head and grits his teeth. He wants to curse the lord's name so loud it bellows through the castle and down the village roads. Having survived this long, he knows better. He grabs his insulting payment and thrusts it into his pocket.

"Sils, see Wemms. Trust me. I'll talk to her."

Silmeir flips him a coin from his pocket and leaves.

Although his pride has been drugged, bled, and pissed on, he still can't bring himself to be seen like this by the masses. He escaped this world's living hell, best to feel good about life and make it worth living. Silmeir knows how to survive, and optimism always helps.

Silmeir makes it back to his hovel cloaked as best he can. He stashes his payment, grabs fresh clothes and makes his way to Wemms'. He keeps his visit as brief as possible, hating his current state. He purchases the flowers, and Wemms promises lustful endeavors to follow upon return. He blows her a kiss and bows.

Silmeir reaches the stream near the edge of the woods. He immediately rips his sullied rags off and walks in. He's needed this for days. His wounds, infections, the urine, and filth that has soaked his pores and his mind need to be cleansed. He soaks and scrubs for nearly an hour. Once dressed, Silmeir burns his old clothes and walks away, his homecoming ritual.

Chapter 8

Over the next several days between kills, Daemos walks the fringe of the deadly Abyss. He studies and prepares, sometimes even delving deeper. Confident as he is, he is no fool. Ignorance will lead to certain death he tells himself. Death has proven to be an ally throughout the years. He wants to keep it that way and not experience it firsthand.

Boils Bogilocus is not the only one with knowledge of the Abyss, either. Daemos learns from a few others, but acquiring their information isn't so forthcoming. Some, he retrieves after fending off attacks, others, he bleeds it out of joyously.

A month passes. The nights are cooling. It's time for the hunt. Daemos knows all the secrets he can. The longer Daemos waits, the more disadvantaged he'll be. The wraith's body count supposedly sways with the seasons. It's higher during the winter. Although it never grows too cold in the barren, desert landscape Viscrucia is located in. The additional rain proves nourishing to some of the deadly plants.

Daemos is the healthiest he has been in a long time. He's kept his hunting to a minimum. Instead, he's been splurging. He trades fresh limbs, some weapons, and jewels for food and water.

He goes out that night carrying his finest weapons, wearing his best clothes. Uglicerous's amethyst necklace hangs from his neck along with the jeweled machete at his side. Many Viscrucian heads turn at the sight and whisper about the citizen of such wealth and experience.

Torches light the macabre entertainment. Daemos savors a fine, blood-tear wine. If it's going to be his last night, he's going to enjoy himself. He captures one assailant, but he doesn't kill any. Now, Daemos sits back and enjoys the mayhem. He loves this city, his home.

The warm sunrise instantly wakes Daemos. He slept little that night in his cave outside of the city. His thoughts were focused on one thing: the wraith, the monster of the deep.

He looks at last night's capture, a drunk who should have kept his guard up. He dangles by his feet from a beam high above in the ceiling. Tied up, there is no hope for escape. The veins from his neck and face bulge.

Daemos is eager. He prepares a hearty breakfast. He cooks some of the meat he cut last night from his dangling victim. It will suffice. One hunt was enough for the day before. No sense exerting himself further by tracking an animal for meat. He will need all the energy he can get.

As his food settles, Daemos plays the attack out in

his head. He reviews the threats of the land and prepares himself of the little-known legends. He imagines the unimaginable.

It's time. He walks naked underneath the dangling man and rips out the man's throat with his talon-like fingernails. Blood explodes from the tracheal spigot and covers Daemos from his shaven head to his toes. He smears it across his scarred body.

Tattoos accompany his scars. Unlike most wanderers of the time, several of Daemos' tattoos are not etched with ink. They're carved into his flesh. Some of his other scars are often confused with his tattoos. With so many wounds, he could easily pass as the walking dead.

The meat bleeds out. Daemos opens his war chest and pulls out his black-painted battle gear. He puts his clothes on and the few pieces of armor. Lightweight bone- and metal-fashioned guards protect his forearms. Knee-high boots protect his legs. Leather gauntlets cover his hands. The animal skin clothing covering the rest of him is light and mobile but still very difficult to penetrate.

Next are his weapons. Daemos wears so many blades he puts any butcher to shame. Knives, swords, axes, and a mass of coiled wire with knives attached to both ends. Daemos throws on his coat and pockets a few vials of a flammable concoction.

He grabs the last piece of armor from his war chest, his murder mask, or what Daemos affectionately refers to as his *face*. The outside is a polished bone. Its subtle curves are painted mostly black and swirled with blood. It covers his face and the sides of his head. Straps fitted with more bone connect it in back. Underneath, a silk lining provides additional protection and comfort, in case of an edged weapon's direct hit. He conceals it inside his coat.

Daemos tightens his hands. The blood has congealed. Its stickiness gives him a better grip and sense of feel on his skin. He grabs a jug of the flammable liquid and walks to the Abyss, eager for the doom.

Daemos reaches the city's border. Dust blows in the wind. Before heading further, he looks back. Petrid, that tall bastard, stands there. He spins a knife with the four fingers on his hand and picks his teeth with a new bone.

Petrid raises his weapon in salute.

Daemos holds up a blade, nods, and walks forward. His greatest challenge lies ahead. Nothing will alter his focus.

"Make it back, Viscrucian, and I will make a sculpture of you, that none will forget," Petrid says. He turns and walks back to his Carving Ground.

Daemos captures dinner for the wraith. It's probably been some time since it's eaten. He grabs a predator creeping in the outskirts. His kind are often drug fiends. He slams him into the wall, knocking him unconscious. Daemos ties the man up, wraps him in a bag, and hoists him over his shoulder. He keeps moving.

He looks over the dark cliff down onto the cursed haze. He feels the drop in temperature. He spits over the ledge and descends to the Abyss.

Slimy vines and plants grow in abundance. Creatures crawl and fly among the shadows. Poisonous, ashen-colored flora swells throughout the derelict land. Fog conceals it. Daemos chose his boots specifically for this danger. They reach much higher than the plants. The leathery outer layer is thoroughly oiled with protectant. Metal guards provide additional protection.

Vultures and crows of ungodly sizes swoop through the mist. They caw, knowing food is soon to come. It calls upon the wraith, awakening it from his slumber, like a boogeyman of childhood fairytales.

Daemos readies his machete taken from Uglicerous.

A wall of fog stands before him. This is it. Daemos removes his coat. He inserts earplugs and puts on his murder mask. Time for the violence to begin.

Daemos steps through the fog into the wraith's dominion. It's pitch-black, and the air is foul. He crouches and waits, giving his eyes time to adapt. He relaxes and breathes easy.

A freakish scream pierces the darkness. The wraith senses the intruders.

The sound wakes Daemos's prisoner. Daemos rips off the bag and kneels behind him. He pulls out one of his vials and douses the man's lower half.

"Stand up!" Daemos demands. He puts the tip of his machete into the man's back. "Move!" Blind to everything, the dreg obeys.

"I can't see!"

"Move! I'll give you enough drugs to make all your pain go away."

"But…"

Daemos digs the blade deeper.

The man trudges forward. He looks everywhere but still can't see. His eyes haven't adapted to the darkness.

Another terrible scream erupts. The man covers his ears.

"Oh, my God! What evil is that? Where are we?"

Daemos pushes the addict forward. Small creatures slither up the men. Others fall from above. The bait frantically slaps them away.

The ground changes. Daemos can't see it, but the difference is noticeable. It's like walking through a swamp. The mire is thick and difficult to traverse.

A huge rush of wind blows above the men, even knocking down Daemos's decoy. The man gasps for breath as he rebounds from the swamp.

"Oh, God! It's the Abyss! You've taken me to the Abyss, you fuck!"

Daemos has heard enough. He sparks a flint and ignites his unique concoction. The prisoner bursts into flames. He screams and curses Daemos. Daemos backs away and trades his machete for his broadsword. He's going to need a bigger weapon.

The wraith wails. The earplugs make the sound bearable. The wraith swoops down again. Daemos can't see it through the gloom but hears it coming. A talon pierces the man's chest, shooting blood onto

Daemos's boots. Daemos swings his broadsword. The sheer mass knocks Daemos on his ass, but something else remains.

The wraith carries the prisoner high into the cave. Daemos finally sees his adversary, the demon itself. The wraith is a fiend of colossal size. Inside its black domain, its four wings spread out across the hellish cathedral. Its body is like tar, a black mass of twisted sludge. Smoke trails it. Slimy talons on the top and bottom of the wings grip the man. Its many eyes peer from all over its body. They are void of color yet, somehow, their absolute blackness is visible in its own spectrum.

An odd growth fills the ceiling and walls. It sways in the darkness like the algae of a coastal reef. Its life adds another disturbing quality to this pit of hell.

Half of one of the wraith's wings is missing. Daemos looks down and sees the piece of the appendage protruding from the murky water. Its residue gloms onto Daemos's armor and sword.

The wraith tears into the man and rips him into four pieces. The consuming fire masks his cries.

Daemos pulls out his bow. He dips three arrows in the flames at his feet and fires them together. One hits the demon's chest, the other his wing, and the third lands in the black life among the walls. The flames spread. It engulfs the winged beast, yet to no avail. The wraith inhales the consuming fire and returns to its onyx color. Its head doesn't bother to look in Daemos' direction. It devours his cooked treat instead.

Daemos figured the fire would not affect the demon, but he might as well try. Luckily for him, the growth isn't so easily distinguished. Its fire stays true and slowly spreads, adding some light to the cave.

He pulls out more arrows from his quiver. Still eating, the wraith plunges. It flies right through Daemos. The blow knocks him twenty feet away, onto hard ground. His bow is in shambles, and his body armor is cracked beyond repair. He pulls up his mask and can't help but cough blood onto his cracked chest plate. He removes his body armor and tosses it to the swamp.

The wraith spits his meal's skull at the armor. It shatters on impact. Daemos tries to catch his breath. The wraith's move puzzles him.

He grabs his battle ax and machete. The wraith screams. The wall growth reels back. The demon swoops down for another pass. Daemos hurls his ax at the beast and quickly readies his machete. The weight of the ax helps it cleave through another wing. Daemos' reaction is not a moment too soon, for the wraith is instantly upon him, one less wing or not.

Daemos stabs forward just in time. The machete spears the demon's claw as it grabs him. The wraith shoots into the air. Its strength is immense as it tightens its grip on Daemos.

The wraith's black head turns toward him. He doesn't want to know what comes next. He turns his blade, loosening the wraith's grip. Daemos plummets to the ground.

He gets to his feet and moves to a better position. The wraith notices and shrieks with frustration. It rips out a large chunk of the wall and hurls it at Daemos's feet. Daemos dodges. The wraith does it again with the same result.

Daemos is surprised by such an easy miss. He looks down. He sees his ignorance and the wraith's demise.

"Blood." His boots are splashed with his bait's blood. Except for his mask, he quickly removes his remaining gear and tosses them to the side.

He stands ready. The old blood from this morning covers him underneath the murder mask from head, to loin cloth, to toe. The wraith sees only pulsing or fresh blood. That may be all the demon can see. The dead blood camouflages Daemos. He won't forget it.

The wraith dives for the armor. The impact slams the ground.

Daemos grabs his coiled wire and buries one knifed end in the ground. He then leaps onto the demon's back and buries the connecting blade into a wing. The wraith shrieks. The living walls cringe.

The wraith leaps from the ground. The wire reaches its limit, and its knife cuts through the wing.

Fire spreads inside this castle of shadows, killing more of the wraith's dominion and illuminating the room. Its connection between his lair weakens. The wraith raises its wings to block out the light.

Daemos hacks through the remaining two wings with his machete. The wraith shrieks in pain as they crash to the ground.

The wraith focuses. It sees its own blood. It covers Daemos and his weapon. The wraith charges through the shadows and grabs Daemos by the throat.

Daemos didn't know it could do that.

The wraith winds back and throws Daemos through the air.

He slams into a wall. The wraith bounds over to Daemos and drives him into the wall again. One of its claws slashes Daemos' left arm. Daemos yells in pain. The wraith answers with a scream of his own. It head-butts Daemos, slightly cracking his murder mask, in the center, shattering his nose. Daemos looks through his blood at the deathly fiend. Its onyx eyes dilate, focusing on its desire.

Daemos pulls the wraith closer. It swings wildly, trying to get a hold of him but only finds the wall. More of it crumbles above Daemos. Light pierces the wall. The wraith reels back in pain. The light burns the demon, searing some of the eyes.

Blood spurts from the wraith's face. Hundreds of fangs beg for fresh blood as it screams. Daemos ignores the ear-splitting sound and grins. He grabs the wall and rips away.

More light breaks through, covering the phantasm and withering its flesh. Daemos punches through its sludge-like body and grabs the most solid thing it can find.

The wraith slashes down. It cleaves across Daemos' chest over his heart, nearly catching it. Daemos stumbles back into the wall again. More caves down.

Daemos grabs and swings the demon with all his might through the wall.

He marches forward, holding it high into the awakening light. The outer fog curtain dissipates. The venomous growth below steams.

A beam of sunlight burns through the clouds, following the wraith's demise. It screams and thrashes. The black sludge of flesh melts. Its blood spills. It covers the warrior's arm and seeps into his wounds.

The shadowy veil of the wraith burns. Only a huge, vomitous oily black spine and skull remain in Daemos's grasp. The last of the onyx eyes extinguish. The growing light ignites the odious vegetation everywhere. Daemos lowers the immense skull. He looks upon his kill as a halo of light shines through the clouds. The black castle burns in the background. Daemos is victorious.

Chapter 9

Lord Villous was an old victim of Daemos. He was a tourist at the time. Daemos was young then, not even in his teens.

The man was a fat, wealthy lord in his thirties from a far-off land. Secretly, he was a sadist and rapist in his kingdom. The easy butchering of his servants and townspeople ceased to quench his thirst for blood and human misery. As always, the addiction grew.

He started hunting and sought more challenging prey. Being the pitiful, *kingly* predator, he was, however, his palace guards were disguised and close at all times. Many times, they prepped his prey for a kill, allowing the lord his easy, quality time.

The youthful Daemos discovered the tourist's dishonorable practices. He thought he should teach him a lesson, the Viscrucian way. He stalked the men, unnoticed from the rooftops. Being such a young age, Daemos couldn't take any chances, especially being outnumbered. He had to strike at the perfect time.

Daemos followed the guards into an alleyway as they set up another toy for their lord. He pounced on them from above and cut them up quickly. He ordered the intended toy to run off, and then he eagerly awaited Villous. The gluttonous lord stepped in and towered over the adolescent. This pleased Daemos even more.

The two fought. The fight was bloody and left both child and adult scarred for life. The lord cut a long gash just behind Daemos' ear down to his shoulder. Daemos sliced off the palm from the lord's left hand. By the end, Lord Villous laid on the ground. This presented Daemos with a devious opportunity.

Daemos sliced the soles from his feet. Leaving his final stamp, Daemos carved *tourist* in the lord's stomach. He wiped the blood from the lord's wound and smeared it down one side of his face in triumph.

Daemos dragged the lord's body out to the desert.

"You don't deserve to die in Viscrucia, kes bag. I've got something better in mind." It was a long haul, but little Daemos was determined.

Lord Villous cursed Daemos's name. Daemos laughed as he filled a cup with the lord's blood and drank it. Daemos journeyed home. The lord attempted to walk away but fell due to the excruciating pain. Daemos left him to bleed out or be eaten alive by the scavenger animals the lord had so much in common with. Either death would suffice.

For a while, Villous laid there in misery, eagerly awaiting his death. Only death didn't come to greet him, it was the vultures. The bloody aroma called to their hunger. The lord made another instinctive mistake of trying to bat them away with his hands and feet. The animals instantly latched onto his skinless extremities and fed. By the time they finished, the lord's right leg was chewed off to the knee, and his wounded hand was pecked halfway to his elbow. He laid there a grotesque mess.

Villous reached out and grabbed the vulture feeding on his other hand by the throat. He slammed it repeatedly into the other feasting on his leg. The birds shrieked, feathers flew, and bones cracked. Consumed with pain, rage, and bloodlust, he ripped into the nearest vulture with his teeth. Like his scavenger brethren, he broke into a feeding frenzy. He needed to kill, to replace his pain and blood. By causing misery, he staved off his own.

Now, the lord wears a shirt at all times to conceal the *tourist* mark Daemos gave him. A thick boot cushions his healed foot, and a golden peg leg replaces his missing one. A golden dagger sits in place of his chewed-off left arm.

He survived that day and, eventually, made it back to his homeland of Kilsan. The encounter with Daemos changed the lord's life. He grew more sadistic. More savage. He cared even less about the people he ruled and only about himself. His speech devolved out of apathy. He vowed to find Daemos and kill him, delivering the most pain anyone has ever endured.

Chapter 10

The trek up the hillside is grueling. The weight of his trophy is staggering. His wounds sting like nothing he's ever experienced. Even his vision betrays him. The wraith's claws or blood must have intoxicated him. Daemos would've liked nothing better than to rest in that palace of shadow, but it couldn't be trusted. Who knows what other demon spawn dwell there? Daemos is in no condition to find out. He has to move.

Finally, he reaches the top of the cliff. He's made it to the Viscrucian border. Not far now. He needs a place to rest and heal as every citizen does after a brutal battle. He needs food, water, and as always, bandages.

A man stands over a kill in the distance. He severs the best currency. Noticing Daemos, he grabs his club and readies himself. The club is respectable. Metal shards dripping with gore protrude from its bulk. The citizen is of average build and size. This suggests he's a formidable killer and agile. He smiles underneath the blood-spattered across his face, ready for another victim.

Daemos walks closer. The man's instincts betray him. He can't help but notice the freakish skull and spine wrapped around the approaching hulk.

"No," he says in disbelief. The men circle each other around the corpse, unaware of the other's intentions. "Daemos? The wraith? I saw the clouds part from the Abyss, but…" He notices the bloody oil dripping from the arm of Daemos' coat.

Daemos looks past the man. He grips a meat cleaver beneath his coat. "I knew it. There is more than one wraith!"

The man turns around. Daemos pulls out his cleaver and throws it into the back of the man's head. He falls to the ground. Daemos drops the skeleton, walks over, and stomps on the man's neck to finish the deed.

"Fool."

He wastes no time and searches the man. Daemos finds water and guzzles it.

He examines the man's victim for food, rags, and bandages. Seeing them, he instantly devours the food. Next, he takes off his coat as it brushes painfully against his wounds. He rinses them off and sews them up. The wraith's blood has stained his injuries like tattoos. He applies what little salves there are. He uses all the wraps and makes whatever new ones he can from the dead men's clothes. Mended a little further, Daemos grabs his things and moves. He needed that. His wounds are better concealed, but he must continue. The wraith's intoxication persists.

Daemos walks the bone-paved streets. He is vigilant as always, but unnecessarily so. He's almost in disbelief. Only a few times in the city's history could this have happened.

Silence surrounds him. Clashing weapons, breaking bones, and the painful screams throughout come to a halt. Daemos walks forward. Everyone steps out of his way.

The news spreads like muscle from a blade. Soon, Daemos reaches the center of the city, a massive circle, over a hundred meters in diameter, surrounded by shops. It's known as the Heart of Viscrucia or Slaughterer's Row, open to the public for murder, mayhem, feasting, and currency exchange in its purest form. The unusable limbs, bones, and rotting meat piles high in the center of it. It stands as a warning to the tourists. Every night, the people set it ablaze and throw their latest victims upon the flaming altar to the god Viscrucians don't believe exists.

Daemos marches up the mound of meat. He's exhausted, but he masks it well. He raises his mythical kill for every psycho to see.

Petrid grabs the man before him and tears out his throat. No one next to him cares in the least. Petrid kneels down and places the dead man over his knee. He rips the shirt from the man's back and uses his flesh as a canvas. He cuts, carves, and scrapes the history he sees unveiling before him.

The deadly woman with raven hair stands in an alley at the edge of the crowd. Her whip wraps around her waist and down her right leg. Her lips part slightly with amazement as she looks upon Daemos. He sees her among the crowd.

Above, standing atop the roof of a shop is a long-haired bard named Lesigom. He pulls out his trusty flesh pad and puts his blood quill to quick use.

Difficult for the rest of the world to fathom, but like many citizens of Viscrucia, Lesigom has a unique talent. He is an exceptional bard. Lesigom's specialty lies in the violent arts. As a Viscrucian, the horrors of reality do not frighten, they excite him. Lesigom bites down on his lip. The taste of blood helps him live in the moment. His creative juices flow, and *this* is a poem that must be told.

The crowd is silent and stares in awe.

"Behold, my fellow Viscrucians. The legends were true. The wraith held dominion over the Abyss. It ruled its dark sanctuary for an untold number of years. That reign is over. I, Daemos, have killed the unkillable! I sent the demon back to the Suffering it came from! Remember this, and those of you pathetic fucking soldiers out there loyal to Lord Villous, I know you're here. You tell Huemic, you tell your lord, that it is done. And if I see anyone of you fucking tourists in the streets of Viscrucia again, I'll do far worse to you than what I've done to the wraith! Do you hear me! The wraith was a true Viscrucian! Its blood ran with honor. It will be remembered."

Daemos rests the skeletal remains on his shoulders. Moments pass. No one knows what to do.

A blade unsheathes. People turn toward the sound. Petrid holds his knife high. The people follow. Petrid pulls out his second weapon and clashes the blades together above his head. The crowd does the same. The pulse of the weapons ring through the streets of the city.

Lesigom loves the sight as he frantically scribbles his new song:

From the pedestal of flesh arose,
A warrior holding skull and bone.
Murderers filled Viscrucia's Heart,
For once did screams and silence part.
The citizens could not believe
That thing that shrieked in the night and was never before seen.
Today it saw the light,
Lost its flight and deadly might.
Guardian and ruler of the black Abyss,
Yet only now and forever more will the wraith be missed.
Daemos, could it be, the *man* to take its killing place?
At this point it's unknown, only time and blood will show.
But there he stands,
Daemos,
The Viscrucian champion.

Daemos walks down from his pedestal of pain. The crowd parts once more. He walks through the streets and disappears.

Chapter 11

The guards open the doors to Lord Villous's chamber. Huemic enters.

"My liege, it is done."

Wine drools from the lord's mouth as he stops mid-drink. "What?"

"Daemos did it. He killed the wraith! Light shines upon the Abyss."

"Baaahhhh!" He throws his goblet at Huemic and hits him in the chest. "Impossible! The wraith supposed to eat, tear him pieces, and swallow his black fucking soul!"

"Apologies, my—"

"Shut up, flesh bag! Great! A plan. We need new plan! Kes! I can't send soldiers again. He'll just kill them."

"Agreed."

Lord Villous slaps Huemic across the face and quickly sticks him with his bladed arm. "Shut up!" Huemic grimaces as little as he can.

Lord Villous thinks for a moment. "Yes. I have ideas, some ideas indeed. We get him, Huemic. His head will be on mantle. His hide will be my rug!"

Daemos sleeps in one of his hideouts far from Viscrucia. Sweat runs down his shaved head. The wraith's damage has taken its toll as a fever grips Daemos. This doesn't surprise him. He expected death or loss of a limb, at the very least. A fever is child's play. Still, this is no ordinary wound or sickness. No one has ever faced the wraith and lived before. At least, not to Viscrucian knowledge.

The next day, Daemos goes through his usual recuperation ritual. He ventures into the woods to find food and water. He is too weak to hunt animals or travelers on the road.

Daemos returns to his hideout. He sets his supplies down and takes a seat. His arm twitches. He carefully removes his bandages and twists his arm back and forth to survey the damage. The wraith's blood has stained Daemos's flesh. The stitched-up wounds are black.

The sight pleases Daemos. Many times, he tattooed himself in the past, but his method is different. He does it the way a true Viscrucian would. He carves his tattoos into his flesh. He uses a special blood dye so the scar remains red on his skin. But this time, the work is done for him. The wraith leaves its mark upon Daemos. Daemos is honored. Still, Daemos is no fool. He cleans the wound and bandages it again.

His fever grows worse. Daemos throws up continually, unable to keep food down. His skin grows pale, and the wraith's wounds still seep blood despite being stitched. Nightmares haunt him. Visions of the

wraith fly past and stab him with its claws. He hears
things: its wailing screams, an evil voice. Hundreds of
onyx eyes stare upon Daemos's soul. Daemos wakes
and swings a knife through the air only to catch
nothing. The fever pain grips him and forces him to
vomit more.

A week of this misery passes. In time, he slowly
heals. The fever fades, and Daemos feels okay, even
though his scars suggest otherwise. He travels to the
town of Yesilmi for a drink, armed and ready for
violence as always.

Yesilmi is a week's ride north of Viscrucia. Being
somewhat close, the town is no stranger to violence, but
it is not commonplace. Having dispatched two
travelers on the road, Daemos has enough coin to pay
his way.

"Welcome, Viscrucian! I hope you had a lovely
journey out of the fallen city," a Sublime missionary
greets Daemos as he reaches town. The Sublime wears
tan clothing, with braided bracelets and headband
adorned with a white stone in the center. The man is
tall and handsome. He has a thick beard and curly
brown hair. "Please, rest your weary soul. You must be
tired of the bloodshed?"

Daemos chuckles. "Save your words, unscarred. My
soul can't be saved."

"All souls can be saved. I am Abrus. I can guide you
to the light."

"The men I killed today disagree." Daemos canters
past on his horse.

"Go in peace. We will meet again. There is always salvation."

"You should hope we don't meet again."

The pious Sublime sticks out like pearls among rubble. They live simply, with few possessions. One thing they lack is fear. They don't hesitate or hide from a Viscrucian's sight. Daemos respects this, especially from peaceful people. Maybe that's why he hasn't slain any of their faith, yet. They're also not worth the effort.

He rents a room for the night at the town inn and heads to the tavern. People passing in the streets make sure to keep their distance. The few children still out stare in wonder.

Daemos reaches the tavern known as Goblins' Gully. Taller than the entryway, he ducks to squeeze inside. Everyone turns upon seeing this giant enter. He walks over to the bar.

"Ale. You can come out, goblin. I know you're here," Daemos says to the seemingly empty bar. He knows the rules are different for him outside his home, and that his scarred appearance raises alarm.

"Can I, Viscrucian?" a wet, invisible voice calls out.

"Seek death do thee?" a similar voice calls out from a different end of the bar.

"Or drink? No blood works here, nor do the Goblin Three wish to see the spilling, nie large, nor wee," a third little voice calls out. Blood works are drinks brewed with blood, human or otherwise.

"Understood, Goblin Three. Now, please entertain me with drink for a fee," Daemos replies, actually playing along. He has a fondness for goblins. There are many kinds, and they always manage to entertain him.

Something rustles underneath the bar. A green goblin spins out from behind the tree, acting as a pillar at the end of the bar, and hops on the goblin's shoulders down below. The third backflips onto the second goblin's shoulders, forming a goblin totem pole bartender.

Goblins are nimble little bastards. Their small stature, usually about two feet in height, demand it. Even stacked together, they didn't equal Daemos' height. A mug quickly gets handed from one goblin to the other, along with a rag to dry it off. Their bodies are perfect camouflage among the woods. Their skin is green and implanted with leaves and thick, bark-looking scales.

The top goblin leans in and opens his vibrant green eyes big and wide. "Can I trust you, oh, vicious one?" Daggers soon spin in all the goblins' hands.

"Aye, green one," Daemos replies and flips him a large gem. The goblins quickly pass it between them, putting their daggers away. Their green eyes light up with delight.

The goblins make Daemos his drink. "Name's Gree," the top goblin says.

"Lorsch," says the middle.

"Mackle!" yells the bottom one.

"Mackle, Lorsch, Gree. Name's Daemos. Nice to meet the Goblin Three."

"Hee, hee, hee." The goblins laugh in unison.

"Daemos...should we know the name?" Lorsch asks.

"A known citizen? Doubtful, even though he the size of a tree!" Mackle replies.

"True, but I am worth remembering, Goblin Three. Ask your cousins, they'll remember me." Daemos has been there many times. Goblins have huge families, and they alternate shifts between them. "I'll be over there, Gree. Keep 'em coming."

The Goblin Three have already vanished. "Tree!" Gree answers out of sight. Daemos figures that meant yes in their wooden language. If not, he'll prune their leaves.

Daemos sits at a wood table in the corner to keep everybody in sight. The tavern mimics its bordering forest. Trees stand as the support beams inside. The bar is built around a few of them. Occasionally, animals race down the trees and steal food. Sometimes, they become meals themselves. The floor is dirt and grass. Vines spread across the interior walls. Lizards, insects, and various other creatures crawl freely throughout the tavern. Tree goblins, nor any other forest creature, would have it any other way. Many of the seats are merely felled trees.

It's a relaxing evening for Daemos. His mind and muscles are at ease. He doesn't have to look over his shoulder in Yesilmi, yet he stays alert out of habit. This can prove difficult for Viscrucians. Once a true citizen, it can be hard turning it off and interacting with the rest of the world.

To pass the time, he pulls out the severed hand of one of his recent traveling victims and makes a bracelet. He cuts off the preserved fingers and shaves them down. He threads a cord through them, connecting the fingers. He wraps them with muscles he's cured, giving it a more polished look. Petrid would approve.

The night rolls on, and the Goblin Three keep the drinks coming. A few of the fellow patrons even engage Daemos in conversation. Enjoying the hospitality, he doesn't end it in slaughter. A horde of sprites take up one table, some ground goblins take another, and humans fill the rest. Usually, more creatures fill taverns so close to the forest. Daemos is surprised gremlins aren't here throwing food around like usual. If mages or wizards show up, they always provide colorful entertainment.

Vine leaves rustle as the tavern door opens. Daemos perks up. A unique scent accompanies the breeze. The raven-haired minx steps inside. She immediately checks her surroundings. Seeing Daemos, she stays her gaze a few extra seconds, and then continues to the bar.

The sight of the seductive killer intrigues Daemos. He did not expect to see her here, away from Viscrucia. Is she following him? Does she think she could actually kill Daemos, the wraith slayer? Could she be so enthralled by his might she has sought him out? He thinks not. Not if she's the citizen he hopes her to be.

She orders a drink from the goblin heap.

"Care to join a fellow citizen for a drink?" Daemos calls out.

Mackle, the bottom bartender looks at Daemos, realizing what this could mean, and perhaps pathetically attempting to dissuade Daemos. The calling out of a citizen outside of the bone streets of Viscrucia has the same possibilities as inside them. Daemos takes pleasure in the openness of his come on. If it translates to a call to arms, bring it on. Let's see what this bitch's got.

Her raven hair swings around as she looks over. She picks up her mug, turns back to the bar, and takes a drink.

Daemos laughs inside. This might be tougher than he thought. She talks to the goblins flipping back and forth behind the bar. Is she jesting on my behalf, mocking the new ruler of the Abyss? Bitch!

Lorsch slides her another drink. She picks it up and walks over to his table. Daemos's mind eases.

"Take a seat," Daemos says, pushing over a chair with his foot.

She sits down and passes Daemos the extra drink. They study each other for a moment, waiting, seeing if the other is going to make a flesh-opening move. Daemos leads and gestures to his unseen weapon underneath his coat, the Viscrucian greeting. The minx responds in kind.

"I saw you in the Heart of Viscrucia. The one who killed the wraith," she says. "You're Daemos."

Daemos takes a drink. "I've seen you and your whip. What's your name, citizen?"

"Faelin."

"Faelin," Daemos repeats. He finally has a name to go with the face. "Are you following me?"

"Why?"

"You said it. You saw me with the wraith, and now you're here, far away from Viscrucia."

Faelin looks into Daemos' eyes. Neither backs down. "No. Probably here the same reason you are. A rest stop on the way out."

"You just got lucky then."

Faelin stares at Daemos, her expression unchanged.

"How long have you killed?"

Faelin takes a drink, letting the tension linger. "A citizen never tells, Daemos."

A come on of her own, Daemos thinks. "To blood then. Forever will it flow." Daemos pulls out a small blade and puts it to his hand.

Faelin waits a moment, and then responds in kind. They each cut themselves on the hand and pour a few drops of blood into the other's drink.

"To blood," Faelin says. They pick up their mugs and cheers.

Intoxicated, Faelin and Daemos stumble into her room at the inn, kissing wildly. Daemos grabs her hair and pulls it tight. He removes the small scythe-like hooks behind her ears as he kisses her neck. As lustful as this encounter is, he needs to proceed with caution. He scanned her thoroughly for weapons down in the tavern.

Faelin grabs his muscular back and squeezes. Her

black-painted fingernails dig in and draw blood.

"So, you like it rough, huh?" Daemos asks.

"What do you think, big man."

She squeezes him tighter. Daemos dives into her lips again. Her other hand moves for the knife on her hip. Before she can free it, Daemos reaches around and grabs her ass, pinning her hand. He takes the blade from her and throws it into the vine-covered wall. Let the seduction begin.

Like two spiders performing a mating ritual, one false step could lead to the other's meal. This is Daemos' kind of foreplay. Maybe she's into a little sadistic carving. How could she not be?

His lips move along her firm, olive-skinned body. He kisses her neck, down to her collarbone, then to the large scar on her shoulder. Eyes closed, this arouses her even more as she moans further. He moves down, kissing the scar just above her right breast.

Daemos reaches between her legs and loosens the knot securing another weapon. Faelin swipes the knife before Daemos can unleash it and throws it into the wall.

Out in the hallway, a goblin crawls on the ceiling, cleaning it of insects and nests. She hears the weapons bury into the walls. She swings back and forth, hanging onto the vines with her feet, and twiddles her little green claws. "Either someone's very unlucky, or just the opposite."

aelin removes Daemos's coat. It drops with a thud from all the weapons.

Daemos rips off her jacket. Only two pieces of her clothing remain: pants and a corset. One side of her pants covers her leg down to her ankle to protect it from her whip. The other side stops high above her knee.

Her corset is armored. Knives are secured on each forearm and bicep. Surprisingly, few scars cover the rest of her body. Daemos pins her hands to the wall above her and removes the blades along her arms.

Faelin pushes Daemos. The cat and mouse game for dominance continues. She slashes down with her nails, cleaving his shirt in half.

"I want your flesh."

She rips his shirt off and kisses his broad chest.

The disarming continues. She pulls his last knife and swings it toward his head. Daemos reacts just in time and catches her wrist. He puts her arm behind her back, spins her around, and buries her head in the leafy wall.

"I'll show you rough."

He uses his knife to cut through the back straps in her corset. It falls to the grass floor along with the knife she held. She moans with the excitement of Daemos taking charge.

He uncoils the whip from her leg. He rips her pants off with one pull, and then spanks her ass. Faelin moans even louder.

Faelin pushes them from the wall. She turns around and tears his pants to shreds before ripping them off.

They clutch each other's naked bodies. Blood smears

from their frenzied scratching as other juices flow. They kiss as much of the other's skin as they can.

They crash onto the bed. The foreplay is intense...but it doesn't even compare to the sex. Position after position. Up and down, inside and out. Their juices flow. They don't break contact with each other even for a second.

After the moaning, screaming, and frenzied fucking finally stops, they collapse. Both breathe heavily. They are exhausted. They lay naked together as their chests expand and contract.

"Careful, big man keep showing a woman that good of a time and she may not let you go. Love may even come to bear."

The statement puzzles Daemos. He's heard the saying occasionally on his travels but never paid much attention to it. "Love? What does *love* mean?"

"What? You've never heard of love before?"

"I don't know what it means. There is no love in Viscrucia."

"You're right about that." Faelin pauses as she catches her breath.

"So, what is it?" Daemos feels slightly annoyed that he has to ask again.

"It's a tough question. You feel for the person. You protect them."

"So, you kill for them?"

"Yes. Absolutely. You...you think of them more than yourself."

"That's not Viscrucian," Daemos says, cutting her

off. Risk versus reward, life and death are always on the line. He has to be swift and focused. Even when lust mounts. "That could kill. Maybe that's why it doesn't exist in Viscrucia."

Faelin rolls her eyes and sits up. "We're not in Viscrucia. There is *life* outside of the city of death. There are good things, pleasurable things. There is more." Faelin reaches underneath her pants, lying on the ground. Daemos springs out of bed and clutches her hand. He grabs the weapon and tosses it across the room. Faelin fends off multiple advances. He eventually moves past her guard and clutches her naked body. He kisses her. Faelin breaks away from his lips.

"Maybe you're right," Daemos says. "I don't know love. I know survival and the kill, the way of the blade. Maybe there's more. Someone would need to show me."

Faelin eases her defenses and gives into his lips. "I've got lots more to show you."

Their carnal embrace resumes.

Chapter 12

Faelin wakes up. She reaches for her murderous companion amidst the stained sheets but finds nothing. She jolts up in the bed. Daemos is not standing over her ready lop her head off, either. He's gone.

"Son of a bitch! That giant...scarred...fuck! Leave me?" Faelin can't think of another way to insult him. The worst she could think of would be calling him a tourist, but she knows that's untrue.

Daemos rides a horse through the forest, continuing his journey to the lord's castle. Acquiring a horse large enough to carry Daemos was no easy task. Not all horses were healthy in those parts. Often, they were stolen from their owners and killed and eaten after they reached their destination.

Daemos enjoyed his little seduction of Faelin last night but kept it at that. Her intentions are still unknown, and she can't be trusted. No citizen can. She mentioned *love*. That concept is foreign to Daemos and, again, can't be trusted. She is cunning and is most likely lying. Spinning a seductive web to catch her prey. Perhaps not. Either way, caution prevails. He'd keep her as a fond memory for now. He may even see her again in the future if she survives that long.

The lord's castle and surrounding village is not much further. Daemos took a longer route to the castle. This gave his wounds more time to heal, and Lord Villous more time to stew. Fuck him. Daemos wasn't on his timetable. Anything to make this so-called lord agitated pleased Daemos.

Daemos doesn't trust Lord Villous. Who is he, really? How does he know about Daemos? Is Daemos well-known past the violence of Viscrucia? He hasn't traveled far enough to learn about such tales and actual histories. The only history Daemos cares about is the one he creates for himself, a history in Viscrucia.

Never has there been such a thing. The thought was pure jest before now. The wraith is known, sure, but his legend was born out of his dominion in the Abyss, and it was no man. A manmade Viscrucian legend, now that is something to behold.

Daemos's body is healing well. He prepares himself for his upcoming encounter with Lord Villous and his minions. Daemos sharpens his blades and readies his poisons. He files his fingernails to make them talon sharp. At night, he surveys the castle walls from beyond the village. He doesn't want to make his presence known just yet. Guards patrol the village and the castle walls more often than Daemos would have thought. Strange. He wants to know why. It's time for a closer look.

Daemos heads back into the forest. He hides most of his weaponry beneath a fallen tree and covers them with leaves and branches. He camouflages himself with dirt and leaves. Finding animal tracks, he scales a tree nearby and hides amongst the branches. In time, Daemos kills two deer. He works quickly and cleans the animals.

He sews the pelts together and makes himself fresh clothes. The skin of one deer would not have been enough. He fashions a large hood to conceal his face. Daemos wraps some of the meat and heads for the village.

Torches illuminate the town and castle walls amidst the night sky. The stars shine bright. Fewer guards would be out at this time. Daemos hunches and moves quietly throughout the village to draw the least amount of attention. He surveys the shops, items, atmosphere, and the people. Before devouring flesh outright, one must observe the appearance and aroma of the meat for quality. So far, Daemos sees this place as rotting meat.

The people are skinny and dismal. The clothing is old, and the food sold isn't very fresh. The town is impoverished. Daemos hears the chuckling of drunk soldiers walking and conceals himself in the shadows. They walk past to the end of the row of shops. The torch lights reveal their heavy armor. It's the wealthiest sight Daemos has seen yet. Fools. The pathetic guards have probably never seen real battle, merely preyed upon the town's people at their lord's behest. Not many children were out, either. Daemos has scarcely seen children for that matter, but he still knows a few things about them.

The guards lumber past. Daemos walks out to one of the communal bonfires of the village. It's as he expected. No song. No dance. The people whisper amongst themselves. The village is shrouded in doom, much like the Abyss. The citizens of Viscrucia have more fun killing each other.

Nimble little feet run up behind Daemos. He clutches a knife at his side and spins around, ready to strike. A young boy stops suddenly in his tracks and drops his wooden toy. Daemos observes. He has never been this close to a child, not that he can remember, at least.

The dirt on the kid's face cannot conceal all his freckles. The child stammers. Daemos looks down at his toy. The kid reaches out, fumbling around before he finally grabs it. Daemos notices a single scar across the top of his hand, like that of a disciplinary lashing.

"You…you…" the boy stutters.

"Yes, child?" He does his best to conceal his true thoughts, something he has seldom done. Normally, Daemos would've stated, "Tell me what you want and there's a chance I won't rip out your tongue, kidnap you, and feast like a king on your tears for as long as your life isn't too burdensome to extinguish," but, this time, he held his tongue.

"I-I haven't seen you around here before, you're bi…" The bonfire light flickers across Daemos' hood, revealing some of his face. "You have a lot of scars."

Unsure how to feel, Daemos naturally grips the handle of his blade tighter.

"I like them," the boy says with a smile. He walks closer and puts out his hand. His little fingers slowly run along one of the long scars on Daemos' face.

Daemos stares back at the child as he touches him. Finished, the child steps back. Daemos smiles. "Come with me," the boy says.

He puts his hand out again, and Daemos accepts. The boy gleefully leads the monstrous stranger through the village and back to his home.

The boy uses all his might to push open the thick, animal skin entrance. "Mama, look, I brought a new friend."

The boy's mother walks in from another room. The child runs to his mother and hugs her.

"Who's your friend, Lemas?" the mother asks.

Daemos walks in from outside. The low ceiling prohibits him from standing fully upright. The mother gasps as quietly as she can. This could be the easiest kill Daemos has ever had. Children…interesting.

"It's late, Lemas. Go to your room and play with your toys. Mama will be in shortly."

"But, Mama…"

"Go!" She pushes her boy into the other room. Daemos looks at the mother. The fire in the center of the room casts a shadow behind Daemos, which shrouds nearly half the room. "Um, my son… I'll get you…" She rushes over to a nearby table with yarn and sewing needles on top. Daemos springs over, grabs her by the throat with one hand, and pushes the needles away with the other. He raises her into the air up to the ceiling.

"Bad Mama," Daemos says, staring into her eyes. She can barely breathe, let alone speak from Daemos's grip. Daemos presents his frightening fingernails to her. He claws deep into the wooden pillar supporting the small home. The mother trembles in his grip.

"Pl-please," the mother manages through Daemos's grip, "I love my son. I'll do an—"

Daemos grips her throat tighter to shut her up. And there's that word again.

"Try again, Mama, and I will tear your scalp off, rip your son's limbs from his body, and drink his blood in front of you." He raises his talons to the top of her head. She nods her head as much as she can.

Daemos places her in a chair in front of the fire. He sits in between her and the entrance to her son's room.

The mother clutches her throat and gasps for air. She then wipes her tears to compose herself as much as possible. Daemos sits and looks at her.

"Apologies, my guest. Something to drink?"

"Yes." He has never said *thank you* before in his life.

The mother sits perfectly still. She looks over at a pouch and cups sitting on a table off to the side.

Daemos walks to the table, pours the liquid into the cups, and hands one to the mother. Her hands shake as she takes the cup.

The boy sings to himself in the other room as he plays with his toys.

Daemos pulls out a knife and sticks it in the arm of his chair. The mother trembles. He reaches into his cloak and pulls out a small package. The mother squirms, nearly at her wit's end. Daemos unwraps the package, revealing the venison.

"Hungry?" Daemos asks.

The mother is at a loss.

"Yes, is it..."

"Deer. Killed today."

"Yes," the mother says relieved. "Grati—"

"I cook. You and your boy sit here. You can move now. Remember what I said."

"Yes." She gets up and goes to get her son. "Lemas."

The three eat in relative silence. The mother and child devour the meat.

"What's your name?" Lemas asks.

The mother's eyes widen, not sure if that is a question that should be asked.

"Daemos," he answers. Daemos looks to the mother.

"I am Cosma," the mother replies in kind.

Daemos sticks a fingernail in the cooking meat and pulls it away from the spit.

"I like your fingernails! Look, Mama, see?"

"Yes, Lemas. I noticed."

"How'd you get them, Daemos?" Lemas asks.

Daemos chews his food as he recounts the past for a moment. "As a boy, my parents took me to a special place. A pool, a bright blue pool. Water fell into it from the stream above. We drank from it. Bathed in it. They told me it had special qualities, that it would make me strong. Said that was the case with the food that grew from the water, as well. It's a peaceful place. That, time, and sharpening."

"Where are your mama and dadda now?"

"Dead. They died a long time ago, Lemas."

"I'm sorry. I miss my dadda. Do you think I could

get nails like that someday?"

Cosma's eyes nearly jump out of her head.

"I don't think your mother would like that, Lemas," Daemos answers. He ponders the child's words. Lemas clearly feels for Daemos. The child is so innocent that he only sees the good in a scarred stranger. He appreciates the differences in Daemos's appearance. It excites his inquisitive nature. He doesn't realize that Daemos has considered killing him. Daemos appreciates the youth's sentiment.

"Good food. No more, Mama." Lemas leans back with a full belly.

"Okay, good boy. Go to bed now. I'll be in later, Lemas."

"But…"

"Now, Lemas. Mama and Daemos need to talk."

"Listen to your mother, Lemas, and we can play tomorrow."

"Okay." He hugs his mother. Cosma kisses him on the lips and sends him into his room.

She looks at Daemos. Daemos stares back.

"What do you want?"

"I was invited."

"Yes, but…now what?"

"I have questions. I never intended coming here, but like I said… Where is your mate?"

"He's dead."

"This place is kes! Misery and kes. Why is it like this?"

"The guard. The castle. That lord, as he calls himself. His guard forces us to work here and takes most of what we make. He scars us to symbolize his property. He often takes our children. It's possible to escape. People have, but not everyone is like you. The surrounding land is harsh and cruel. Usually, those who try and escape are found, dragged back over the land, and made an example out of whether they're alive or not."

Daemos picks venison from his teeth with his nails. He sees why the lord is so enamored with Viscrucia and why he's probably never had the balls to go there himself. "What does he look like?"

"He is a husk of a man, missing an arm and a leg. Replaced them with golden blades," Cosma says.

Then again, sounds like he *has* been to Viscrucia. One time, at least.

"A fat, wretched man, and stinks, too, at least from what I can remember," Cosma continues. "I've only seen him once."

"How many guards?"

"Dozens. Mostly by day. They prey upon us by order and choice. Some of them used to be children from the village, but no longer. It's rare to cross their path and not be trampled over."

Daemos recalls the scar on Lemas' hand. "Are they good?" he asks.

"Yeah, they're good. Good at tormenting the village! Not much else. Nothing close to the guard of a real kingdom."

"What do you know of the inside?"

"Whatever's going on in there, it's evil. You hear

screams. I avoid the castle as much as possible."

Satisfied with the information he's received, Daemos stands up, puts his coat on, and moves toward the entrance. Figures he has caused the poor mother enough panic. He never intended to be there to begin with.

"You're..." Cosma blurts out, wishing she had just let him leave like a passing nightmare.

"Yes," Daemos replies. "Keep the meat. Tell anyone of this, and I'll be back collecting meat instead of providing it. Keep your son quiet." He turns his hand slightly, and a dagger drops into it from his sleeve. Cosma clutches her seat, having no idea he could arm himself so deftly. He slings it into his chair. "It's superior to knitting needles. Conceal under clothes on your thigh or forearm. If you ever fear harm to your son or self, bury it in their stomach without hesitation, and lift until their ribs stop it and their guts warm your feet."

"Th-thank you, Daemos. I'm scared...and grateful at the same time."

Daemos leaves. Cosma looks over at the shiny blade. She has never seen a weapon like it. The subtle contour in the handle, the unique oil, resin, and blood mix applied to it for superior grip, the minimal, yet sufficient cross guard to protect and maximize concealment, and the curved blade, sharpened fine enough to separate all flesh in its path.

This is the first Viscrucian weapon she has seen. Luckily, Cosma is too naive to ponder the vast number of lives it has already cleaved from the land.

Chapter 13

Daemos follows up on what Cosma said. He speaks with others, gaining information on the layout of the castle. He kills one of the informants for good measure. He took an unnecessary risk letting the family live but felt confident Cosma wasn't stupid enough to inform anyone of his presence.

It's time to meet the lord of the land. He puts on his regular clothes, gloves, weapons, coat, and throws the wrapped skeletal trophy over his shoulder. He carries a tarnished, wide-bladed saber in the other.

The menace walks through the center of town. A path clears before him. He stands as tall as most huts. Word spreads like a shock wave.

A guard rushes toward Daemos and blocks his way. "Halt! You…" he says.

"Your lord is expecting me. Escort me to him now or die," Daemos says.

The sentry smirks as he reaches for his sword. Daemos thrusts his saber through the man's face, through to the back of his helmet. The nose guard did nothing as always. Blood squirts across Daemos's face. Screams erupt. He yanks his sword out of the man's head, and then hacks it off, sending it spinning into the air. It falls onto its former body. Daemos holsters his weapon and grabs the guard's seeping head by the back of the helmet and moves forward.

The horror swarming the streets titillates Daemos. He smiles upon the bedlam. It's not often he witnesses such innocent fear from the masses.

Daemos walks steadily toward the castle. Four guards round the corner, securing their equipment when the head of their fallen comrade greets them. Blood drools from the gaping mouth and severed neck onto the dirt and Daemos's boots. The guards back up as they draw their weapons.

"Good. You're smarter than your friend here. If you wish to stay that way, take me to your lord and put your weapons away. He is expecting my gift."

"Cass, check it out!" a guard says.

"Cass, I don't wait. By the time you get to his chamber, I'll be carrying at least three more heads. We all go now, or you all die. These are pretty much the last words this head heard before it left its body."

Daemos steps closer. The guards peer up at their adversary. They are in new territory. *They* are the ones who abuse the people. Their intimidation always ruled, until now.

"OK. We will take you."

"Good. Stay in front of me."

The guards lead Daemos to the castle gate in two by two formation. The two in front lead the way while the two behind them walk backward, bumping into each other like fools, trying to keep their eyes on Daemos. Daemos conceals his laughter. He stares right at them to keep them on edge. If one of them does happen to fall, however, Daemos will surely kill him for such pitifulness.

Villagers watch from the edge of the street and shop entrances. Everything has stopped to behold the spectacle. Parents hold their children. Daemos carries the head by his side. The sentiment of the crowd changes. Horror persists, but not by all.

Daemos notices Cosma and Lemas standing among the crowd. Lemas is awestruck. Cosma immediately crouches and grabs her son, turning his head toward her.

"Lemas, look at me!" she says with a hushed authority. "Do *not* wave to him, say his name, or make any movement or sound at him! If you do, the guards and people will see, and they will *kill* us! They will kill us! Do you understand?"

"Yes, Mama," Lemas says quietly, clearly too afraid to defy his mother.

"Good. The only time you can speak of him is to me alone in our home like I told you. Do you understand?!"

"Yes, Mama."

Cosma kisses Lemas and stands. No one in the crowd notices. Lemas looks at Daemos silently, hiding all emotion. Trepidation fills Cosma's gaze. Daemos looks elsewhere, content the small family understands.

Ten soldiers accompany Daemos by the time they reach the gate. The portcullis is raised, and the gates are open. They walk through into a grand bailey. All guards stand at attention. The workers stare.

The castle used to be great at one time. Negligence has sullied the walls, and the ground is unkempt. The smell isn't what it should be, either. The picture is painted all too clearly for Daemos. The lord has plagued this once prodigious city. He is either the miscreant spawn of once proper lineage or a tyrant who seized the city in a coup. Neither matters now.

Chapter 14

"Huemic, the lord's kes boy," Daemos calls out. "I wondered if you ever made it out of Viscrucia alive. Considering how informed your sad brothers are here, I figured not."

Huemic stands tall before five underling guardsmen. He is well-groomed, and his armor shines. He is much more comfortable in his home setting compared to Daemos's. He commands respect and is used to people knowing it. Outside the city walls brings a quagmire.

"I was going to say the same for you and the Abyss," Huemic retorts. "I didn't think you were Viscrucian enough to whimper out of there in one piece. Figured you were no more than wraith kes down in the Abyss."

Daemos squeezes the helmet in his hand. Blood oozes out from the pressure. His eyes burn inside. Huemic grins, looking down at the freshly spilled blood. Daemos is in Huemic's world now, and he is the one surrounded.

"More alive than you'll be, tourist."

"Whatever you say, Daemos." Huemic motions to the head Daemos carries. "Hungry? You needed a snack before facing royalty?"

"Viscrucian hospitality. Thought I'd teach you some of our ways since you left so early last time. You sure you're using the word *royalty* correctly?"

"The city of suffering. Where ghouls walk the streets and children can't be within a five days' ride. Yes, quite the home. Did you succeed, Daemos? Is that it that you're carrying?"

"Take me to him."

"My guards will carry that for you. No need to—"

"Don't bother, little ones. Lead the way, Huemic."

"Kill your walk, Daemos! We're not in slaughter city anymore. Your weapons. Release them to my guards." Daemos stares silently at Huemic. "That or leave. Enjoy your journey home. We're not in Viscrucia. Get used to it, you walking scar."

Moments pass. The guards stand ready. Daemos drops the head to the ground and carefully lays the wraith's remains beside him. He walks over slowly to the guard closest to him. Wearing gloves, Daemos cracks his knuckles and proceeds to pull out a hidden knife by the hilt. He places the handle in the guard's bare hand. The blade is surprisingly rusty and dull. He turns to the next guard and does the same, each time brandishing an unseen weapon well beyond its prime by the hilt and puts the handle in their bare hand. Reaching Huemic, Daemos hands him the smallest blade in his arsenal, a meager hook.

"Satisfied, Huemic? I'm naked now."

Huemic scans the weapons Daemos relinquished.

"You call that head and these rusty blades wealth?

Pathetic. Guards!" He turns around and walks away. The men follow their captain.

They lead Daemos through the keep's grand doors and up the main stairs.

Silmeir walks the castle halls going about his regular duties. He looks significantly better since he returned to the city. He is cleaned up and well-dressed. His wounds have healed, and he doesn't wear the look of defeat he previously did. He hears the grand clamor of footsteps coming from down the hall. Silmeir peers out from behind the wall. Daemos appears, carrying something very large.

Daemos, Silmeir thinks. *He defeated the wraith…and survived! Is it possible?* After hearing Daemos and the guards reach another level above, Silmeir slinks around the corner and ascends deftly behind.

The guards stop on the fifth level as Daemos had planned. Too high to jump for an escape.

Two sentries stand before a grand wooden doorway. "The lord's prize awaits," Huemic says. They nod to their captain, and both reach for the door. Daemos smirks at Huemic's authority. They pull with all their might as the massive doors slowly unfold.

A noble throne room is revealed.

Huemic leads the way down the ten steps to the main level. Pillars line near the outer walls, creating corridors. Torches are fixed to the pillars. Only a few tapestries and murals, covered by cobwebs and dust, hang on the walls behind.

A large pool shimmers in the center of the floor thirty meters from the entrance. A grandiose marble sculpture of the lord rises from the center. He bears all his limbs and a sinister smile. Light shines directly upon it from a window high above in the entrance wall. *This isn't the original effigy that stood,* Daemos thinks.

The party walks around the pool. At last: Lord Villous. He sits upon his throne. Ten steps lead up to it so he can look down upon everyone else. Two more guards stand at the bottom of the stairs. He is more grotesque than Daemos imagined. He knows pain well. Daemos smiles at the thought.

Silmeir walks up the outside stairwell and passes the sentries. The throne room floor is crafted of fine stone, but the outlining walls are simple wood. He creeps along the outer hall to his favorite hole in the wall, one that he carved. He extinguishes the torch closest to him. Silmeir's spyhole gives him an excellent vantage to see and hear. An escape path is also nearby.

The guards line up next to each other, forming a semi-circle at the foot of the throne steps facing Daemos. He stands ten meters away, distancing himself. The effigy cloaks Daemos in its shadow, a pathetic excuse at displaying power. Perception and command are strong customs in this city.

Before the lord can muster a single word, Daemos tosses the guard's head to him. The lord moves his bladed arm in front of him. The blade pierces the fallen's eye, sliding into the back of the skull. The sound is palpable. The head becomes a pincushion of entertainment. Perhaps the guards will use it for sport later.

The lord studies the severed head and laughs. "You must be Daemos. You are bigger than I imagined. What is this?"

"The answer."

The lord spits phlegm to the floor. He pulls the head to his mouth and bites off a piece of skin from its cheek. A few guards squirm from the sight as their lord chews one of their own. "To what?" he asks, vitriol laced in his words. Daemos fails to be intimidated by the lord's snack.

"To your soldiers who stand in my way. Educate them before you run out."

The lord looks at the head briefly, and then slams it down on the throne's armrest. The pincushion head pops off his blade and bounces on the floor beneath. He spits out the chewed flesh and grits his teeth, groaning as quietly as he can. Anger burns within as Daemos smiles. He enjoys seeing the lord's sentiment divulged so readily.

"The wraith!" the lord bellows. "Man-heads do not impress me, Daemos. I have a room full of them. Did you complete your task, Viscrucian, or can you only kill mans?"

"My reward."

"What do you want?"

"Enough games! State the reward Huemic offered

me! I didn't travel this far to civilization to talk. Do I look like I like to talk?"

"You look like you like to bleed."

"Your headless soldier's body still bleeds in the village."

"A body bag size of coin and jewel. Not your size! That's enough for a lifetime."

Daemos looks at the lord. "That's a start. I also want a room in your most fortified tower. Two women a night, food every day, a death challenge with one of your guards upon my request, and a slave."

"What!?" the lord blurts out, spitting on himself. "No trophy is worth that! How dare you claim such worth, you filthy Viscrucian scar bag!"

Daemos smiles. "That's the minimum of what I'm worth...and I said no more games. Why am I really here? You don't even care about the wraith. You haven't even looked at it."

The lord's lip slowly curls up, and drool escapes. Huemic stands true. The rest of the guards grow restless. Their hands fidget. Sweat permeates. The lord's breathing wheezes out.

"The wraith will be good trophy, but you, Viscrucia man, a better one. Huemic."

"Yes, my lord," Huemic answers.

"Take him to the removal rooms."

"Guard!" Huemic calls out.

The guards brandish their weapons and step forward. A few guards stumble. Daemos quickly sets the bag carrying the wraith down behind him and rips off a portion of it. The first guard charges at Daemos, holding his sword ready to the side. Daemos swipes the bag piece across the water and pitches it at the guard. Surprised, the guard swings at it but misses and gets hit in the chest. The water splashes in his face, and the guard falls clumsily as Daemos parries. He smacks the side of his helmet on the pool edge. Daemos raises his foot and stomps down on the guard's face, breaking his cheekbone and separating his jaw.

Other guards charge while others wobble in place. "Get him!" barks the lord.

Daemos snags the guard's sword and hurls it through the stomach of another. A third guard swings his mace up at Daemos' head. Daemos evades. The guard swings again, but Daemos moves in and catches it by the handle. He opens his other hand and punches his talons into the guard's throat. The guard gurgles blood. Daemos clenches and rips down, shredding his throat.

Daemos takes the mace, spins, and ducks to avoid the oncoming sword of his next attacker. The fourth guard misses but manages to slam it into the third guard's arm, hacking it off. The guard falls to pieces, unable to scream through his open throat. Daemos slams his mace into the fourth guard's spine, paralyzing him. Daemos stands with open arms and spattered in blood, ready for the next wave of attackers.

"Leps!" the lord yells, insulting his failing guards. He slams his fist on his throne and stands. "Huemic! Bleed him! What are you doing?"

One guard vomits. Another drops to his knees and itches himself feverishly. Others move warily forward.

Huemic staggers. He holds out the hooked weapon Daemos gave him and opens his hand. Sweat drips from his nose as his eyes widen. The handle and his hand are covered in a fine black dust. An infection spreads up his wrist. His skin is gray and pale. His veins look black underneath. "My lord, he poisoned us." Huemic looks up at Daemos. Daemos smiles in return.

Silmeir's amazement continues at the sight of the spectacle. The only word he can muster is: "Daemos."

Huemic throws the hook at Daemos but misses badly.

"Bleeding time, Huemic!" Daemos calls out.

"Sentries! Guards! Bring him in pieces!" Huemic orders. The throne room doors open, and the sentries run to their captain's call. Huemic wipes his hands off on his armor, covers them in cloth, and rushes up to the lord. "Lord, we must go. Your guard will cleave him."

The lord swings his bladed hand at Huemic's head, but Huemic manages to grab him by the elbow and stop him.

"Huemic, you fool!"

"For your protection. We must."

The lord spits in Huemic's face. Huemic merely looks back as sweat and spit run down. The lord turns to take his leave. Huemic wipes the spit off his face, and they walk behind the throne to a secret passage and make their escape.

"Tourists!" Daemos yells out. "The removal room? Ha! You only play with pain, Lord Villous." Daemos raises his blood-soaked fist in the air and clenches it. Tracheal pulp squirts and oozes from between his fingers. "I am pain!" He opens his hand and smears the blood across his mouth while licking it off. "The rest of your guard will know!"

"A retreat?" Silmeir questions. "Daemos made the lord retreat from his own throne room?!" Silmeir laughs, but the sound of the soldiers' stomping feet drowns it out as more enter the throne room.

It's time Daemos made his escape. In time the entire chamber could be swarming with the lord's ill-trained guards, too many for him to handle alone. He takes a blade from each of the two closest guards and throws them into the legs of two sentries who just entered.

A guard carrying an ax wipes the vomit from his lips and lumbers toward Daemos. Bile and the black poison remain. He raises the ax but gags. Daemos grabs the weapon and kicks him in the stomach, sending the filthy contents rocketing to the floor.

Daemos grabs the bloody mace with his other hand. He looks at the death prize lying by his side, the most sacred spine ever to be seen. He bites his lip. He wants to hoist it over his shoulder again and take it on his bloody journey as he murders his way out of the castle, but better judgement dissuades him. The clamoring of the foot soldiers outside the castle windows and down in the levels below caution him otherwise.

"Dark God of the Abyss, in time, your rightful resting place will be by my side. But for now, I have more people to kill." Daemos makes his way behind a row of pillars to move among their shadows. He reaches the entrance to the throne room and stands behind the closest pillar.

"He should be in... Oh kes," the first guard says entering the room and seeing the carnage.

"I don't see him," says the second. Daemos grips his weapons tight, ready to swing around for the kill.

"You take that side, I've got this one," the first guard commands. They run forward down the steps and to the sides of the room. Daemos quietly slips out the entrance into the corridor, semi-displeased he didn't collect another pair of kills.

Only a few torches shed light down the stretch of the corridor. Dark and ominous. Whether the lord gave any thought to the look of the castle, or if it naturally took on the anxiety of its workers, is arbitrary. Daemos flies toward a pair of stairwells. Just as he steps toward the left one, a scratchy voice speaks behind him.

"That's not the way you want to go," Silmeir says.

Daemos turns around. Silmeir moves toward Daemos from a distance with his hands raised, indicating that he's not a threat.

"I speak the truth, Daemos. I know of a better way." Daemos lowers his weapons, allowing Silmeir to move closer. A good three meters away, Daemos makes one big step and swings the mace between Silmeir's legs, stopping just at the point where Silmeir's genitals meet the shaft of the mace. Silmeir takes a deep breath and looks behind him. The bloody head of the mace is mere inches away from his ass. "Uhhhh," Silmeir stammers.

"Why should I follow you? I know how to get out of here. One move and you'll never bear children," Daemos warns, lifting Silmeir with his mace.

"There's no time. I'm no fool. I would never get this close to you if I meant you harm." Daemos leans in and peers into Silmeir's eyes. "Please," Silmeir pleads as his balls press into his pelvis.

Please. Daemos squints at Silmeir. He has heard that word before, but he's not entirely sure of its meaning. He lowers Silmeir and removes the mace from between his legs.

Silmeir takes a deep breath and moves past Daemos, descending the right stairwell.

"This way."

Chapter 15

The lord hurls food across the room. Huemic avoids it as best he can.

"How, Huemic?! How this happen? The scar was surrounded!"

"He just killed the wraith, my lord. He's bound to have a few tricks up his sleeve," Huemic explains, raising his bandaged hand as evidence. He tears off the bandage and dunks his hand in a bucket of water and scrubs feverishly.

Two sentries guard the door. The lord walks up to one and grabs him by the arm. "Go out and get every guard to hunt him down, understand!?"

"Yes, my lord," the guard answers.

"Everyone you can find. Even the villagers! Bring him to me. Go!" The guard takes off immediately. "You stay here and guard the door!"

"Yes, my lord," the other sentry answers.

Huemic dries his hands with a cloth. The lord screams again and overturns the table in front of him. "Calm yourself, Lord." Huemic says. "This isn't the end. It's just the beginning. We have other measures."

The lord looks at Huemic and slowly calms down.

"Yes. Finally, you're right about something, Huemic. Now stop wasting time and find him!"

Losing patience, Huemic tosses the cloth to the side and exits the lord's chamber.

Chapter 16

Silmeir leads the descent, ushering Daemos down the steps, across a hall, and into a new stairwell in the back of the castle.

"Where are we going?" Daemos asks as he enters uncharted territory.

"Underneath the castle, there's a way out. We'll avoid most of the guards. Only a few know about it, and no one would dare go this way."

Daemos places the ax in his other hand and grabs Silmeir by the back of his throat. "If no one would go this way, then why are we!?"

"I told you. Less guards. Do you want to fight four or forty? You'll basically go unseen. If anyone can survive, you can."

"What's the danger?"

"The creatures. But we both know you can handle creatures."

"If this doesn't go well, little man, I promise you'll die much sooner and more painfully than me."

"I know the secrets."

"One more surprise, and it'll be your last."

"No more surprises. Now hurry."

The unlikely pair descend to the dungeon. The commotion of troops rings throughout the hallways of the castle. A single guard stands watch over the dungeon. The guard readies his sword. "Guard! It's me, Silmeir. The one the lord is after, I just saw him back that way. Go!" The guard brandishes his sword and moves toward the impending danger.

Something is wrong. The torches are out. Soon, the guard is shrouded in darkness. The subterranean dark stone walls only exacerbate the guard's dilemma. He listens closely. Nothing. He strikes his sword hard against the wall. Sparks fly, shedding some light. He creeps forward making no sound, then stands still.

He hits the wall again. The sparks barely show Daemos a few meters away, throw something shiny before the shadows reset. The guard quickly strikes the wall again to reveal the threat. Just as the sparks shine once more, an ax cleaves into the guard's chin, throat, and collarbone. He falls to his death.

Daemos's loud steps pierce the black hallway. His hand feels the whereabouts of the body, and then dislodges the ax. His footsteps continue.

Silmeir walks first into the dungeon depths, followed by the bloody hulk behind him. Silmeir peers at the condemned. The ones who recognize him back away from the bars. Today is not the day. Perhaps he will disregard past transgressions. Silmeir extinguishes each torch they pass. The prisoners remain silent.

Descending a few more levels of the dungeon and further below, the two reach their destination.

"This is it, the entrance to the exit. The beginning of the end," Silmeir says.

Daemos pushes him to the ground. "You sound like an idiot." Securing his mace to his side, Daemos takes Silmeir's torch from him.

He walks around to study his surroundings. Finding another unlit torch on the wall, he lights it and hands it to Silmeir. The ecology has changed. A stream of water, maybe a meter deep and wide, runs at their feet and leads into a dark tunnel. The dark stone rock of the dungeon is interlaced with softer soil and some vegetation.

"Hello," an odd female voice echoes from down the earthen tunnel. The sloshing sound of legs traversing water makes its way closer. Daemos and Silmeir look at each other. Silmeir sets his torch down and puts his finger to his mouth, signaling Daemos not to speak.

"I can hear. Hello," the vaguely feminine voice calls again. A woman emerges from the darkness. Her clothes are dark and wet. Her skin is pale. Long, dark wet hair hangs off the side of her head while the rest of her face is covered in a dark shroud. Her visible eye finds Daemos and makes contact. She looks soft and frail, but her body is oddly plump underneath her wet clothes. "Why you here. See what I to show," she continues, not making much sense. She moves closer to Daemos. Still holding his ax and torch, Daemos is ready.

"Look…" she says when Silmeir suddenly jumps down from above and smashes her head with a large piece of the black stone.

Her body crumples into the water. Silmeir raises the rock again and crushes her skull once more for good measure. Daemos watches Silmeir's handiwork. He rarely interferes with another's kill. He rather enjoys the sight. He can't be the one doing all the killing, after all. Silmeir jumps out of the water and dries his hands on his shirt.

"This is where you'll escape, but there are many dangers. Follow the water until you're free. They'll never suspect you went this way."

"The dangers. Now," Daemos demands.

"The water: do not drink. The berries and plants: do not eat. The forgotten people like this, and the creatures: kill."

"Simple. Why? What else?"

"The berries and the water turn people into lifeless hosts for the creatures. They lose their bodies, minds, and the creatures break free when they've grown. But that is not the end. The creatures get big, very big. They are slow when they are young, but greater in size and speed when they are adults. Large, usually white, but sometimes different colors. They live in the walls. They are a death sentence. The worst of the prisoners are banished down there and given to those…those things." Silmeir gulps, looking away in thought. Regaining composure, he looks back at Daemos. "You can survive and pass through where the others, already at death's door, have failed. Move fast. Kill quickly."

"That's how I live," Daemos says with a smile. "You're not coming?"

"I don't think I'd survive. But you can. I'll make my way back or hide here until nightfall, depending on where the guards are."

Silmeir moves his hand behind his back. Daemos sees the Viscrucian gesture. He's motioning to a concealed weapon of his own. Silmeir is full of surprises, and now, even honor in Daemos's eyes.

"Viscrucian?"

"Not exactly"

Daemos nods, understanding Sil's message. Silmeir has seen the delights and ventured through the city enough to survive but doesn't pretend to be one of its citizens.

"Your name."

"Silmeir."

"Silmeir. I'm Daemos." Daemos chucks his ax down. The head of the ax sticks into the ground with the handle raised in the air, ready to be wielded again. He unfastens his mace and holds it out for Silmeir to take. "Move fast. Kill quickly." Silmeir takes the mace from Daemos and nods.

Daemos pulls the ax from the ground and raises it along with his torch. Ready for another journey into a dark and unknown dominion, Daemos jumps onto the remains of the woman in the water. Her body bursts with ease underneath the subtle current. Silmeir was right. The woman wasn't really human any longer. She was something else. Daemos treads the water with a smile on his face. This is the first surprise he's enjoyed in quite some time. A new challenge. A new escape. A new enemy.

"Daemos," Silmeir calls out before he disappears into the darkness. "Come back. Kill the lord. He deserves to die."

Daemos looks back. "Death may be too merciful."

He moves steadily down the stream. If what Silmeir said is true, then he doesn't need to worry about a swarm of guards following him, only the unique threat ahead. He thinks about his recent social encounters: Lemas. Cosma. Silmeir. People with information and knowledge about him. People who still breathe. In Viscrucia, they'd be dead, but not here. When Daemos travels outside of the city, he reminds himself that things are different. Not everything is a threat, nor is everyone a liar and a murderer. Silmeir is, Daemos knows, but he likes that part about him. In the outside world he has allies, but very few. Silmeir may be one now. All that depends on if he survives his escape.

The tunnel grows wider. The things have made room down here, no doubt. Condensation occasionally drips from the tunnel ceiling. Algae and some foliage grow along the rock. Daemos sets his torch to it, but the flame doesn't affect the moist algae. The leaves sometimes light for a few seconds, but then die out, doing little to help with visibility. Daemos wades forth. He moves his torch all around with each step to scan his surroundings, looking for the inevitable.

Fifty meters or so in, he finally comes upon a warning. A single berry. Bright, robust, and strikingly beautiful. The blue skin faintly radiates light. Daemos moves closer and lifts it slightly with the blade of his ax. It's luminosity shines across the blood on the blade. Daemos raises his weapon back up, ready to strike.

More and more berries appear: red, green, orange, black, yellow, purple, and so on, different shapes, sizes, and textures. Daemos has entered a vineyard. The berries' subtle fragrance in the air soothes his nasal passages. Their faint glow lights the way. Their beauty is mesmerizing.

Daemos wades over to a patch of green berries. They are perfect. Their texture, flawless. He lifts them with his ax to get a closer look. He has never seen their equal. What could the harm be in having just a handful? He's slain many today. A snack couldn't be more welcome. He smells their delightful aroma when it hits him, his scarred reflection in the congealing blood upon the blade. His stark contrast against the beauty jolts him from his intoxicated trance.

It's a vineyard alright, a vineyard for the damned. Daemos backs away from the wall with some difficulty. The toxic air has even permeated his muscles. Daemos looks down. A large creature rises out of the murky water from between his legs. It's wrapped itself around Daemos's boots without him realizing it. He swings his ax between his legs, slicing a meter-long trench through the creature's amorphous body. Its opaque blood looks like semen and drifts through the water. The creature's scream gargles beneath the water.

Daemos steps quickly and swings frantically through the air and into the water, trying to cut anything in his immediate vicinity. He looks back. The giant gelatinous white blob of a creature lies dead in the water. Daemos checks his surroundings. Nothing else appears to threaten him at the moment.

He sets his torch to a small patch of berries on the wall. They fizzle slightly and pop. The flame dies from their wet juices. Bad idea. Last thing he wants is to be without light or for the juice to shoot into his mouth. Gross. Daemos spits from the thought of it. He's wasting time. He moves faster and regains his focus. *Move fast! Kill quickly!*

A soft voice mumbles in the distance. Daemos stops. "The berries," it says. Daemos smiles. No more lackadaisical, drugged up, Mr. fucking nice guy. If he's fighting monsters, Daemos thrills in becoming one.

"Yes. What about them?" Daemos responds, inviting the forgotten to come out and play.

"They're delicious," a second voice chimes in from behind Daemos, surprising him.

"What's...name?" a third voice asks.

This is getting interesting. A forgotten comes out of the darkness. Not much for conversation, Daemos swings and decapitates it. The semen-like blood cascade's down the body's chest. The head spins on top of the water as one of the white creatures oozes out of the head and into the water. Daemos's eyes widen. He did not expect that.

"Why?" the third voice questions. Daemos turns ready to swing when he finally sees the face of the forgotten, or what's left of it. A gaping chasm, roughly ten centimeters wide, runs down the length of his face to the middle of his chest. The creature dwells pulsating within. It moves its body to flap the tongue that remains on the right half of the face for speech. Most of the forgotten's teeth have fallen out. The surrounding flesh has wilted away. What's left has a consistency closer to porridge than skin. The person that once was is long gone, hence Silmeir's term for them: the *forgotten*.

Daemos's face contorts as he averts his gaze. The sight even offends Daemos. He has never seen a feeding of this kind. He does what any good person would and puts them out of their misery. Seeing the guiding path, he swings down hard through the facial crevice, cutting both the forgotten and creature in half. The infant creature's death cry is odd; somewhat aquatic. The husk of the human makes no final sound.

Daemos hacks through the remaining forgotten. He doesn't give them a chance to attack. Anything could be possible from the creatures that gestate beneath their human husks. Daemos doesn't want to find out. He's outstayed his welcome. It's time to find the light of day.

A berry nearly killed him. Pathetic. Daemos chuckles at the thought. One of the many great lessons to be learned. *Anything* can be a predator.

He moves fast. The berries provide some light, but their numbers are dwindling. Daemos continually checks his surroundings. Periodically he stops to listen, but not for long.

The tunnel opens up to a cave. Its magnitude cannot be conceived due to the sparse amount of light. Daemos trudges through the water, looking for its exit. Gooey bodies lay slumped over in the vast pool. This is a hatching area, and Daemos is not alone.

Water ripples toward him from multiple directions. The cave is so great Daemos can't see his enemies in the distance. He looks back to a large pile of bodies. He walks over and sets them ablaze. Daemos is relieved it worked. Enough of their clothes have dried long enough to ignite. As the fire grows, so does the threat. A dozen forgotten walk toward him like zombies. Their state of dissolve and change varies. A few of them sputter their stupid attempts at speech. A young boy, maybe in his early teens, has even become host to one of the creatures. The lord's cruelty knows no bounds. Some of the forgottens' eyes have sunken back in their heads. Others' bodies have become bloated with their creatures squirming inside them. They close in on Daemos and he chops them down.

The next forgotten tries to speak when its tongue falls out of his head. The creature worked its dying host one too many times. Its body starts to shake. The creature swells inside and rolls its lower extremity up from the forgotten's intestines to its chest cavity. Daemos knows what's coming.

He thrusts the tip of his ax into its shoulder, pushing it into another forgotten. The creature hatches from his host. The face and chest of the forgotten crack open. The creature spills onto the incoming forgotten like a newborn calf, taking it down to the water. The young life is free from its egg, but like most newborns, it lacks strength. It crawls over the body and away from Daemos like a worm.

"Warrior," a newly turned forgotten calls out to Daemos from behind him. Daemos spins around. "Kill us. All of us," its remaining human inside pleads to Daemos. Daemos nods and immediately lops off his head.

He cleaves down his assailants with the same zeal he did before, but his actions don't go unnoticed this time. A large creature in the cracks of the cave wall unleashes its aquatic cry. A rat, the size of a beaver, hears this and scurries along the wall to escape. The creature rolls out and over, absorbing it instantly.

The rat's screams are silenced by its consumer, yet its fear is palpable. The beast slowly pulls it apart. The brown fur and blood expand giving new color to the once white creature. The creature dissolves its prey during their final moments. Billowing out of the wall, the creature reveals it's over four meters in size. Daemos looks up at his formidable foe. Its body surges as it continues its consumption of the rat.

Daemos turns to the forgotten closest to him and hacks through its waist. He drops his torch onto the body of one of the fallen. He picks up the mess of a torso by the back of its shirt and heads into battle with the creature. Using the chest as a human shield, Daemos opens the beast with the first swing.

The rat spews forth into the water below as the creature quickly rolls along the wall to escape. It hisses as it launches a portion of its body at Daemos. Daemos kneels and blocks the oncoming attack with the forgotten's torso. The creature grabs and pulls it away. Daemos slashes again. The creature reels. Its milky blood pours onto the rock and water below. It convulses in pain.

Daemos charges and cuts it in half. It falls from the cave wall into the water. Daemos breathes heavily and checks his surroundings. One forgotten remains, no other creatures in sight. He runs over and lops it in half, lengthwise. Daemos grabs his torch and builds its flame among the pyre of bodies burning.

Seeing where the water exits the cave, he forges ahead. He's survived too much at this point not to make it out alive.

He follows the water through more tunnels, killing creature after creature. Silmeir was right, this place is evil.

Ahead, he sees it, the light at the end of the tunnel. Daemos smiles. He runs forward when, suddenly, he stops. Water drips all around him. He looks up. A massive creature, seven meters in diameter, descends upon Daemos. Its center expands, ready to consume its prey.

"Kes!"

Daemos ducks and holds his ax and torch above him. The creature closes in when tremors shudder through its body. Its slimy exterior blackens from the torch. It screams. Its meal is right there yet it can't feed. The fire bubbles its flesh. Daemos wastes no more time. Holding the torch above, he crawls through the water to his freedom amid the monster's screams.

Chapter 17

Days later, Cosma and Lemas watch the frenzy amongst the village streets. The people have never seen such insolence. Flustered guards runabout. Their demeanor varies now. They don't all possess the bullying arrogance they once did. The action taken by the outsider did not change everyone, though. Others grew worse.

Tar surveys the carnage: the broken bones, the dismembered limbs, and the vast amounts of blood.

"This is heresy," Tar says. "The outsider must suffer to maintain order, Kilsan order." Knowing well his lord's predilection for torture, he can't think of a punishment for fitting.

Tar is a far cry from the rest of his brethren. He's beautiful. Piercing blue eyes compliment his strong jaw line. His golden hair is long and thick. His fingernails and teeth are clean. He even bathed this morning. The flower pedals he uses give him a pleasant smell. He conceals all his scars. He takes great pride in knowing his looks far exceed any of those in Kilsan. His vanity is second to none.

Tar spends days searching for the lord's prize. He

finds the next best thing to Daemos, something he's sure the lord will like. This will be his moment. He can feel it. He fidgets with his hands. He pushes back his cuticles and bites his lip. Now is his time. He walks up to the throne room and tells the sentries that he has vital information the lord must hear at once. Granted access, he makes his way to the lord. He sees Huemic standing next to him.

"What is it, Tar?" Huemic asks.

"I didn't find Daemos, but I have the next best thing. I have the one who helped him escape." Huemic and Lord Villous look at each other. "Please, follow me."

Tar leads them and a few accompanying soldiers down to the dungeons. The dungeons are oddly quiet. In one of the cells, Silmeir lies beaten on the ground. Three guards: Grock, Jommutin, and Beypiscomous, watch over him.

"Silmeir," Villous says, smiling. "Sweet boy. You're in pain again. Without me this time? I don't like that. Tar. Why, Silmeir?"

"Daemos disappeared. The rest of the guard couldn't find any trace of him, but I did. There was some blood in the dungeon halls, and the guards were missing."

"There's always blood in the dungeon halls, kes bag!" argues Silmeir. He spits up blood to further his point.

Huemic looks at Tar. "Every guard was told to search for Daemos, so they left their post. Fool!" He pulls out his sword.

"Wait!" Tar pleads. "I looked further. There was

some water spread all over at the stream below. I think Silmeir or Daemos used it to cover their tracks. Daemos escaped down there."

"Guard! Seize him!" Huemic yells. The guards who came with Huemic and the lord grab Tar immediately. Tar's three guards reach for their weapons. Huemic immediately raises his sword to Jommutin's throat. "Stand down, or you'll live your remaining days down here!" The captors stand down.

"No! That's not all! Look, look!" Tar says, pointing to another cell.

Huemic and the lord walk over to the other cells. The prisoners hang, strung up. One has been skinned alive; the others had their throats slit. No survivors. The lord smiles with delight. "Yes?"

"They didn't talk at first, but I made them. I knew they would. One of them mentioned a man, someone like Silmeir, helped Daemos to the water below. Daemos must've escaped or died down there. I heard Silmeir knows the water. Most don't. My lord! They told me. I skinned them, and they told me!" He smiles and twiddles his fingers.

The lord looks over Silmeir and Tar. He slowly cuts Tar's side below his ribs with his bladed arm. Tar cries in pain. "Did you like? You like skinning those men?" the lord questions.

Tar gasps from the pain. His heart races. "Yes, Lord. Yes. They are prison kes! Their lives don't matter. I liked skinning them, giving them what they deserve. I can help you, Lord." Tar clutches his fresh wound.

"Maybe you can. I like what you done here. Good torture. Give me more."

"Yes, Lord Villous. With pleasure."

"Take your men. Find Daemos for me. Our special someone can help you. Hurt him plenty, but not too much! You hear, Tar? No limb removal!"

"Yes, Lord."

"Then bring him back so I can hurt him more. If you not, I skin you and *worse!*"

"Yes, Lord!"

"What should we do with him?" Huemic asks, motioning to Silmeir. "Do you even need him anymore?"

"No. I don't," says Lord Villous.

Huemic smiles. "I have an idea."

Silmeir screams, seeing his fate. Huemic holds a bowl of the luminescent berries and a cohort carries a jug of the stream water. Tar forces Silmeir's mouth open.

"It looks like this will be the last time, Sil," the lord says.

"I know you're hungry," Huemic says.

"Time to feed!" Tar adds.

Huemic drops the berries into Silmeir's mouth. Tar and Lord Villous pour the water into Sil's mouth to help wash it down.

Huemic, Tar, and his goons continue the ritual for days until they are fully satisfied the change has taken place. They drag him down to the underground stream and into the tunnel. Beaten and barely conscious, they leave Silmeir to the forgotten.

Chapter 18

The sun shines brightly through the clear sky. The slight breeze feels good against Daemos's skin. Being a few days ride away from the castle now, he takes his time.

Upon escaping the cave in the lair of the creatures and the forgotten, Daemos retrieved the weapons he hid outside of the castle. He bartered a few of them for a horse and rode fast.

Daemos has not seen a soldier since the last one he killed in the dungeon. He escaped and feels content about his latest mission. He will revisit the lord someday to rip out his spinal cord as he did the wraith's, since that's what the lord took from him but, for now, there is nothing to be done.

Daemos embarrassed the lord at every turn. He killed his men in Viscrucia and the lord's own land. Only by his own accord did he agree to the lord's challenge and walk into his own house. Daemos slaughtered his guards, threw one of their heads at him, and showed the villagers their disgusting lord is not as powerful as they feared. He also survived the insidious creatures and learned a new way into the castle.

Yes, Daemos is content. He travels to different villages. He eats good food and sleeps well in the inns. People are polite. Daemos responds in kind by not hurting anyone. He has traveled to many lands. Although it can be difficult, he knows how to adjust to the different people's social customs. His body is healthy. There is no sign of the lord's soldiers, no threat of danger. Perhaps that is what Daemos needs again, or at least the view. The Death Pit could be just the entertainment he needs.

Over two weeks pass before Daemos arrives back in Viscrucia. The sight excites him. He's missed his home. He smells its lingering death from a thousand meters out. He is armed and ready. His weapons, some newly acquired, are cleaned and polished. It's been awhile since Daemos has killed anyone, too long. He misses the thrill, especially from worthy foes, from *family*.

This homecoming is different. He returns not from mending the usual wounds of Viscrucian play but with more esteem than ever. He is the wraith killer. He shamed an entire kingdom. He survived the tribulations of another new species. The name *Daemos* spreads across the lands.

The citizens who recognize him show him the sign. He returns it in kind. He seeks out Petrid, Boils Bogilocus, chef Aemeggur, and others to share recent adventures and kills. Daemos relishes their tales. He enjoys seeing Petrid's new art, tasting Aemeggur's cuisine, and hearing of Boils' latest kills as pus leaks. Daemos is home.

Daemos visits the Death Pit as he promised himself. People give him space, not wanting to unleash his nasty side. He savors a piquant blood tear wine as the spectacle of death shines before him. One warrior even dedicates his upcoming deathmatch to Daemos. He wins gloriously. Honored by the killer's gesture, Daemos donates his winnings to him.

Daemos's homecoming couldn't be any better. He grabs his bottle of wine only to find it empty. That's when he hears the uncoiling of a weapon. He knows its unique signature well. He turns his head to find its raven-haired owner standing with a fresh bottle of blood tear wine. Faelin smiles. Wasting no time, Daemos stands up and walks over to her. She secures her whip to her leg and holds a blade instead.

"A citizen of your ferocity makes no mistake in arming herself at all times in a place like this," Daemos says, pouring on the compliments.

"A killer of such sizable stature has apparently earned some respect among those who have none," Faelin says. She playfully scratches her nails across Daemos's arm. "Join me?"

Daemos checks his surroundings: the bottle doesn't appear to be tainted, the light scratch from her nails feels fine, the patrons are not eyeing him preparing for a kill, no oncoming commotion, or threatening sounds nearby. She grabs the wine and moves toward Daemos's table. Daemos grabs her forearm and pulls her in close. "Follow me."

They walk through the dark streets. Within a minute

they've already picked up a pair of stalkers. It's bound to happen. No night can go that well in Viscrucia. Alas, Daemos sees an opportunity before him. Boils Bogilocus leans against a wall a few meters beyond an alleyway entrance. Daemos reaches into his coat.

"Boils, hungry for a fine blade and a pair of kills?"

"Always."

Daemos smiles. He pulls out the jeweled machete he took from Uglicerous and stabs it into the wall before ducking into the alleyway. Ornamental jewels shine from the polished femur handle. "My gift, citizen. Happy slaughtering."

The two men following the couple gain speed as they see Daemos and Faelin escape into the alley. The bulky armor the men tried to conceal within their cloaks only slows them down. Boils' eyes light up at the sight of the killing instrument. "Try and have as much fun as I will," Boils says as he moves toward the blade and grabs it. Daemos leads Faelin down another alley as he hears the dance begin between weapons and flesh. "Fucking soldiers! Not even tourists. I'm going to enjoy this."

Boils' call out of the soldiers; clearly sent on a mission, perks every killers' ears up within the vicinity. This carries with it several factors. It grants an audience. Everyone wants to see soldiers die. And if by some miracle they prevail, that audience will finish the job. Plus, they'll be well equipped with armor, weapons, and possibly forms of outsider currency, so their bounty will be great; great for Boils that is.

Daemos extinguishes any torches nearby as he maneuvers through his city. Reaching his chosen destination deep in a back alley, he stops and checks his surroundings for any followers or violent vagrants. After a few seconds of satisfied silence, he opens a hidden entrance and enters. Faelin follows as Daemos checks inside.

Daemos closes the entrance and grabs a flint lying in a niche next to the door when he hears Faelin's footsteps rushing up behind him. He ducks and parries as Faelin claws through the darkness. This bitch really likes to scratch. That's fine, he has claws of his own.

She swings again, but Daemos evades it with ease this time separating himself among the shadows. Daemos throws the flint against a stone in the wall. Sparks drops onto a pre-oiled torch just below, igniting it and lighting the room. The sudden light catches Faelin off guard. Daemos swings down. His fingernails tear her shirt in half, and her breasts jump out. Faelin tries to reach for a blade, but Daemos sweeps in and grabs both her hands. He moves them behind her back. She struggles as Daemos grabs the bottle of wine lying next to them and pops off the top.

"I see I made an impression," Daemos says. He puts the bottle to her lips and pours wine into her mouth. She closes her eyes and drinks it, spilling some down her body. Daemos moves his head down and licks the wine up from her chest to her lips. She purrs from the sensation. He takes a swig from the bottle.

"You have no idea," Faelin responds. "My body has

ached for yours. Now it's my turn. You'll never forget this night."

"Show me your worst."

Their sex is wild and sweaty.

Daemos wakes up groggily and looks around with blurry vision. Faelin sits fully dressed in the corner. Daemos moves to the entrance and opens it slightly to get an idea of what time of day or night it is. He opens the door and slowly sticks his head out. The moonlight shines down upon him. This pleases Daemos. He wasn't out too long. But what happened? Why did he fall asleep? He didn't intend on that happening.

Suddenly, the moonlight disappears. Daemos looks up. A man jumps down from the top of the building and hits Daemos on the head with a piece of wood, knocking him unconscious. The man drops the wood and fumbles with his thumbs.

"Found you," he says. He looks inside the hideout at Faelin. Faelin blows him a kiss.

Chapter 19

Daemos wakes up. He lays nearly naked, bound, and gagged on a table in the middle of some basement. Six wooden beams hold up the ceiling. The floor is made of slate. No sunlight shines in from the walls or ceiling above. With no apparent holes for ventilation, sound will not travel far. It's the perfect abattoir. There is no mistake about it. Daemos knows what's coming. Otherwise, he would already be dead.

He tests the knots of the ropes that bind him. No luck. There's even more rope than necessary. His captors are well aware of his strength. The rope holding his hips down barely conceals his genitals. The table that holds him is sturdy.

Another table against the wall holds an array of weapons ready to dish out just about any form of sadistic punishment desired. Hooks, blades, hammers, cleavers, saws, and jars full of insects and various concoctions, sit at their disposal.

"He's awake," Tar says, standing at the head of the table. He bites his lip, eager for what is about to come. Six other guards accompany him: Grock, Jommutin, Beypiscomous, and three others, Nays Sim, Pall, and

Espinkin, hand-selected by Huemic, of course. Daemos scans his crowd. From the looks of them, they've done their fair share of killing. The most skilled of all of them, Faelin, walks in from the shadows to the foot of the table.

"We got you, in your own home of all places. I knew it would work," she boasts. She raises her hand and spreads her fingers. A faintly tanned powder sticks to the inside of her fingernails. "This isn't like the black powder you used at the castle. It works slower. Puts you to sleep like a charm."

She places her hand on a dark jar signifying they have plenty more of the sedative. Daemos stares back at her. He merely takes in the information she presents him.

"You know what's coming, Daemos. Your agony will be legendary. It will call out to the Suffering itself. But this isn't the end. It's just the beginning. After days of torture, Tar and his men will take you back to the castle; my father's castle. There, Lord Villous will take his time in making you suffer. No one knows how to inflict more pain on the human body than him. Not even you. Eventually, your bones will be on display above his throne as a warning to all the lands, that he is the most powerful lord and conqueror of all."

Daemos glares at Faelin and bites his tongue. He feels personally challenged and insulted by the bitch's claim that the drooling Lord Villous knows how to inflict more pain than him. No one knows how to deliver pain better than a Viscrucian. It's how wine is made.

"My father remembers you. He remembers the pain you cut into him."

Daemos can't help but laugh inside. He has no clue what in Suffering she's talking about. This should be entertaining.

"You cut off his arm. You cut off his foot. You left him to die out in the desert years ago when I was a child."

Daemos remembers. The story brings a fond memory back to Daemos. He wasn't even in his teens back then.

"He survived, as lords do. But when he came back, he was filled with more hate than ever. He went mad. Many died because of it. Too many, including my mother. My father killed his own wife out of madness."

She moves around to the side of the table and pulls out a serrated knife. *Fuck,* Daemos thinks. It's time.

"I'm here to pay it back. And let Lord Villous cut your name from this land forever!" Faelin puts her blade to Daemos's skin and slowly pulls it along his body, raking his flesh. She intermittently spins it, cutting into him. "Grock, Jommutin!" The two walk over. "His hand," she says. The men punch down onto Daemos's hand and wrist to soften him up and finally get his hand outstretched.

Here it comes, Daemos thinks. Faelin saws into the base of his ring finger. Daemos jerks violently from the pain. In five seconds, Faelin frees Daemos of his phalange. Dark, nearly black, blood spurts onto the table. Grock and Jommutin look puzzled. Daemos breathes heavily underneath his gag.

"I'll keep this as a souvenir," Faelin says. "Until I see you back at the castle. Remember, don't kill him! No limb removal. And, Tar, my father warned specifically not to harm his genitals. He wants the pleasure of removing them himself."

She dries the dark blood from Daemos's severed finger. She kisses it, winks at Daemos, and puts in a small pouch she carries. Daemos isn't surprised by her choice. He gave her a lot of pleasure with that finger. She responded in kind then, too. Of course, now, Daemos wishes it were still attached so he could gouge her eyes out with it. A fleeting thought that only slightly helps cope with the pain.

Faelin walks over to Tar and kisses him passionately. She bites on his lip as she pulls away, foreplay Tar undoubtedly loves. She walks up some stairs and leaves. The fact that Faelin is with Tar, at least from time to time, does not surprise Daemos in the least.

Daemos was careful. He kept his eyes peeled, evaluated the situation every time, and disarmed her appropriately. That new sedative drug, though, was unknown to Daemos. He never had need for something to put someone to sleep. What was the fun in that? He wanted his victims to know who their deaths were coming from and how, right then and there. There's no point in subtlety.

It's time for the others to join in on the fun. Tar looks over the roadmap of scars that is Daemos's body. "We might be too late," Tar jests. The others laugh more than necessary. Beypiscomous drinks heavily from a jug and passes it around. "Don't worry, Daemos. I have plenty of fun ideas. You won't miss a thing."

The torture begins.

The destruction of Daemos's body lasted four days. He experienced a living hell the likes of which no one ever had before, nor after. His finger was merely the start. With six men, their cruelty varied. He was beaten. Fingers and toes were broken and severed. A shoulder was dislocated. Toenails and some of Daemos's precious fingernails were ripped out. He was pierced dozens of times with sliver-like pins and stabbed with knives numerous times for good measure.

Chunks of flesh were randomly carved out. They burned him, as well. The searing of his flesh was often a necessity to keep Daemos from bleeding to death. If the men failed to deliver the lord his prize, their outcome would surely equal that of Daemos's. For this, they made sure to give him water to keep him somewhat functional.

Blood was everywhere. The chopping spat it on the walls and wooden support beams. It caked and congealed on the tables. None of the original wood was visible. The cutting filled the floor with it. The floor became a swamp of murky, near-black crimson. Often, the tormentors stumbled, trying to move through his sludge of suffering. The men, not planning enough ahead, didn't bring aprons and were covered with blood.

The few rags they brought were already black and hardening. Flies buzz in droves. Bloodsucking insects burrowed in through the walls. The holes they made let in sporadic beams of light where the walls met the ceiling. The air was thick and sickening.

Tar was the ringleader, of course. His sadism led the charge. He was like a tourist in a flesh peddler's weapon shop, giddy as can be. He paced the feats he put Daemos through, to elongate the punishment his body would allow. Beating, cutting, breaking, carving, and burning was often the system of torment used. However, the skinning was the worst.

Tar pulls out a long skinning knife, smiling ear to ear.

"Tar, you mustn't!" Pall objects.

Glaring at Pall, his head and hands twitch. "You dare interrupt me!"

"You'll doom us all! You were supposed to hurt Daemos. You've done way worse! Any more damage and the lord will be jealous you took that away from him!"

"Agreed," Espinkin says.

"Have you seen what Villous is truly capable of?" Pall questions. "Have you ever seen him at his worst?"

Tar looks around.

"I have. Not his usual killings and torture in the dungeons, what he does in his private chambers. He feeds on his victims while they're still alive! Sometimes cooking them, sometimes biting their flesh right off their bones! Other times he'll bring in their loved ones and feed on them. Those are the screams that haunt the villagers at night."

Beypiscomous grimaces and covers his mouth.

"That will not be my fate!" Pall takes a deep breath and raises his hands. "You've had your fun. We need to fulfill our duty. We captured and tortured him. Let's head back to Kilsan. We risk our lives every moment longer that we stay. Come on. Let's not suffer the wrath of Villous."

Tar seethes. He looks over his companions. His men shrug their shoulders. Huemic's soldiers nod their heads.

Tar steps away from his torture slab and breathes deeply.

"Pall...Pall, you're right." He says and strolls toward the man. "We do not want to finish the lord's prize possession."

Pall sighs and loosens his shoulders. Tar extends his hand. Pall reaches out to shake it when Tar buries a knife in his lung with his other hand. Pall gasps for air. Tar removes the blade and continues stabbing him. Pall slumps down into the blood beneath him.

"I'm in charge here! I say when we're done!"

Espinkin shakes his head and turns away.

"We're not going anywhere."

Skinning was Tar's personal touch. It fit perfectly. His vanity was the only thing stronger than the pleasure he derived from removing the skin from others. His direction was sound. He jumped throughout the body to disperse the agony and inflict maximum pain. He skinned the top of one foot, and then would filet the opposite calf. Pieces of his chest, stomach, and back were carved up like a turkey. The worst and what took the longest was the removal of Daemos's face. Half of it, anyway. The cuts were shaky, and a little back and forth as Daemos writhed in pain. His lips were cut in half, vertically, along with the rest of his face. His nose was bisected. Moving up, the men peeled back Daemos's scalp from the top to the back of his head with their fingertips.

The torture took its toll on everyone. Every man, including Tar, threw up at some point. The sounds, the sights, the thick, sticky pool of blood they waded through on the floor or the smell of open and charred flesh. At some point, the men's senses revolted the contents of their stomachs. They consumed massive quantities of alcohol to sustain the sadistic pace Tar set. They ate little. After all, who could eat as they choked from the ostensible stench of suffering in that human slaughterhouse?

The pace slowed by the fourth day. Even Tar knew there had to be some of Daemos left for them to take back to the lord after all. This concerned Tar's fellow butchers. No one wanted to be on the lord's bad side.

The thought of leaving continued to eat at Tar. This was his moment. He was having such fun. The wreckage of Daemos would prove to Lord Villous the power of his will and his commitment! Tar was mad. The inhuman escalation took hold of him and brought him to new heights. It was his turn to kill the unkillable! He needed something more. This gave him his latest idea on how to leave his final mark.

Daemos laid there, the embodiment of pain. He didn't know how long it had been at this point. He couldn't believe he was still alive. Perhaps, he wasn't. Perhaps, the transition to the Suffering is seamless, and he didn't even know he'd already arrived. Tar moved above and opened one of Daemos's eyes.

"Daemos. I can tell by your breathing that you're still with us." Tar says unable to keep still. He quickly rubs his fingers together. "This means a lot to me. We're going to take you to the castle soon so the lord can personally have his fun with you. I have to say these are the best days of my life. I wanted to let you know I am personally the cause of this. I found Silmeir. I tortured the prisoners beneath the castle, and I led him to his end, which is almost as bad as yours." Tar runs his fingers through his golden locks.

Daemos's eye opens partly. "Silmeir. What did you do to him?" he asks.

Tar can't hold back his smile. He answers. "I discovered some of the secrets beneath and threw him into the trench you escaped from. He's one of the forgotten now." This awakens Daemos more. "Now that you see me clearly, remember me, and remember this face!" Tar immediately stabs Daemos in the eye. Daemos screams horribly. Tar scrambles the knife around, and then removes it. Tar opens Daemos's other tightly clenched eyelid suffering from the pain. He jabs a spoon beneath his other eye and pops it out. Daemos's screams continue.

Nays Sim wretches again in the corner. Beypiscomous and Espinkin pass a bottle of alcohol between them to dull the sight of the anguish that permeates their senses. Daemos's screams die down. He breathes heavily, managing to stay alive. Tar is satisfied.

"We're doomed," Nays Sim says, shaking his head in his hands.

A door opens above. Esim, an immense Viscrucian man riddled with scars, walks down the stairs holding a sack in his only hand. Grock stuffs severed pieces of Daemos into a bag.

"What happened?" Esim asks. He looks at Daemos's mangled body. "I see," he says. Grock and Esim exchange bags. Esim provides them with food in exchange for the blood money for rent.

"Any changes out there?" Tar asks.

"Still good. No one is gathering. No one knows. There's been talk, though."

"Talk doesn't scare me. We're almost done here."

"Fine. I'm heading back for some skin games."

Beypiscomous looks at Esim's missing hand and motions to Espinkin. "You sure? Looks like you've played enough." He and Espinkin laugh. Esim drops his bag of flesh and swings a blade between Bey's legs. Beypiscomous immediately stops laughing.

"Let's play roll the cubes, instead," Esim responds. "Since none of you have cubes, we'll use your balls instead!"

"Apologies, Esim! Apologies!" Beypiscomous quickly responds.

"Apologies, our Viscrucian friend," Tar intervenes. "Beypiscomous sometimes forgets where he is upon having too much drink. Grock, Jommutin, go with him. Grab supplies for our journey back."

Grock nods.

As Esim removes the blade, he makes a slight cut in Beypiscomous' inner thigh. Bey reels back. Esim grabs his flesh bag and ascends the stairs as Grock and Jommutin follow. Tar and the others have a drink as Daemos passes out.

Over an hour later, Grock and Jommutin return with supplies, inebriated. Tar, Espinkin, and Beypiscomous play cards at a side table. The two rush down the steps, jabbering to each other. They drip sweat and blood. Daemos's body twitches.

"Did you get everything? We head out in the morning," says Tar.

Grock and Jommutin drop their bags. "Yeah, we got everything," Grock answers, out of breath. "Guys, you gotta try this game!"

"Yeah, the Skin Game Esim talked about!" Jommutin adds. "We watched him play it. Bloody good!"

"*Skin Game,*" a dark voice says to Daemos. Daemos's body twitches again.

Grock pulls out some cups with colored cubes inside from his pocket. He and Jommutin sit down at the table. Grock explains the rules of the game. Jommutin pulls out his knife and stabs it into the table. The basics were simple. One can wager whatever they want, typically a location on the body and the size of the cut. Whoever has the lower score must cut into their skin the wagered amount, hence the name: Skin Game.

Failure to cut the agreed upon amount results in his opponent finishing the job. Usually, they don't take too kindly to this. The simplicity of the game is often the appeal to people of similar nature. This also allows for the game to go on for hours varying on the crowd.

Tar smiles. This is his type of sadism. Only his vanity competes. He would never wager his face. Should he lose, the cost would be too high. However, small cuts to parts of his body he can conceal could be worth the risk.

Grock and Jommutin demonstrate. Cursing and cheers erupt, followed by blood. Daemos's body twitches, unknown to the players of chance. It doesn't take long before everyone is drunk and wild with bloodlust; it never does. The Skin Game escalates at a fever pitch. Its climax is always an event.

Over two hours pass, and the once clean table resembles the coagulated slab that confines Daemos.

"All right, enough!" Tar says, slurring his words as he pulls back from a fresh slice. "Bandage up, you fucks! Then get some sleep. Long journey the next few days."

The men compare wounds before poorly trying to bandage them. Blood spills everywhere as they stumble back and forth, adding to the thick pool beneath them. Most of them take an extra drink to dull the pain as they lay in their cots. The sound of their blood dripping lolls them all to sleep.

Chapter 20

Huemic sharpens his sword with a whetstone inside his castle chamber. Polished blades, shields, and armor adorn the walls. Huemic counts the strokes. He is meticulous. He cleans up, puts his tools away, and dries the blade with a cloth. The weapon gleams in the sunlight shining through the tower window.

He hears footsteps coming down the hall. Based on their sound, he has a good idea who it is. His chamber door opens, and Faelin walks in. "Huemic," she calls. Huemic keeps his focus on the sword. He blows off any dust that might remain.

"I see your Viscrucian manners cling to you like the stench of that kes hole," Huemic says.

"Still bloated with your failures of Daemos escaping?" Faelin responds. "How much longer do you think you will hold this rank before my father throws you down in the dungeons?"

Huemic stands up with his chest out and secures his sword in its scabbard. "I was born here, Faelin," he asserts. "Raised here. I've protected Lord Villous longer and better than anyone. I've dealt with your hollow offenses year after year. No one threatens my position. Who else would do it? You? You two can barely be in the same room together. I keep his soldiers in line. *I* keep your father in power. If not for me, the people could break his doors down and feed him to the dogs in the village square. Is this all you came to do? Waste my time and patience, like usual?"

Faelin walks up to Huemic. "I'm here to tell you...that I got him." Huemic looks into her eyes. She pulls out a damp cloth and unravels it, revealing Daemos's bloody finger. Huemic looks at it, and then to Faelin. "I told you that you failed. I didn't. I got him in Viscrucia. Tar and his men will bring him here in a day's time."

Huemic has trouble believing the severance in front of him. "If you actually caught him, why did you leave him with Tar?"

"I can't carry him out myself, fool. And you know well what happens when a group of soldiers walk side by side in that place. They're going to soften him up and then bring him back so my father can have his own fun with him." Faelin walks to the door. "I'm going to his lordship now," she says, just before exiting through the door.

Huemic closes his door and catches up to her as she walks through the castle halls. "You want to be there when he hears the news, do you?" Faelin says, with her hubris flowing.

"Congratulations, Faelin. That is, if Tar doesn't die first. I bet he doesn't even make it out of Viscrucia. Then what will you tell his lordship?"

"Daemos was bound and bloodied when I left him. Tar and his men are savages. They got into Viscrucia just fine, and they will kill any fool in their path who tries to stop them."

"They're not dealing with fools, Faelin. They're facing Viscrucians. *They* are savages. Your pet, Tar, has never tasted the rotten fruit of that place. Never choked on the death hanging in the air."

"I have been there. *I* have killed there! It was my ways that captured Daemos!"

"You're not the only one to have killed there and survived, Faelin. Don't forget that."

Faelin and Huemic reach the two sentries standing guard before the throne room. Faelin nods to them and smiles. "It's my father you need to worry about, Huemic." The guards open the grand doors.

The opening of the doors echoes through the hall. Faelin and Huemic walk down the staircase to the grand hall. As they reach the fountain, they walk around it on opposing sides. The lord looks at the two of them while he touches the tip of his golden dagger appendage.

"What news you bring?" the lord belches out before anyone else can say a word.

"I have done it, your lordship," Faelin says, lifting her chin confidently.

"What have done this time?"

"What you have always wanted. Your daughter, Faelin, has captured Daemos, the scourge of Kilsan. Tar and his men have him and will bring him here in a day's time. This is my gift."

The lord stares at her. "Huemic. This true? You help her? Why do you not bring him to me now!?" It only takes seconds for the lord to lose his curt patience. Huemic knows this unbecoming trait better than anyone that remains.

"My lord, Faelin says it to be. I was not with her. Tar will bring her here."

"I hope so, for her sake."

Faelin clutches Daemos's finger tightly with contempt and conceals it behind her back. "Father, Daemos will be here—"

"I heard you'd said," the lord cuts her off with his broken speech. Huemic walks forward to the foot of the lord's throne and turns to face Faelin.

"Thank you, Faelin," Huemic says. "We look forward to Daemos's arrival. Let his lordship, and I, know when he arrives."

Faelin looks to both of them. They say nothing further. She turns around and stomps away. Reaching the doors, she looks over her shoulder. Huemic and the lord smirk at each other. Faelin slams the throne doors shut behind her.

Chapter 21

Ominous clouds swarm above Viscrucia in the early hours of the fifth day. Thunder rumbles. Lighting strikes in the distance. The winds pick up, kicking dust and sand off the streets. The Viscrucians look around. They know a heavy storm is coming.

"Listen," the dark voice calls again to Daemos. This nudges Daemos from his slumber. He awakens to the pain that embodies his life. Did he hear something? Was that a voice? The dripping sound becomes clearer. He can hear it all around him.

It drips on his own blood beneath Grock. It seeps through Espinkin's bandages. Beypiscomous's cot dampens from it. Blood trickles down Nays Sim's flank. It sticks to Tar's hands. Daemos can see the bright crimson shine through the black void.

"See," the dark voice calls. Daemos's body jerks. He definitely heard the voice that time, but it did not come from the room. It came from within. He opens his eyelids as he used to. Stinging air fills his open eye sockets. He shuts his eyelids immediately and squints. Old habit.

That bastard took out his eyes. No sense in trying to use what he doesn't have. He now must live what's left of his short life in darkness. He cannot see...yet he can. Daemos tries to relax and concentrate. The pulsing red slowly comes back into focus. He sees the fresh, uncoagulated blood. It calls to him; the rivulets of crimson radiate through the darkness like a moving spider web.

Daemos cannot believe it. How is this possible? What is happening? Daemos breathes. He calms himself amid the pain and thinks. Flashes of his torture run through his mind: the severing, the skinning, his eye removal, and so on. He thinks back further: the creatures, the berries, the lord, Faelin, his healing from his battle with the wraith...the wraith!

"Yes, Daemos," the dark voice returns. Daemos moves his arm that the wraith wounded. His tormentors had trouble cutting through the unusually tough skin with the black scar, so they moved on and skinned his other arm, instead. That black scar. His sickness. His dark new blood. Daemos thinks back to his battle with the wraith. Yes! The blood!

Daemos covered himself in his captured prey's blood before he ventured down into the Abyss. It was his war paint. He went unseen by the wraith until he was wounded. The old, coagulated blood camouflaged him. It was not until he was wounded that the wraith sensed him. It saw his fresh blood. That is what Daemos sees now: the blood vision of the wraith. A vision of life, yet death. The vision of the dark ones. It is a gift.

"Lord," Daemos speaks within, calling to the wraith with the utmost respect.

"Daemos," the wraith answers. *"Go forth. Kill. Exact your vengeance!"*

The first smile in days crawls across the half of Daemos's lips that remain. The wraith is right. Now is Daemos's chance. Daemos moves his left hand. They skinned part of it. The rope tied around that wrist is weaker than when they started. Daemos has struggled against it for days now. It's damp with blood. Yes, the blood will help Daemos, his blood.

He twists and turns his wrist and hand against his bindings. The grating brings fresh blood to lubricate the rope. With a finger severed and having lost skin on his wrist and the outside of his hand, Daemos's hand is more pliable and smaller than it once was. He wrenches against the ropes. He's never been so happy to sense his blood or feel pain.

Daemos frees his hand and breathes deeply. He works at the rope tied around his other hand. His dripping blood helps him see more clearly what he's working against. After freeing his other hand, he proceeds to remove the rest of the rope holding him down.

At last, Daemos has liberated himself from his blood-caked bindings. He tries to sit up, but the pain sends a shockwave through his body, preventing it. He has not moved in days. Aside from muscle and skin being removed, the simple act of them not moving suddenly takes its toll. Daemos catches his breath and forces himself to sit up, facing the pain. He stretches his body as much as he can. The simple movement brings forth more blood and more sight.

Daemos has embraced pain before, better than most, but this is different. He opens his eyeless eyelids and looks at the blood he sheds. He smiles. He has experienced such anguish and suffering that he now realizes it's a part of him. It has changed him. He sees it in his mangled new body. He is not the Daemos he used to be. He is a disfigured husk of his former self. His pain is immeasurable, and now, he kind of likes it. He jerks his arms, scattering his blood. It sticks to his surroundings, revealing them to Daemos. Yes, he does enjoy the pain.

The ground cracks in and outside of Viscrucia. The fissures widen. Rancid odors leak from below. Ominous sounds stir from within. Most people within hearing distance run. The storm begins. Rain falls upon the city of the damned.

Now, the real healing begins. Daemos moves over to the table with the containers. He feels around for the jar containing the drug Faelin used on him. Going off his memory, he thinks he's found it. He smells it. Nothing. This should be it. He marks it with his blood. He checks the other containers to be sure. The sound of maggots squirm in one, the subtle smell of black peppers in another, and so on. He finds the jar he wants.

Daemos grabs a knife nearby and uses it to pick up

the sedative. He places the drug just under the sleeping men's noses so that it's inhaled quickly, and then on their wounds, so it absorbs into their bloodstream. The sedative, mixed with sleep, alcohol, and blood loss, should be all he needs. He needs uninterrupted time, time for retribution, time for vengeance, time for pain.

He walks to another table and finds a pitcher of water and drinks it as fast as he can. Next, he finds the bag of food Esim brought and devours a sizable portion. The food and water help immensely. He needs nourishment and sustenance. He hasn't eaten in days.

Daemos selects Grock first due to his thunderous snoring. The others follow in time. He ties them all up to the six wooden support beams. He binds them at the ankles, waist, chest, and neck, with their hands tied behind the pillars. With the stage set, Daemos drinks more water and eats more food. Moving the dead weight of those idiots around is exhausting in his current state. Having rested a more and regained a little strength, Daemos is ready.

One by one, he pounds stakes through their wrists and into the support beams. The pain and screaming jolt them from their slumber.

Tar gasps for air and as his head whips about.

"Oh god, oh god, oh god!" Grock wails.

"Tar! What did you do?" Jommutin questions.

"My hands! My hands," Nays Sim exclaims. "I can't move!"

"No! Daemos, no! This can't be!" Tar shrieks.

Daemos impales their ankles next. The fresh blood

spreads across the thick muck of his own and brightens the room. The men scream. Daemos sits calmly at his torture table.

"This is nothing compared to my suffering," Daemos reminds them. "You fools have no idea what is about to come."

Tar shakes his head back and forth.

The screams of the six unleash the dead beneath the land. Skeletons and mangled corpses burst from the cracked earth. Demons and other entities possess their bodies. The first person they can get their hands on they kill. Upon their initial kill, their rib cages crack open and spread out into wings. The demons scream. Somehow, they feel pain in their possessed transformations. Their outlying flesh stretches and bleeds. The skeletons rip the skins from their victims and slap it across their extended ribs to create their own fleshy dactylo patagium for their wings. Some spectators stare in awe. The sights would melt the sanity of bystanders anywhere else in the world.

After thirty seconds of screaming, Daemos cannot take it anymore. He cuts out all their tongues. Although this will not silence them, it will quiet them. He has no need for any of their words or pathetic attempts at begging. He wants them to gag on their blood as they endure their violent demise. Next are their eyelids. They should experience the sight of their horror. Daemos knows he could very well drop dead at any moment.

He grabs a hammer, pliers, a small skinning knife,

nails, and a handful of long pins and sets them on his center torture table. Taking the hammer, pliers, and skinning knife, he walks over to Tar and stabs the skinning knife in his ass. He cups his hand beneath the wound to collect the blood, and then smears it across Tar's face. He stands in front of Tar so he can see him.

Daemos wears no expression. He calmly sees the man who ruined his life through his blood vision. The expression on Tar's face is the opposite. Terror consumes it. Being no surprise to Daemos, he simply stares back with his same serenity.

Moving around Tar, Daemos cracks him in the hands with the hammer. Once they are sufficiently broken, he takes Tar's finger and rips most of their nails out with the pliers. Daemos, then rips the skinning knife from Tar's ass and slices off the remaining fingernails. He kneels and alternates between smashing Tar's toes to a pulp with the hammer and cutting them off with the knife.

Daemos looks at Tar's face again. He has seen better days. He's lost a lot of the color from his once tan face. Concerned for the worst, Daemos grabs an iron rod from the small firepit in the corner. He cauterizes the wounds in Tar's wrists, ankles, and a couple fingers and toes to prevent death from blood loss. He allows a little blood to escape, however.

Daemos grabs a double-tipped pin from the table. He opens Tar's mouth and stabs it into the floor of his mouth where his tongue used to be, forcing Tar to keep his mouth open or risk stabbing himself in the roof of his mouth, possibly stapling it shut. The effort of breathing, keeping his mouth open, and continuously swallowing his blood will be exhausting. Daemos gives his other five prisoners the same courtesy he showed Tar.

The demons' shrieking screams pierce the lands. At time it sounds as if they're speaking to one another. The Viscrucians are amazed with wonder. They have never seen anything like it. The demons fly through the rain and sweep up Viscrucians, soldiers, and tourists. The citizens look on and smile. The demons carry their victims up into the dark clouds above and rip them to pieces. The clouds grow red as crimson rains. The Viscrucians open their arms and mouths as the blood of the unworthy cleanses their sacred streets. Now, the thunder above comes from the bodies bursting and screams piercing the clouds.

"Isn't this glorious, Petrid?" Aemeggur the butcher says.

Blood rains down on Petrid's face. He smiles at Aemeggur. "Absolute pain," he answers. Pain is Viscrucian slang for beauty. He looks around at the supernatural chaos when his smile fades. The realization hits him. Daemos. He is not here. He looks around. This is because of him. Something is wrong.

An odd sensation grows inside him. It is so foreign he cannot remember having felt it before. He feels…sadness. It is the first time in years. For Daemos, this must be his death.

Exhausted already, Daemos sits to have a drink and eat. Sweat runs down from the skin he still has to exposed muscle. The maiming of six prisoners is a lot of work for a single man on his deathbed.

"Good," Daemos says. "Now that we're all cozy, we can get started," Daemos explains.

The men frantically look at each other.

"Get started?" Grock sputters without his tongue.

"Can't be! This is only the beginning?" Beypiscomous says.

Daemos walks over to the table and grab hooks and small weights. "Nays Sim," Daemos says, "let's start with you." Nays Sim mumbles in his attempt to speak and spits up blood. Daemos makes a lateral cut along his arm, just beneath his shoulder. Having cut all the way around, he slices down his triceps to the elbow. Daemos makes the same cuts along his other arm, forearms, calves, and thighs.

"Now, Nays Sim, comes the fun part. I encourage everyone to watch while you still have eyes." Daemos hooks the small weights into each of the cuts. The additional weight pulls at the burgeoning flaps of skin. Daemos hooks the last two weights into his balls and penis. Nays Sim screams, so Daemos uppercuts his jaw through the pin into his mouth, stapling it shut. It doesn't eliminate the screaming, but it helps.

"Don't worry, everyone. I won't do that to the rest of you. I'll give each of you your own personal suffering."

Daemos grabs a piece of wood and breaks nearly every bone in Espinkin's body. He makes small cuts at the bottom of each wound to ensure Espinkin will slowly bleed to death. He punctures holes all over Jommutin's body, and then fills them with the flesh-eating bugs kept in one of the jars the men forgot.

Daemos disfigures Grock with an ax, hacking off his nose, ears, lips, chin, elbows, and kneecaps. He slits Beypiscomous across his stomach and removes the spike from his wrists. Bey gets his hands around just in time to cover his stomach and prevent his intestines from spilling out. This brings him to Tar.

"It's time, Tar. Your torture of me was exceptional. I've never been through anything like it, but it was still very sloppy." Daemos grabs Tar's genitals with one hand and severs them from Tar's body with a blade in his other. Tar gasps as the lower pain sucks the breath out of him.

"Too impatient," Daemos goes on. He holds Tar's manhood in front of his face before throwing it against the wall. "It lacked focus. You jumped from one body part to the next without reason." Daemos wipes his hand on Tar's chest. "You see what I've created? That's focus. That is thought and execution. You see Nays Sim's skin as it tears away? Hear Jommutin's body being eaten away from the inside? Those bugs are hungry! Now it's your turn."

Daemos slowly slices from the back of Tar's head, up over the top and down to his forehead. At the same casual pace, he grabs the open flesh and pulls down, splitting his face in half. Tar unleashes a scream the world has never known, which seems to last ages. It divides down the back of his head while bisecting his nose, lips, and chin, down to his neck. Daemos tightens his grip around the skin and rips it clean from Tar's neck.

"Glorious."

The demonic savagery continues across the city. Blood rains from the sky. Chunks of human meat hail down. The cracked earth from whence the dead escaped now glows red with blood. A multitude of smiling faces walk the streets, perhaps the only time in Viscrucian history. It's prosperity, the apex of the city. People hold out chalices and cups and fill them with bountiful blood offerings from the sky. They drink the pain. They drink the death from above. As they do, they savor the suffering, for it is the best blood tear wine Viscrucia has ever known. No one goes thirsty. No one starves. Screams howl through the air like a symphony from the Suffering.

Petrid hears Tar's harrowing scream. He looks around to where it may have come from.

"Daemos lives," Petrid says. "At least, for now."

Daemos grabs the back of Tar's skinless head and pushes it down. "See it!" Daemos demands. "Face your new reflection." Tar stares at the abomination before him. The faceless horror reflects in the ocean of blood.

"Remind you of anyone?"

The six dying men scream. Their end is near.

"I can feel all of your flesh. I see your blood. I feel your pain." Daemos grabs his table of torture and hurls it off to the side of the room. "Now," Daemos says before reaching up to Tar's face. He digs in and pulls his eyes out. Tar is given yet another reason to wail. Daemos takes a step back and places the eyes into his own sockets. "Bleed for me. Each of you are a sacrifice. Give in to the anguish. Give in to your pain. That is what I am now. I...am your God...of pain."

The undulating pool of blood beckons him. Daemos kneels and sinks into the center of the torture chamber. His tormentors quiver in agony. Their blood billows and spills onto Daemos. A blood cocoon of pain, anguish, suffering, and torment encases him. One by one, they all die.

Chapter 22

By the time Silmeir healed enough to begin his journey, the flying horde of demons and the dead had surrendered their possessed bodies and left their mark upon Viscrucia. Some got their fill. Others screamed in defeat, relinquishing their search. All of the possessed barreled toward the streets from the crimson sky. They slammed their bodies, some merely bones, others a little meatier, into the roofs and walls of buildings and into the streets themselves. The crashing impact embedded their bodies within. Even Petrid never imagined such art. Demonic murals painted the city. The rain stopped, and the night sky overtook the crimson clouds, covering the city in darkness.

After waking in the bowels of the castle surrounded by the forgotten, Silmeir gathers his strength and limps forth. The creatures and the forgotten let him walk past without intervening. Silmeir fears the worst.

He makes it back to his hut. Gathering fresh clothes and some coins, he makes his way to the outlying woods and bathes. He scrubs and scrubs and scrubs. Cleaned and dressed, Silmeir revisits Wemms and buys what herbs, medicine, and bandages he can, praying it will make a difference. Back at his hut, he applies the herbs and salves, bandages his wounds, packs a bag, and arms himself with weapons. Then he passes out.

Silmeir wakes up groggily the next morning. He has rested long enough. He does not know how much time he has left. Regardless, he must make it count.

"I must find Daemos. That, is, focus. What? Why?" Has his mind deteriorated that much already?

"Daemos."

What possibly could Daemos do to help him, other than kill him? How could he help Daemos? He is not sure. He doesn't care.

"Must find Daemos."

Chapter 23

On the fifth day after Daemos's torture started, and everyone died, the pool of blood coagulated. Nothing moved. The revolting stench of death was palpable.

On the sixth day, the Viscrucians feasted. They cooked the flesh of the fallen. The blood storm and screams that echoed throughout the land would undoubtedly keep any outsiders away for days, if not weeks. Those unholy sights could last a lifetime. Why rush to kill when any kill would be nothing by comparison? So, the Viscrucians feasted. They ate and told stories of the horrors they beheld. Fires burned throughout the city.

Esim, lights a fire on the top of his building below the night sky. He enjoys cooking up there. He can see the city and any attackers that approach. While cooking his meat and slugging down sangloshe, he discards any pieces he doesn't want by tossing them off the roof.

One such bone, wrapped in fat, catches fire and so he tosses it. It bounces off the ground below and into a hole at the base of the wall. It finds its way down to the basement and lodges into the thick, gooey blood against the pillar Tar died upon.

The flame slowly builds along the wooden pillar. The blood heats and liquefies, spreading out from the pillar. A piece of Tar's burning flesh falls from his body and onto some of Daemos's black blood. It ignites somehow, and burns across the pool to the next pillar, and then the next, and then the next, until it comes full circle back to Tar's.

All the wooden pillars ignite. A ring of fire burns through the blood around the cocoon at the center. The six corpses burn. The blood bubbles. The cocoon heats. It slowly unravels, layer upon melting layer. Daemos's body becomes visible inside the womb. The flames around the pillars have risen, and the pool sways.

The cocoon is now gone. Daemos's body floats among the gore, but it's different. It has changed. Before, it was mostly skinned, open muscle tissue breathing the outside air. Now, some sections have been replaced with the skins of his sacrifices. They found a new willing host while gestating within the cocoon. Yet, parts of his body are still flayed and open. He is the epitome of pain.

"Rise."

The fires burn, the bodies cook, and the blood billows. The vision of blood surges back to Daemos. Its magnitude jolts him back to life. He opens his mouth to gasp for air. He gets it, followed by a mouthful of blood. Daemos spits it out and unleashes a primordial scream that exemplifies the anguish of his resurrection. It booms through the streets like a shockwave. Esim hears it but cannot place its location albeit right under his nose.

Daemos raises himself upright to a sitting position. Blood soaks him. He sees his body with his eyes closed through the blood. Daemos slowly feels the new skin on his body. He reaches up to his face and feels his eyelids. Moving his hands away, he opens his eyes. His old sight returns, human sight. New eyes see for him. They are the same color as his old eyes. They are no longer the eyes of another. Daemos blinks, and the pupils turn black. He blinks again, and they turn red, restoring his blood vision. He blinks again, and his human sight returns.

"I-I can see. I'm alive," Daemos says, and then looks himself over. "Sort of." He stands up, looks around, and inspects himself more. He notices his skin tone is slightly red, even underneath the layer of blood. "The pain…it feels…good," he says, and then stumbles. He grimaces. "At times." He clenches his fists. Skin remains on one of them. He regains his focus.

"Move," the wraith calls to him. Daemos listens and searches for clothes and weapons.

The first thing Daemos can find is a ratty coat. He throws it on to cover himself. He looks for other clothes when the door at the top of the stairs opens.

"Kes!" Esim exclaims.

Daemos quietly moves underneath the stairs.

"What are you fools doing? If you were hungry you should've said something." Walking down, Esim waves the smoke from his face. He reaches the bottom and cannot believe his eyes.

"Kill him!"

Daemos lunges from behind the stairs to strike. It is his worst attempt since he was a child. He stumbles forward and swings, but most of his muscles have atrophied while others have been severed completely. The surprise attack still gives Daemos the advantage, however. His attempted slash at Esim's throat becomes a sharp gouge into the man's eye.

Esim stumbles back against the wall. Daemos attempts similarly with his other hand but fails again to deliver a killing stroke. His nails gouge into Esim's ear this time. Somewhat confused, and feeling very weak and stupid, Daemos rips Esim's eye and ear free and lurches up the stairs as fast as he can. Staying any longer and Esim would most likely kill him. He's not ready for a straight up fight.

Having lost partial vision, hearing, and depth perception, Esim tries to regain control. He grabs the broad ax from its sheath on his back. "I'm coming!"

Esim marches up the stairs. He finds a trail of blood leading out the front door as the smoke continues to rise around him. He pushes open the door and waits a second, in case his assailant stands within killing distance, setting a trap. Nothing. Esim slowly pokes his head out of the doorway and sees his enemy.

The large man hobbles in a bloody, ragged coat. He reaches the corner of the alley and turns his head to Esim. The man is missing half of his face, and his eyes are entirely black. This grotesquery surprises even Esim. Is this the man they were torturing? The man disappears down another alley.

Esim's emotions turn. "I'm coming, ghoul! I'm going to chop you into pieces!"

Daemos stumbles down the alley from one wall to the next. He is so weak that he can barely move. He doesn't even have a weapon. Any decent killer who finds him like this will have no problem carving him up. He must get out of the open!

"I see your blood, ghoul!" Esim continues shouting. "Nowhere to hide!"

Fuck! Now Daemos's *enemies* see his blood!

A tan flesh curtain sways in the breeze ahead. The words *Weapon Shop* are scrawled in blood next to it. This is Daemos's only chance, grab a weapon and kill Esim!

Daemos throws open the flesh curtain entrance to the weapon shop and collapses onto the counter, dripping blood. "The Black Fangs," he says, gasping for air. He slams a bloody eyeball and ear on the payment scale. The few fingernails he has left are chiseled into talons. "Now!"

"That's not enough," the large flesh peddler says. Holding a bloody scythe, he crosses his burly arms. Daemos knows the posture and stance the peddler takes. Feeble attempts at bartering are pointless. He's ready to cleave Daemos in two without a second's hesitation.

"I'm no tourist."

"Then you wouldn't be buying a weapon. Viscrucians *acquire* their own."

Daemos eyes the Black Fangs across the wooden counter. The dual-bladed weapon is forged of black iron. It's two black hooks resembling fangs precede two spoons, guaranteed to scoop out whatever the teeth rip through.

"Death is knocking," the peddler adds.

Coughing blood, Daemos grabs the Fangs. The peddler tightens his grip on the scythe.

Daemos slices off his two end fingers with one of the teeth. Grimacing in pain, he pushes them over to the peddler. Laughter soon permeates the grimace. "Consider it a down payment. More's coming, I promise."

Esim opens the entrance. Blood runs down the side of his face from his missing eye and ear. The brute is riddled with scars. A stump lies where his right hand once did. His left raises a stubby ax, eagerly awaiting Daemos's flesh. "I'll feast like a king selling your flesh, Ghoul!"

The ax races toward its victim. Daemos spins away and puts his new weapon to work. The Black Fangs tear through Esim's testicles, scooping them out along the way. The brute's breath escapes him as he plummets to the ground. Daemos steps over him. He rams his razor-like fingernails underneath the base of Esim's skull in the back of his neck. Daemos pulls his head back toward him and slams the Black Fangs into his eyes. Esim wails. Using the top of his skull as leverage, Daemos snaps the Fangs back, cracking open the top of his head.

Daemos breathes deeply. He steps back to the counter and presents the additional payment. "Here, one brain and a set of nuts." Both squish as he places the bloody matter on the scale.

The flesh peddler stands there. "That's enough."

"Good, because I want my fingers back."

The peddler chuckles. "What for?"

Blood and sweat run down Daemos's face. He stares at the peddler. "What'd you say to me?"

The peddler leans in, staring right back. "What do you want them for, bleeder?"

Daemos slides his bleeding hand toward his severed fingers. His stumps touch his fingers. Blood spurts onto them. His blood and tissue slowly reconnect. The peddler's eyes widen with disbelief. The blood seeps back into his fingers as if rewound in time. Not even a scar remains. Perfect. Daemos raises his hand and wiggles all his fingers. Before the peddler can muster a word, Daemos rips his throat out with the Black Fangs. "Don't ever question me."

Daemos grabs a blood jar from the counter and sets it in front of him. The peddler collapses. His gaping neck lands on the jar, and blood spurts from its former owner.

Daemos walks outside. He scrawls the word "Closed" with his bloody hand across the curtain entrance. Limping back in, he slams the wooden door shut behind it.

Chapter 24

After dispatching Esim and the arrogant flesh peddler, Daemos collects his new earnings and finally has some time to rest. Discovering his new healing trick is a gift he never imagined possible. He did not know why he even attempted it at the time. It felt natural when nothing else did. While he performed that miracle of healing, the rest of his injuries linger. Not all of his affliction regenerates like the wind. Pity. He is still adapting to his new body.

He drinks all the water he can find in the store. Thirst adds to his pain. Next, the blood. He grabs the jar and guzzles it. His dehydrated body craves more.

An hour passes. He lies there in agony. He cannot sleep, the pain prevents it. He tries to stay on guard. Daemos must be more careful now than ever.

The place is not safe. Daemos must move. He needs clean bandages, lots of them. He needs to get as far away from the city as he can to rest safely without the constant threat of death. However, more than anything, he needs more to drink. *Parched* does not even begin to describe it. Too much blood loss. Too much sweating. Anything! He must drink. He has rested at the blacksmith's long enough. Someone could burst in at any moment.

Daemos puts on his new clothes, courtesy of his last victims. For the first time, his size is a disadvantage. The clothes are short and tight. Cutting slits down the middle provides some breathing room. He sewed their skin and other fabrics to the short ends, but this only makes it more visible. He looks like a hobo, even by Viscrucian standards. His weapons and new currency bulge at the seams. A few drinks, then he can escape to one of his hideouts, consume his water reserves there, and sleep before making his long trek across the deadly sands.

The blood-stained entrance springs open. Daemos grips his weapons tighter than ever before. He must be cautious. Citizens will quickly pick up on his wounded manner. Dying now would be insulting after what he had survived. He peruses the streets. Dusk will soon be gone. His destination is clear, the Death Pits. He doesn't want to, but it is on the way to his next stop. He cannot wait any longer. Daemos shrouds his face with the small, ill-fitting hood as best he can and limps forward.

He is right, the Viscrucians sense his weakness instantly, like vultures hovering over their next meal. Daemos knows. The sword and Black Fangs he wields speak for him. The roar of the crowd grows with every step he takes. Perhaps this is a bad idea. Fuck it. You only die once...or so Daemos thought.

The crowd is rowdy. Violence consumes the air in the arena. Two quick drinks, maybe three. Anything.

Daemos slides through the crowd as best he can. Weapons are a little too close for comfort. He hunches down to avoid attention and finally arrives at the bar.

"Sangloshe," he orders.

His eyes race through the bar. He sees the fights, the mangled regulars. Crimson and worse trails leak from wounds. His shabby coat grates against his skin and skinless portions of his body. Blood slides underneath his coat and down his arm. Still no service. What in Suffering?

"Sangloshe!"

A one-armed bloodtender turns his head. Eyes around the room catch Daemos.

He wants water more than anything but resists the urge. Ordering water in his condition sends too clear of a signal of his desperation.

The ugly bartender hears and proceeds to pour. The spigot pukes a murky liquid into a cup. Daemos throws four fresh fingers onto the counter. Daemos snatches the drink before the bloodtender can even set it on the bar. Blood drips from his palm. The bloodtender looks down. Daemos slams the empty glass on top of the blood. "Another."

The bloodtender grins. "Thirsty?"

Daemos scowls back as murderous thoughts race through his mind. The bloodtender grabs the cup to accommodate his patron.

A filthy hand slams down a severed one. "I got to hand it to you," the man belches, "how you made it this long. Your insides bleed."

Daemos takes a deep breath to prepare for the beating he'll give. He turns to the commenting asshole. "Who the fuck are you, handsome?"

"Quilgorsch. You're almost big enough to feed a mox. And you're ripe, too! Bleeding you out will take half the time." Sangloshe runs down the side of his chin. Drool runs down the other.

Mox is a term for a small tribe of five to ten nomadic warriors of the Ssagaecian clan. They are skilled warriors originally from the Ssagaecian mountains, but nothing that gave Daemos trouble, at least before.

"Offering to buy me a couple rounds. I didn't know the Ssagaecians were generous," Daemos responds.

"I didn't know you were funny, bleeder. I just wanted to end your stench before it infects anyone else."

The bloodtender returns with Daemos's ale. Daemos grabs it and chugs it as fast as he can. He looks to his antagonist, and then around the room. The floor is damp from the betting. Flesh has been won and lost all day. Citizens kill flies out of instinct.

"One more, bloodtender," Daemos says.

"You're not the only killer here, bleeder," says the bloodtender.

"I might be soon, you one-armed maggot," Daemos grumbles under his breath. A man from the same mox, judging on his hairstyle and clothing, makes his way around the bar behind Daemos. "Quil—" Before Daemos finishes, he stabs Quilgorsch in the stomach and smashes his cup in Quil's throat. As Quilgorsch collapses, Daemos grabs the meat cleaver from Quil's pants, spins around, and slams it into oncoming mox member's throat. Daemos rips out the cleaver to finish the decapitation, but the one-armed bloodtender breaks a cup over Daemos's head.

"Throw the bleeder into the pit!" yells the bloodtender. Two eager men next to Daemos happily oblige.

A bar brawl ensues as Daemos is tossed into the pit. He lands with a *splat*, narrowly missing the severed elbow jutting from the ground. The gore comes in and out of focus as Daemos adjusts his eyes.

The two combatants look at the new prey. Daemos slowly rises to his feet. Barely able to stand, his eyelids are heavy and begin to close. The blood light comes into focus. The pulsing blood of the death pit warriors shine forth. "The wraith," Daemos mumbles to himself. The facial tissue rises in his cheeks to form his new, mangled smile.

"Death! Death!" the crowd chants. It rises to a fever pitch.

"Death?!" Daemos mocks with his eyes closed. "Is that the best you've got? Not by what little blood I have left!" He tosses off his cloak, revealing his true self to the crowd.

The chanting stops. The embodiment of agony has taken aback even the bloodthirsty crowd of the Death Pit. Daemos spreads his arms wide, holding his weapons.

"Pain! This is the spectacle I give to you! Let me

show you," Daemos calls out. The bloody warriors before him look at each other, then march toward Daemos. Daemos feels the warriors' pain from their wounds with each step they take as it surges through their bodies. Recognizing the opportunity, he puts his new powers to the test. He drops his weapons and claps his hands together. The two men slam into each other, back to back.

Daemos raves. He separates his hands, and then slams them back together. Each of the warriors' weapons stabs through themselves and into the other. They cry out. "Yes. I will show you pain."

The crowd can merely watch. Daemos begrudgingly pulls his hands apart as if something is trying to hold them together. The men scream with torment. The man on the left's eyes suddenly spurt blood and are pulled out of their sockets. The man on the left's legs quiver. Blood splashes beneath them. His screams reach a higher pitch. His bloody testicles descend beneath his kilt.

The crowd's eyes bulge and their mouths hang open. Some question the sight before them.

"What is happening?"

"How is this walking corpse still alive?"

"How is he the tormentor?"

"Impossible!"

Daemos circles his hands in the air and brings them to a close. Blood seeps through his fingers. He feels his victims' suffering. The eyes circle the men and replace the other's missing testicles. The nutless man gasps. His old testicles circle and enter the bloody eye sockets of the other man. He screams in horror.

The sight induces vomiting amongst a small portion of the crowd. The two, humiliated warriors collapse, unable to take any more.

"How was that Death Pit patrons?" Daemos questions. A few men flee the vile scene. Two men shoot arrows through the fallen men to end their suffering. "That is the opening to my play of torment. The Suffering opened up and spat me back out! It has a new dominion here and seeks a new following! I am the name and face of pain! If you want more, I beg you to stand in my way."

The wind howls. Only a few whispers are audible amongst the crowd. Daemos wastes no time. He throws on his coat, grabs his weapons, and hobbles off through the exit. The crowd raves.

Chapter 25

Waess, a young Viscrucian woman, creeps along the alleys of the city. Her skin and clothes are caked with dirt, sand, and blood from the previous night's rain, blending for near-perfect camouflage. She is a savvy thief and killer but still an adolescent among the citizens. She sneaks about, concealing herself to avoid attention.

Smelling an unusual fragrance of death, Waess moves forward. She sees the smoky source. Pulling out palm and foot claws from a bag, she puts them on and scales the wall behind her to get a higher view, wondering if it's a trap. Reaching the top, she sees no one.

Waess has been careful but knows this is still odd. It must be due to the blood feast all day and the night before. She climbs back down and puts her scaling claws away. She pulls out a piece of cloth and wraps it around her mouth. Ready for the smoke, she grabs a long butcher's knife and enters the building.

The smoke has died down considerably. Only a few small fires persist that light the room. Seeing nothing of interest in the main level, Waess quietly walks to the staircase that leads to the basement. She pauses at the top of the steps and listens. She hears only the crackling of flames, nothing more. Waess descends as her mouth hangs open in awe underneath her protective cloth wrap. She thought the carnival of carnage the night before was a sight, but Viscrucia never ceases to amaze.

Looking around, Waess sees no survivors. She breathes deeply and holsters her butcher knife. She takes off the cumbersome cloak she wears and sets it on one of the tables. She looks over the inhumane instruments and other means of torture.

Waess steps down into the pool of blood. The fire keeps it warm and liquid. She wades into the center of the pool and looks at each of the bodies. Waess has never beheld such suffering. She inspects and touches each of them. Their blood mingles with her own crimson camouflage.

The pool swirls around her. Wind blows in through the holes in the walls. This excites the fires that remain. The room brightens. Fear sets in and rightly so. She pulls out her knife. A deep, otherworldly sound reverberates from below. Waess trudges toward the stairs. The nearest pillar adorned with a charred body splits and falls, impeding her exit. She changes direction.

One by one, the pillars respond in kind until she is fenced in. Limbs from the bodies sway in the blood. The deep, moaning sound grows. The wind quickens and howls, blowing and spreading the fires. Soon, all the outlying blood beyond the pillars catches fire.

Terror consumes Waess. She looks down for the first time. The blood bubbles as if it were boiling. It suddenly surges and explodes. It engulfs her and pulls her below. She thrashes and bursts out of it as soon as she finds the floor beneath her feet. Waess screams in horror. Flames engulf the basement walls. The six slain men are soaked in blood once again. She grabs one by the shoulder to pull herself out. It's skinned head springs up. The mouth opens and bellows in pain. The eyelids open but only blood drains out.

"Hel..pf..me," The charred, mutilated, toothless husk mumbles. The lack of tongue and blood discharging from his mouth make his words nearly indiscernible. Waess pushes herself away when one of the other bodies grabs her. Screaming, she spins around and lops off the hand that held her. All the men have reanimated now. Waess moves to the center of her undead prison to avoid their reach.

The ghastly moaning grows louder. Something is coming. The walls shake. Soil crumbles. A black, tar-like substance emerges impossibly throughout the burning walls. It bubbles and swells along the walls and ceiling, consuming the flames. Its surface reflects the mayhem that ensues. The room goes black. Something horrible is here.

Waess sinks into the blood. She fights and swims away. How is she swimming? Suddenly, there is no floor, no bottom to the blood. It swirls in a circle. A vortex swells from the center, sucking everything to it. Waess grabs one of the men's arm and pulls herself out of the vortex and up to a splintered beam. The undead six cry out in pain and new terror.

A flame slowly rises from the whirlpool, illuminating the basement once again. The blood rushes around faster as the center spreads and deepens, giving way to the growing fire within. The fire reveals the onyx flux among the walls: beautiful and mesmerizing at the same time.

The black mass acts as a barrier to the burgeoning Suffering beyond. The damned creatures contained across the threshold reach out, pushing its envelope, but they cannot break free from its dominion. Unknown appendages, tentacles, tongues, fangs, and other nameless horrors make their attempt at the fresh offerings. The surface is reflective in parts, purely obsidian in others and, yet reveals the infinite distance of time and space among the rest.

The undead scream at this abominable sight, their impending doom. Their screams change in tone, transitioning from terror back to agony as the burgeoning fire melts their already disfigured flesh and muscle. Waess cannot muster a sound as the shock of the sight unfolding is too much for her to grasp.

The vortex has opened underneath. The pool of blood empties into an abyss. Beyond is the cataclysm of the Suffering. The fire rises above and opens, finally revealing its host: a woman. A demon woman with fire for hair, hovers in the air. Her naked body is pure perfection. Her skin is silken and flawless. Her breasts and ass are bountiful. The demon's fiery red hair is lavish and dances in the wind. Its magnitude changes on demand. It spirals around her body down to her feet, then suddenly burns back up and dances only two feet above her head.

The whirlpool rages, pulling the melting men down into the Suffering.

"You were told," the demoness explains. "You are a sacrifice."

The vortex swallows them. Their screams disappear into the void below. The tables, weapons, and all that remains gets sucked down. Waess screams. Her clothes burn off. Her skin soon follows. She disappears beneath with the blood.

The cataclysm vanishes. The room is now clean and silent. No bubbling onyx horde. No blood. No bodies. Only a demoness.

Chapter 26

A headache started an hour ago. Is it from the labor of his journey or is he too late? Is one of those things growing inside of him? The thought is too bleak. Silmeir tries his best to ignore it. His horse tires. He needs to make camp for the night. He still has far to go.

Silmeir rations his water as best he can for his horse and himself, yet his thirst lingers. He did not make up much ground during his first day of travel. It is disappointing, but it doesn't matter. He is happy to be alive another day. The fire he made burns bright and gives warmth. Millions of stars light the night sky. It can always be worse...and soon will be. He tries to enjoy his last moments.

Odd dreams come to Silmeir at night. They move slowly. At times the visions are bright. Most of the time, the dreams come in a dull gray. He sees faces. He hears whispers. He remembers neither.

Rain wakes Silmeir up in the morning. He grabs his things, quickly jumps on his horse, and continues his journey. The rain is light and clears out in time. Days pass. Silmeir hunts what he can for food and finds a decent amount of other sustenance along the way, but he still has much distance to travel. His pilgrimage has just begun.

The trip lacks conversation, so he starts one up with his horse, Mr. Brown. It's pretty dull at first. Mr. Brown doesn't seem to pay much attention. Is Mr. Brown not much of a talker, Silmeir wonders, or is it because Mr. Brown requires more stimulating topics? Perhaps it's the exact opposite. Maybe he's not an intellectual, but a fool, a prankster.

Silmeir puts his theories to the test. He broaches subjects of all matters, eager to discover what Mr. Brown fancies. Silmeir's scientific prodding prevails. Mr. Brown responds with neighs, whinnies, and various movements, large and small. Silmeir is pleased. This trek was starting to dull in his mind.

Chapter 27

Step by step, the demoness ascends the cellar stairs. Silence. The mangled wood does not creak underneath her subtle touch. Her hair of flame whips across it, igniting it with grace, and silence still. The fire rages inside as she walks out of the broken-down hovel. With only a few steps into this world, she creates a path of destruction. Her intentions are clear.

The demoness steps naked through the alley. The cool breeze gently moves her flame. Her skin is flawless, not a single scar marks her. She stands over two meters tall. A wanderer steps into the alley ahead and notices her. He drops the knife he carries and his mouth gapes. He stands frozen. The demoness walks past the shorter man without paying attention to him. Her steps leave no tracks within the sand. She disappears down another alley.

Commotion sounds ahead. The demoness turns another corner. Two dirty men circle each other. Her presence disrupts their concentration. The feud that positioned them moments from murdering each other disappears. The men stand next to each other, blocking the demon's path. She stops. All three of them stand roughly the same height. The men peruse her body.

"You lost your clothes. I like that. Less work for me," the perverted man says as drool runs down his mouth. "Should I kill him so I can have you all to myself, or let him join in?"

"No," the second man says. Deep scars spider web across his face. "She is mine. I'm going to be the first one to scar that perfect skin of hers. I'm going to leave a mark she'll never forget. She'll suck me real good after I've had my cutting fun with her."

The demoness stands calmly. The scarred sadist makes the first move and jabs his blade toward her flank. The demon's hair of fire lashes out from behind her and grabs her assailant by the wrist. He shrieks. The drooler stumbles back. Her hair melts his hand into a single, bloody ball around the blade's handle.

The demon's face shows no emotion. The man doesn't know what to do. Another attack could bring about the same repercussions, or worse. The woman moves a free hand up to the man's detained forearm. With her fingers outstretched, she pushes her hand through his arm. Blood spills as she separates it from its host. The cretin screams in horror. The demoness looks at the drooler. Taking the hint, he bolts in the other direction.

The one-armed menace falls to his knees. The demoness looks down at him and considers whether to kill him or not. She decides. Moving down, her hair laces her hands and lips. She opens her hand in front of her mouth and blows him a kiss.

"As you wish," whispers the demon.

The man's lips bubble and dissolve. The disintegration continues: teeth, tongue, throat, burrowing out through the back of his head. The man keels over, quivering. His heart finally stops as the demoness pulls out his intestines. She does not use them for her clothing, the smell awful. She simply experiments with the human's body.

She strips the muscles from his legs and removes the skin from his back. She incinerates the sweat, blood, oils, and whatever filth that remains with the heat from her hair. Grabbing his clothes, she cuts and fashions them together with his skin and muscle tissue.

The demon's new outfit is one of a kind. The fabric is crimson from the blood of its late owner. The connecting muscle is a bright red, and the flesh is much lighter. Where her hair is at affects the brightness of the hues across her clothing. She debones the femurs and loosely fastens them to her hips as maces. She takes other bones for knives and hides them within her clothing.

The demoness puts on her prey's sandals, as they are close in size, and walks through the alleys, into the streets, and exits the city of the damned. She mesmerizes every Viscrucian who sees her. Her visceral garb is the most unique and elegant they have ever seen, let alone the rest of her. Any normal person would retch at the sight of the walking gore.

"Petrid, look!" A Viscrucian shouts to another.

Petrid turns his head to catch the view. His jaw drops from the sight.

"Such fashion," he says, wiping drool from the side of his mouth.

She asks a few questions along the way. She questions them about the epitome of pain that wanders the streets. They answer honestly, too dumbfounded to do anything else. A few other fools that stroll up to her receive broken jaws and arms. Only one man's foolishness results in fatality. Then she disappears from the city. Only three people die from the demon's first day walking among the living. Not bad. History reveals this to be a light day. Death means nothing to her. She has lived it for eons. The paths before and behind her are paved in it.

Chapter 28

He did it. Daemos managed to escape Viscrucia. His muscles nearly atrophied. He closes the entrance to his nearest hideout outside of Viscrucia. He opens a secret compartment hidden in the wall. Two large jugs and a wooden chest fit inside. He grabs one of the jugs of water he's stashed and guzzles it. He grabs the other, much nicer crafted bottle.

"Help me again," he pleads. "Give me the strength. Heal my wounds." He drinks the blue, luminescent water. Finished drinking, he pours the rest of it onto his wounded body. Relieved for the moment, he collapses onto the dusty stone of the cave.

Daemos wakes. He can't move. Pain is everywhere. He sighs with relief, knowing he's still alive. He falls back asleep.

The next time Daemos wakes, he moves. He bandages himself with the few supplies he has in the cave and grabs the additional weapons. He must keep moving, far away from his home. It will be some time before he can return if he survives that long. He exits the cave with his weapons drawn. Satisfied no one is near, he covers the hideout entrance and leaves.

Daemos limps to his next hideout. He sees a few travelers along the way but keeps his distance. Interaction is too risky. He has nothing of value to trade for a horse or any other travel beast, so he limps onward.

He makes it to his destination, a desolate area, much like the desert of death where Viscrucia flourishes. It is the closest and most barren place Daemos could reach at his feeble rate. He stumbles between the stone walls, dragging footprints and smearing blood. The walls are subtle at first. Starting as rocks, they are shallow in height. But soon, the rocks become boulders. Deeper and deeper, the chasms give birth to the Halls of Stone.

The whispering winds serenade Daemos like a lullaby as they pass through the halls. The height of the stone walls cast deep shadows now. Daemos lacks the strength to look up to guess what time of day it is. He fears vertigo will overcome him if he takes his eyes off the ground. He feels the smoothness of the stone on his hands as he tries to stay mobile.

The halls open to a small clearing. Perfect, Daemos thinks. He walks to the center and collapses from exhaustion. His food is nearly gone, and he is out of water. He can barely move. Death is close...again. He still has a chance, however. He chose this path of least resistance for a reason. People rarely venture this way, and that's what he needs to avoid, people. A little-known creek runs through the Halls of Stone. It can be his salvation. He needs to find it, just not now. He passes out.

The cellar. The table. The torture. The memories torment his sleep. Daemos wakes to the pain of his night terrors. He hopes it will be the last time.

He finds the stream. Water never tasted so good. After bathing and cleaning his ravaged body, he eats whatever possible. Daemos follows the stream. The halls rise higher and higher, blocking out much of the light.

"Escape…"

Daemos stops and listens. He checks behind him. Has someone been following him? The breeze picks up. It's probably just the wind he thinks. Maybe his mind is playing tricks on him. Daemos treads forward.

"Escape…" whispers through the gathering blue mist.

Daemos halts and raises a weapon. That was no trick. Someone, or something, is with him. "Who goes there?"

A cold wind rushes past. The chill brings goosebumps to his skin. Daemos hates the sensation. Even his flesh senses doom.

"Escape…" a voice hisses behind. Daemos turns around. "…is hopeless."

Daemos marches on, gritting his teeth. If another fight comes, so be it.

"No one…" a different voice calls from above. Daemos follows the sound but finds nothing.

"Returns…" says another.

Daemos limps faster. How many of these damned things are there? Is he surrounded? He rounds a corner and freezes. The passage is narrow. A faint blue light emanates past the wall. Something drifts behind it. Daemos thought he would be safe hidden within the halls. He is wrong.

Weapon ready, he steps forward, but something pulls him back. He turns and slashes through the aqua haze. Nothing. Wailing echoes through the halls.

Daemos storms ahead, swinging. The mist curls around his movements. He slashes nothing but air. Laughter joins the taunting voices. They are everywhere, yet nowhere. He can't find his assailants. This continues intermittently…on and on and on. The blue fog grows. The haunting works on Daemos's mind, chipping away at him. Daemos is used to a straight up fight - seeing his enemy and facing him as combat is intended. Hours of torment later, he can take no more and passes out again.

"You are here now…"

Daemos jolts awake. Night has fallen, but the blue fog swells beneath. It creeps in from the edges of the halls. The fog glows on its own, providing the only light within the halls.

"In time…"

"Time…time…time…" The cries increase.

"Does this haunting have no end?" Daemos wonders.

Glittering vapor whirls past. Shapes form within. A decayed face looms in the mist. "You will join us…"

Daemos gets to his feet. "Leave me!"

More spirits emanate. "No one leaves..." There, forms vary and transform. Partial faces, limbs, torsos, sometimes whole bodies appear. Some look normal, some even look beautiful at times, but the mist gives shape and takes it away.

"This is your home now, Daemos..."

"How do you know my name?"

"The dead know..."

They float and swim around him, above and below. Some spirits appear to be male and female, others are horrifying monsters.

"In time...you will know..." More contorted beings soar around. They appear in the stone. They form in the sand. The phantasms reach for Daemos. He swipes through them. Laughter accompanies the wails. Daemos treks ahead. "Keep walking..."

"Walk for days..."

"Walk for years..."

"There is no salvation..."

"No one escapes the Halls of Stone..."

Hall after hall, passage after passage, Daemos journeys forth, hounded by the fallen that never found deliverance. His sanity wanes. He finds another clearing and drops to the ground. He glimpses the stars above the ethereal plane as his consciousness drifts.

Chapter 29

The temptation is too great. Death follows her everywhere. The sight of her is appallingly intoxicating. Like a siren's call, anyone who partakes in the malicious arts is beckoned to her. Then death follows. They slow her down a bit, which surprises her.

The cursed souls of the Suffering know better, or, at least, can avoid it. The trail of bodies lays clear as footprints. However, unlike the standard Viscrucian victim, these lambs are left intact. She does not strip them of their flesh, and their belongings stay behind. The demoness has no use for them now. She is already clothed, not entertained by their weapons, and apparently, not hungry.

Distancing herself from Viscrucia, the demoness continues her hunt. Her trail is still clear. No more assailants attack. The only thing that remains is time…time until she finds what she seeks.

Chapter 30

The terrain plays tricks on Silmeir. Is he lost? He cannot tell. A pounding headache disrupts his thoughts. He does not remember the trees ever looking like that. Their color is different. The bark crawls. Mr. Brown presses onward. He is getting closer, he thinks. Daemos. He must find Daemos.

The land ahead is strange. It rises high above, but this does not faze Mr. Brown. Mr. Brown knows what to do. He canters and jumps across the islands of land floating high above the terrain below. Mr. Brown knows all. In the shade of the trees, over the rock, through the haze, Mr. Brown will pass through the terrain like a ghost, carrying Silmeir with him.

Mr. Brown finds a stream. Is it floating or grounded? Silmeir cannot tell, but what does it matter?

"Good man, Mr. Brown," Silmeir says. "I was getting a little thirsty myself." Silmeir steps down off his companion.

They enjoy their drink. Water ripples through the gentle stream. He sees his dirty reflection in the water. The days of travel wear on him. He dips his hands into the water and splashes water on his face. He rubs his hands on his face to clean the dirt off, but it isn't dirt. It feels different now that he touches it. It's not going away. Silmeir looks at his fingers. Blood and some other mucus-like fluid are there. He doesn't think he's still bleeding.

Silmeir cleans his hands in the water and waits for the ripples to dissipate. His reflection comes into focus. It is not dirt at all. It has begun. His face is massively swollen. A dark line of flesh loosens across his cheek. Blood and puss permeate. Silmeir touches it but cannot feel it with his finger.

It has taken over. Silmeir did not notice. He looks around. Images. Landscapes. Location. Mr. Brown. These things are a mix of memory and confusion. He knows where he is headed…somehow. He will find what he seeks. Something. Someone. Silmeir looks back to his reflection. He sees himself, but he sees something else as well. He sees the nuances. He sees the minuscule tremors within the flesh. Subtle palpitations. His fingers shake as they graze against the swollen and permeated fissuring divide. A tear runs down it. No sensation.

Silmeir closes his eyes and clenches his fists. He erupts, unleashing a scream that scares Mr. Brown. The force of his scream rips his facial crevice open an inch. Silmeir thrashes and attacks the water, cursing what he has become. The din echoes across the land. The crows caw. Camouflaged creatures notice. He falls backward, screaming. He pushes himself back a few feet until he gives up. Silmeir closes his eyes and weeps. Water, blood, flesh, and tears slide down his face. His body twitches. He falls asleep when his mind can take no more hatred and fear.

Silmeir wakes in the middle of the night. His vision is blurry. Thousands of stars illuminate the dark sky. He rubs his eyes. His vision of the stars blurs further. As he looks out beyond, the vision takes shape. A star shoots across the sky. More stars catch fire. It forms a woman in motion. The hair burns bright. She is looking for something.

"A woman."

Chapter 31

Searing pain wakes Daemos. The stars blur above. Frozen, he accepts the pain. It washes over him in waves. He slowly comes to manage it. A light appears from the stone hall leading to his sanctuary. Daemos raises his arm. He feels warmth as the light grows red. Daemos opens his eyes as best he can. Fire emerges and moves closer. The center of it sways. The sound rolls off the stone. The demoness appears from within the traveling inferno.

Daemos has never seen anything like it before. Fire. Power. Perfection. With her target in sight, she slows her pace. Her fire breathing hair unwraps from around her and rises back behind her shoulders. Daemos stands, never taking his eyes off her. He's mesmerized like the others. If this is how it ends, Daemos cannot think of a better way to go.

They gaze upon each other for the first time. Fire surrounds their fluid reflections within the stream.

"What are you?" Daemos asks, not knowing whether they'll be his last words or not.

"You are dead," the demoness says. "You owe your soul to the Suffering. Nothing denies it." She walks around him, observing.

"I will not be taken," Daemos states, standing his

ground. "Nothing will stop me. I will send a hundred more in my place. I have a new place among men. I am their bringer of pain."

The demoness smiles. Her eyes flash red. "I like that. I have never seen a man capable of such death. I have watched for ages. You were mistakenly born here, instead of with me among the Suffering."

Daemos believes her origin. Nothing could be truer in his eyes. Where else could such power and deadly beauty come from?

"Why stay? Just to survive, because that's all you know? What further purpose do you have?"

Daemos reflects on her interesting question. No one has ever asked him that. He looks at her and answers, "I am not done here. There is *more*. More for me to kill. More suffering to bring. More punishment to deliver. More souls are not worthy of this land. And now. there is more." Daemos pauses and looks at himself, at his body. "There is more to me. I have changed. I have died. I have grown." He notices his missing flesh.

The dark voice deep inside him calls out. *Pain.*

Daemos clenches his fist, remembering how he got here. "I said I will send one hundred more in my place. I shall. But there are a few, a few I must send to the Suffering personally. They will feel what true pain is. They will beg for their place in the Suffering before I am done."

"Revenge," says the demoness. "That is your remaining purpose?"

"Revenge…yes, and no. As I said before, *more*. There is more to my purpose. I feel it, I know it, but I do not know all of it. Like my flesh, there are pieces missing."

"Interesting. Seems like there is more to you. An unknown."

"Are you here to take my soul?" he asks.

"Yes, Daemos," the demoness smiles. "You died that day, yet here you remain. Then the great storm came to claim you. You resisted further and sent more in your wake. This horror woke the dead, reminding them of the agony and betrayal they felt, giving them an unquenchable thirst for more pain and blood. They hunted and searched for you, but again, you evaded, trapped between here and your rightful destination. Now, I am here. *I* will usher your soul to the Suffering ahead. This world couldn't kill you, so *I will*."

"This demon bitch is from the Suffering, alright."

Neither flinch, as they stare at one another upon the unholy promise.

"How will you take me through to the Suffering?"

"I will take your soul back through the Pain I came, at the bottom of that shit heap of the building supposed to usher your death. I've sent many through my arrival. And many since. Yours will soon follow. The other souls will join me when I cross. But you… I'm taking you there myself."

"What is the Pain?" Daemos asks. He has never heard of it. Another man would not have picked up on it at the time.

"The Pain is the portal to the Suffering. The only way."

"Then I'm not going anywhere."

The Demon's eyes engulf in flame. "What makes you think that?"

"We're near the center of the Halls of Stone. We can't

get out. I've been trapped for days. It's said that people use this place to escape. They escape, but never return. Their spirits haunt this place. You are stuck here with me. You can't kill me."

"Sad attempt at a lie."

"I wish I was lying. I don't want to be damned here forever, either."

The demoness looks back through the hall she came. It appears the same. She smells the air…but she smells nothing. She turns back to Daemos.

"The winds lift any trace of smell. The stone helps with the cleanse. The sand below changes along with it. It's a maze, a damned labyrinth of lost souls."

"Why did you come here then?"

"I had to escape Viscrucia. I needed to rest. I didn't intend to go this deep within the Halls. I was dying, and I had a feeling that something, not someone, was after me. I trailed my blood along the rocks, but it's probably been swept away by the winds by now. Then the phantoms found me. If you can find a way out, do so. In the meantime, I'm going to rest."

"There is always another way."

"I believe you, but I don't think we'll find it. Not for a long time, if that. So, that gives me time to heal."

She stares at him defiantly. Her eyes are blacker than the night's sky. She could cleave him in two with a swipe of her hand. Daemos stares back.

"What is your name?" Daemos asks.

"Vel-Syn," the demoness answers.

"Vel-Syn…I shall remember it as long as I live…and after," Daemos replies. Vel-Syn extends her hand and places it on his chest, skin covering most of it. She senses his pain, his pulse, and what remaining life he has left. Her fiery hair moves around Daemos, yet it does not burn him. It feels warm and soothing. She removes her hand, and her hair returns behind her shoulders. Daemos lies down and looks at Vel-Syn one last time before he closes his eyes. He has time. He still needs to heal.

"Your body is quite a sight, even to one of the Suffering's children," she says and then looks around to observe her surroundings. "Do not worry, though. I will show you death. I will find our way out. Through, above, or below, one way, I will find it. I do not require some mortal's help."

Vel-Syn looks above and studies the stars. She kneels to feel the sand at her feet. She touches the stream and observes its movement. The Demon's incendiary mane lights the stone walls. They are oddly smooth. Enough precaution and thought. She looks to Daemos. She left the Suffering and traveled through time and space to find him. Now, she's leaving him already. Can this be? The demoness worries not. Nothing will stand in her way, least of all some maze. The Suffering is a puzzle of pain. She has navigated it for thousands of years. This new exit will simply take time, nothing more.

Vel-Syn kneels and wipes Daemos's skin with her finger. She smells it and licks it to inhale and take in his scent. She walks to the stream and follows it the direction from which she came. The stream will lead her out from the Halls of Stone. Its subtle current flows the opposite direction. This will not even take her a day. *More*, Vel-Syn thinks. Daemos is right. There is much *more* to come.

Chapter 32

It's been hours, and Vel-Syn still hasn't reached the end of the Halls of Stone. She walks through a narrow, stone corridor. The stream is substantially thinner at her feet. She could've turned a hundred times by now and selected a different path but continues to walk along the water. The Halls haven't decreased in height, either, as if the maze has trapped her in its center.

Vel-Syn sees the water flow in the direction she's walking. That's impossible. It was flowing in the opposite direction when she started. How can this be? The current cannot simply change direction, can it? Vel-Syn looks above to the night sky. She'll use the stars.

She searches for a familiar pattern but can't find one. She keeps looking, but the stars seem to move. Anger boils inside. Her flaming hair amplifies, burning hotter and brighter. Vel-Syn takes a deep breath to catch a recognizable scent, but that fails, too. The gusting wind howls by as if it were mocking her.

She looks all around. Each vantage mirrors the other: shadowy obsidian. Her flame somehow only lights a couple of meters away from her. This labyrinth of insanity blinds her senses. Ages amid the pandemonium of the Suffering and even she had never experienced this. She is a master of psychological torture. Thousands of victims writhed from her malignant mind games, yet somehow, she finds herself in new territory.

The mist gathers. The cries call to Vel-Syn now. Sensing their presence, the demoness screams. Fire explodes from her body, nearly incinerating her clothes.

"Ghosts don't frighten me," she warns. "I will send you to a dominion far worse than this."

The fog and voices retreat.

Vel-Syn's eyes burn red. She slams her fingers into the stone wall closest to her. She reaches higher and slams her other hand into it. She continues and scales up the wall with brute force. Meter after meter, she climbs and climbs. She did not think the walls were this high. She sees nothing below. The night has shrouded the bottom in darkness.

It matters not as she soon reaches the top. Vel-Syn pulls herself up and stands atop the Halls of Stone. She cannot believe it. The madness continues. The night sky above that previously held the stars is now consumed in fog. No stars remain. If not for her illuminating tresses, absolute darkness would shroud her.

The Halls defy Vel-Syn at every turn. They are a fortress of illusion, above and below. The thought that Daemos is right pleases her almost as much as it incenses her. He continues to intrigue her. He may be worth the trip after all. However, if she doesn't escape this prison, she will show him real suffering, the likes of which even he has never fathomed. Daemos. She must find him again. He must be hiding something. She will rip it from him.

Vel-Syn steps off the ledge from atop of the Halls of Stone and falls to the darkness below. She slows her descent by gripping the rock wall. Shards break free as she claws down. She lands at the bottom. The broken rock falls to the stream. She walks a few paces back the way she came, or at least thinks it's the way she came. The wind howls from behind her this time. The rock crumbles. Vel-Syn turns around and walks back. Her claw marks that were so prominent just seconds ago have reduced to subtle indentations. She runs her fingers over the marks. The edges crumble to dust in front of her, now erasing all remnants. She spins around and slams the back of her fist into the wall. More fragments fall but, surprisingly, much less than her previous markings. Is this cursed place adapting? Is it answering her every call and test? *So be it,* she thinks. This is only the beginning. She walks back through the halls.

The sun rises hours later. Luckily, she finds Daemos again. The halls must have willed it. This thought annoys Vel-Syn to no end.

"Any luck?" Daemos asks, still lying on the ground.

Vel-Syn kneels next to Daemos and extends her hands over him. Daemos's body tenses.

"I might need you alive longer than I thought," she says. Daemos convulses, trying to breathe. She loosens her fingers and lifts her hands. Daemos's body eventually relaxes. The strain is over. "Your bleeding has stopped." She wipes a small trail of blood from him and tastes it. "Too bad. It tastes good."

Daemos breathes heavily. He lifts a couple of his bandages to see she's telling the truth. "I'm glad you enjoy it," Daemos says. She has extended his chance for survival. He is grateful for her painful intervention. He's dealt with worse. He crawls over to the water and gets a drink.

"We will get out. It's just a matter of time," she says.

"Good. I look forward to it when that day comes," he says.

She walks away down another stone hall. This continues for days. Daemos heals while Vel-Syn tests the labyrinth. She makes fires at night.

Daemos sleeps more soundly than most nights he was alive. Oddly, he is safe, trapped with a demoness in a prison they cannot escape. His body heals. He feels better every day, and his mobility increases.

Deep sounds echo through the halls. Daemos and Vel-Syn rise. The sounds continue. Large footsteps walk down the stream. An animal breathes heavily. Vel-Syn raises the fire, casting more light on the hall entrance. Mr. Brown appears trudging slowly while carrying Silmeir. Silmeir hangs his head, swaying back and forth, barely able to stay vertical

Daemos puts his hand out to Vel-Syn, signaling it's okay. These intruders are not a threat. He walks over to them. "Silmeir, is that you?" he asks. Silmeir turns his head and looks at Daemos. The fire reveals that his condition has worsened. The milky creature moves subtly within him. "Silmeir...no," Daemos says sadly.

"Daemos, is that you?" Silmeir asks.

"Yes. It's me."

Silmeir's face trembles. His lips curl up attempting to smile. "Daemos...I found you. I wasn't sure if I would ever see you again. If...I would make it."

"Silmeir. You said you would be fine. Look what they've done to you." Daemos helps Silmeir down from his horse and to the fire.

"What?" he says. "What have they done?" His head bobbles around, looking in many directions.

Vel-Syn steps forward. "He is not what he once was. His mind has...decayed. The thing inside him has influence."

"Thing inside?" Silmeir asks. He feels his face with his hand. His fingers touch the edges of his flesh before it caves into his host's dwelling. "I can't feel anything."

"That's good," Daemos says.

"Daemos...I had...to find you. I've been...looking for you..."

"Why?"

Silmeir's lips curl upward again. "I don't know. I don't...remember." Daemos looks at the progeny of his enemy. He escaped and killed those hideous things. He thought that terrible part of his life was in the past. Daemos taps the creature in Silmeir's face. It squirms, moving Silmeir's head. "Something told me I have to find you." He looks over to Vel-Syn. "Who is this?"

"I am Vel-Syn. A descendant of the Suffering."

Silmeir turns and looks at Daemos. "She's pretty. I like her. Is she going to kill us?"

"No," Daemos says. "At least, not yet."

"Oh. Okay…that's good…maybe."

"There is something I can do," Vel-Syn says, moving closer to Silmeir.

"What?" Daemos asks.

"Yeah, what?" Silmeir returns.

"I can remove it. Your blade or brute force would fail. It's probably his only chance unless you want him to die."

Daemos thinks for a moment. Is Silmeir better off dead? Is he of any use to me, or will he just slow me down? Do I *want* him to live? This kind of pondering usually only lasted the time it took to deliver a killing stroke, but life is not like it used to be.

Three of them stand there among the Halls of Stone, four if Silmeir's horse is included. None of them fully human, if they ever were. The demoness among them is not of this world. This is intriguing. Perhaps she can save Silmeir. Daemos looks at him, seeing the shell of his former self. "Silmeir?"

"Yes, Daemos," Silmeir says.

That's all Daemos needs to hear. There is a part of him left inside.

"No, he can live," Daemos answers. "Remove the creature."

Vel-Syn kneels next to Silmeir and whispers an incantation. She reaches out toward Silmeir's face. The creature quivers. She inserts her fingers into it. It shakes and releases its grip on its host. Vel-Syn continues her incantation as she pulls it out from Silmeir. Daemos grimaces from the sight.

More and more of the creature is revealed. What Daemos initially saw was just the tip of the iceberg. Long and thin malleable tentacles come out limp. They might have reached down to the top of Silmeir's legs. Vel-Syn holds the creature out over the fire in one hand. It flails about in pain. With her other hand, she places it on Silmeir's open face. His features slowly mend. The edges of his wounds come together and reattach, for the most part. Like Daemos, he is not the man he used to be

The creature's slippery skin blackens from the fire. It melts in Vel-Syn's piercing grip and falls into the flames.

"Thank you, Vel-Syn," Silmeir says, breathing deeply. "I feel better...I think. I don't feel pain, I think. Is that good?"

Daemos looks at Vel-Syn. He says nothing. He never knew how to say *thank you*. Vel-Syn believes she understands his minute gesture. Daemos reaches to Silmeir and feels his new face.

"How do I look?" Silmeir asks.

"Better than me," Daemos says. Given his mangled state, the ugliest person ever born may hold that over him, as well.

"Did you hear that, Mr. Brown? Not too bad." Silmeir says, standing up.

"Who are you talking to?" Daemos asks.

"To Mr. Brown, of course. You remember Mr. Brown," he says, walking over to his horse. Mr. Brown drinks from the stream. Silmeir pets him on his head and signals he can rest for the night.

"No, Silmeir. We haven't met."

"Oh. That's strange. Mr. Brown is my horse, of course. We guide each other."

"You guide each other?" Daemos asks.

"Yes," Silmeir answers. "We found you, didn't we?" Daemos and Vel-Syn look to each other. Silmeir grabs a blanket from his saddle and lays down on the ground to rest. "Since I may live to see tomorrow, I am going to sleep. Rest, Mr. Brown. Rest, my friend." Mr. Brown neighs in return.

Vel-Syn walks over to her side of the fire. "Humans," she says.

Chapter 33

Silmeir wakes to an odd mumbling sound. He sees Daemos writhing on the ground in his sleep. His eyes flutter beneath. Sweat runs across his brow.

"Daemos," Silmeir says, shaking Daemos awake. His eyes jolt open as he pants. "You were having a nightmare."

Daemos catches his breath. "You have no idea. My tortur...I used to...it matters not."

Vel-Syn plods about. Her fiery mane whips about, occasionally striking the stone walls. Silmeir walks over to Mr. Brown and joins him for a drink from the stream. Daemos looks over to him. "How do you feel, Silmeir?"

"Good...I think," Silmeir answers. "I don't feel much."

Daemos realizes that will probably be a consistent response from Silmeir. He'll need to get used to it or stop asking the question.

Mr. Brown neighs and shakes his head. Silmeir pets his companion's mane to calm him. "Mr. Brown doesn't like it here, Daemos. Now that we've found you, Mr. Brown thinks we should leave. I agree with him."

Daemos looks at Vel-Syn as she tries to hide her anger. Daemos chuckles. He already appreciates the fact he spared Silmeir's life. It's been awhile since Daemos felt any levity. This could be a beneficial arrangement.

Daemos stands, stretches, and joins Silmeir and Mr. Brown for a drink. After his drink, Daemos reaches out to pet Mr. Brown, but Mr. Brown backs away a step and whinnies.

"Easy, Mr. Brown," Silmeir says. "Daemos is our friend. He's the one we were looking for. You frighten him, Daemos. Vel-Syn, too. He has never seen anyone like you before. He just needs to get used to you is all."

"I'm used to it," Daemos says. He looks at Vel-Syn. Her beauty radiates past her gruesome human clothing like the flames from her hair. "Is that your form down in the Suffering?"

Vel-Syn glances at her body. "No. I chose this form, something more human to adapt to my time here. I've seen many human women. I did not like how most of them entered my dominion. I felt this is more suitable."

"You can do that? Change your form?" Daemos asks.

"Demons can do many things. Everyone's form changes when entering new realms."

"Good choice," Silmeir says.

Daemos keeps his thoughts on Vel-Syn to himself. "Mr. Brown doesn't like it here, huh? I can't blame him. I don't know if you know this or not, Silmeir, but we're in the Halls of Stone. We're trapped here."

"The Halls of Stone? Oh." Silmeir checks his surroundings. He then looks into Mr. Brown's eyes. "That's okay. Mr. Brown wants to leave. We will take you out."

Daemos looks over to Vel-Syn, and then back to Silmeir. "You know how to get us out?"

"Yes."

"Okay. Lead the way."

"How do you know how to get us out?" Vel-Syn questions.

"I see the way. Don't you?"

"You can't see kes! You have a hole in your face."

"I see you, Vel-Syn."

Vel-Syn's hair burns bright red as she purses her lips and her eyes widen.

Silmeir climbs atop his saddle. Daemos walks over to Vel-Syn.

"You think this human husk can find the way?" Vel-Syn asks.

"Not really, but what do we have to lose?"

"Mr. Brown may lose his head."

"Silmeir, Mr. Brown, lead the way."

Mr. Brown starts walking. Daemos and Vel-Syn follow behind. Her hair burns bright.

Chapter 34

A guard's fist pounds on Faelin's chamber door. "Faelin. Your lord wants to see you in the throne room right away."

Faelin picks up two daggers and conceals them underneath her clothes. She walks over to her door and opens it. Two fully armored guards stand in the hallway. They take a step back and give her room to walk ahead.

"After you, Faelin."

Faelin looks at them. They stand calm and still. She walks ahead, and the guards follow behind.

Is there news? Has Tar and his men returned? Or have her worst fears been realized? Are they dead? Did Daemos escape? No, that's impossible. He was trapped in that cellar of suffering, surrounded by too many bloodthirsty, sadistic brutes. They must have finally returned. Perhaps they were attacked as they tried to escape Viscrucia. Who knows? Countless scenarios have played out in Faelin's mind, day after day. The days kept adding up. The wait must be over. They've returned with their prisoner. It's the only reason her father would call for her now.

The sentries push open the grand doors to the throne room. The view surprises Faelin as she sighs. The hall is filled. Over one hundred people stand in attendance: nobles, the elite, and even some commoners. Their chattering dulls to a whisper as they look at Faelin. She is surprised that her father let the likes of them in. This will be a lesson for them, something they can witness, the success of royalty.

Faelin walks down the steps and across the hall. All eyes gaze upon her. This is it. Her time of greatness is here, and they've all come to see it. The lord's most prized possession is here and Faelin, his daughter, has given it to him. She walks around the pool with the great statue of the lord standing tall in the center. Even Faelin doesn't like that statue of her father. Numerous guards stand in formation at the foot of the steps leading up to the throne and the lord. Of course, Huemic is there. The lord sits still for once. The crowd quiets.

"Faelin," Huemic says. "Thank you for joining us."

"I am at my lord's service," Faelin says.

"Yes. Because of your deeds in service to the lord, he has requested an audience." The lord spits to the side of his throne. Saliva hangs from his chin.

Disgusting, Faelin thinks. Even during a time like this, her father can't manage to act regal. It is a little odd that he isn't dominating the conversation already.

"He wants everyone to know what you did," Huemic adds.

Faelin looks among the crowd. She doesn't see Tar

and his men. Faelin clears her throat as anxiety builds.

"What information do you have? Where is Tar?"

"What information have you heard lately, of the villages nearby and others further out?"

This is an odd question, Faelin thinks. Local news and politics are her father's concern these days?

"Tell me what I should know, Huemic."

The crowd stirs. They sense the growing tension. Why did the lord bring them here?

"Things are the same here. Calm, peaceful, as always," Huemic says. "The villages and town nearby are the same, as well…" Huemic turns and meanders away. Faelin is highly annoyed at this point. She opens her mouth ready to question why she's here when Huemic continues. "Further away. Many days ride, it sounds like things are different. Off near the wasteland of Viscrucia."

"You went there again, Huemic? Maybe you should stop wasting everyone's time and let us know what you saw."

"No, Faelin. I did not go there. I've spent my time there and won't be going back. I've heard from other men. Have you heard the tales?"

"No."

"Your men have not returned. No one has gone this long to the city of death and returned. No sign. No word. During this time, more men have died. A…storm. A storm is told to have risen. A bloodstorm. Men in Yesilmi saw the rain."

Faelin gulps.

"You failed your lord!"

Three guards rush in from each side. Faelin reaches for her knives. She grabs one and swings. The oncoming guard dodges the blade. Another guard grabs her other hand. A third guard barrels in and grabs her by the neck. Faelin struggles. The crowd gasps. They came for a show, and they're getting it.

"Huemic," she gasps. "What are you doing?"

"You failed, child," the lord exclaims. "Failure needs punishment."

Two guards emerge from the crowd. Each holds a young female hostage. Faelin recognizes her two friends instantly: Ness and Ensa. Their hands are tied behind their backs. Knives press against their throats. Their faces stream wet with tears.

"You're dirty," says the lord. "Your stench disgusts. Clean her."

The guards pull Faelin into the pool. They kick the back of her knees. The third guard grabs her hair and plunges her head beneath the water. Faelin struggles as best she can. She splashes water frantically as she tries to escape.

"Faelin! No!" her friends plead. The lord smiles at the sight of fear...at the sight of his daughter drowning.

"Put them on their knees, too," Huemic orders. The guards each pull out a blade and sever the tendons behind their knees. They drop instantly.

"Good, good," the lord mumbles.

The crowd squirms. Some turn away, closing their eyes.

The guard brings Faelin up for air. She chokes. After catching her breath, she regains a little composure. "Father! Don't …there's still…"

"You heard your lord," Huemic interrupts. "Failure deserves punishment."

The guards force her back into the water. It's difficult for her to see underneath the water. She can barely think, barely concentrate. The water darkens. Blood pollutes it. The guards pull her out from the water again. Her friends cry. Their wrists and femoral arteries have been cut on the inside of their thighs. Faelin cries with them. Ness and Ensa are friends she has known since she was a child. They are innocent. They are good women. This is what being friends with Faelin brought them.

"Clean her, I said!" the lord spits out. The guards dunk Faelin again. She chokes on her friends' blood. Many crowd members weep. They know her. She is a friend to most.

By the time Faelin emerges, both of her friends are dead. Their skin is pale from blood loss. The entire pool is now crimson. The guards let Ness and Ensa's bodies drop into the water. Faelin weeps. She is exhausted. The guards drag her to the edge of the pool.

Faelin looks up. Huemic smiles. The lord salivates from the sight. She is soaked and humiliated in front of everyone. Two of her best friends were bled out on display for her mistake.

"There. Cleaner. Good," the lord says and smiles. "Learn this, Faelin. There not be second time."

Huemic steps out from his position near the lord. He addresses the audience. "Daemos, our enemy, is still alive! There is no other explanation. Faelin...said she captured him and left him in the hands of her men. She said they were going to bring him back here to your lord. Weeks have passed. No one has returned. Now...it rains blood. Well, blood deserves blood. Faelin knows this. If anyone hears rumor or whisper of anything, tell your lord's guard immediately. You know the consequences. Now I, Huemic, the captain of the guard, will deliver Daemos. I will make your land safe again."

Huemic nods to the guards detaining Faelin. The guard behind her quickly pulls Faelin's head up by her hair and smashes her face down on top of the pool ledge, breaking her nose and knocking her unconscious. The guards leave her draped over the edge of the crimson pool.

Chapter 35

Ripe red sangloshe pours into a wood mug. Boils Bogilocus rolls two severed fingers to the bloodtender. "To blood," Boils says, as he raises his mug. Bone bracelets wrap around his wrists. He takes a sizable drink. A fresh wound has been stitched up on his shoulder. Other than that, his flesh is its usual, ugly self.

Boils drinks alone. This house of food and drink is small and less crowded compared to others in Viscrucia. It's a lesser known establishment. As close to a locals' bar as there is in Viscrucia, one might say. The bloodtender is a scarred mess. Boils likes that about him. They've shared many tales. They've seen each other kill many times.

The door opens. An immense shadow looms into the pub. The towering Petrid ducks under the entryway and walks to the bar. He sees Bogilocus and motions to an unseen weapon he carries. Boils returns the greeting. Petrid pulls up a chair next to him, yet still over an arm's distance away. He maintains his guard.

"Petrid, you look as good as the day I last cut you," Bogilocus remarks.

"That bad, huh?" Petrid answers. "That's a nice cut you have."

"Ha. 'Tis a scratch. The citizen is paying for my food and drink."

The bloodtender motions to Petrid. "Sangloshe," he answers. The bloodtender pours another thick red sangloshe. Petrid grabs his beverage and drinks. "Did you enjoy the rain, Boils?"

Boils takes another drink. "The blood storm. It was the most amazing thing this sack of rotting flesh has ever seen. Blood...bodies...demons..."

"And screams," a voice adds from the shadows in the corner.

"Above or below, Lesigom?" Petrid asks him. His presence did not escape Petrid.

"Above, of course. That's where the demons played. Brought red to the clouds. Blood to the ground. Anyone near that screamed on the ground, I cleansed and drowned." Bogilocus smiles, hearing the verse. "Seems the Suffering has a choir, too. Music for the few. So many it slew." Lesigom takes a drink of peth, a bitter alcohol crushed from organs, much stronger than blood wine. "And you, Petrid? Did you enjoy the blood wetting? The shower of pain, with no drain...just red...red rain?"

"I did. It was...the Suffering. Here. I still have trouble believing it."

"Believe it, Petrid," Boils responds. "It was an offering. A gift...to us...to Viscrucia. Maybe never before, maybe never again."

"The mud turned to blood," Lesigom continues. "Pain to rain. Flesh to kes."

Boils laughs and takes another drink.

"Why the gift?" Petrid asks. "Why the blessing to Viscrucia? Why did the demons come?"

"Demons or *the* demon?" Boils returns.

"Hair of fire. Body of desire."

Petrid rolls his eyes and gulps his ale.

"Share your thoughts, tall question man. Boils said believe it, but what do you believe?"

Bogilocus looks at Lesigom, and then to Petrid. Lesigom is onto something. Boils didn't catch it earlier as he enjoyed his drink, and the memory of the rain wetting his face.

Petrid tightens his grip on his mug. He plans his moves and weapons to use if necessary. The bloodtender stands back watching, ready with a concealed blade. Bloodtenders always sense death before it strikes, like vultures throwing their own dinner party.

"That day. It was pain...absolute pain." Petrid often uses the Viscrucian slang for *beautiful*. "Such a sight. Everything I saw that day. But what I didn't see...was Daemos."

Boils and Lesigom take in this new perspective.

"I didn't see a lot of things that day. I didn't see priests walking Viscrucian, either," Lesigom jests. Boils and the bloodtender have a laugh.

"But did you see him later? That thing in the Death Pit?"

"That was no man," Boils says. "'Was a demon. Cast from the Suffering that day. Still feeding on the living."

"Are you sure?"

"Viscrucian champion, killer of the wraith, Daemos may be, but he's still a man, indeed."

"It is a dark time," the bloodtender says. "A time…like the beginning of Viscrucia. Birth is bloody. A wave of blood and death, unlike the usual days. The death has been growing. Blood is boiling. The Suffering has risen. A new time has come, and with it, change. This is not the end. This is the beginning. The dawn."

Cryptic words from a proprietor of blood, even for this crowd.

"I won't miss it," Bogilocus says. "If there's more to see, I will see it. I will be a part of it. I'm not going anywhere."

"I will ride this wave, too," Lesigom says. "I will tell its tales. Scribe its history. Sing its story." Lesigom raises his peth. "To the blood that comes. To the new dawn. To…Viscrucia." Every man raises his drink and imbibes.

"Still, Daemos is not among us," Petrid says. "That is not like him. He would not miss something like this. If it is a new time, my gut tells me Daemos would be a part of it. That he would be basking in the center of it. Possibly, even be the cause of it." The men listen.

"Even if that cause was his death?" the bloodtender asks.

"It could be," Petrid replies.

"We don't know. Not yet, at least," Boils says. "Knowing Daemos, he would kill us if anyone shed a tear for him. Then guzzle it in a fine blood wine. Raise again. To Daemos, death or not, a true Viscrucian." The men toast a final time.

Seconds pass.

A woman bursts through the door with black fangs raised, ready to claim a new prize and hoping to capitalize on the surprise. She swings down. Petrid narrowly dodges the fangs as they slam into the bar. The woman pulls out another blade and spins around. Petrid whips out a small sickle and catches her wrist. It severs her tendons, and she drops the blade. He slams her face onto the bar, breaking her nose. He kicks the back of her knees, dropping her to the floor. He grabs her by the hair and chops her head off with the sickle.

Petrid quickly raises his weapon and faces the rest of the group, ready for an attack looking to exploit his defense. Boils now holds a knife yet has not moved. Lesigom holds a blade in one hand and his drink in the other.

"Another sangloshe, Petrid?" the bloodtender asks.

"No. Keep the body," he says. "Consider it your tip." Petrid grabs the woman's head and walks out with it.

Chapter 36

Faelin awakes in the pool of blood. Only the moonlight illuminates the room in a few spots with a blue hue. Shadows cover the rest of the hall. Her movement sends ripples across the water. She rolls her head over and reaches for her nose. It's shattered. She tastes blood. She pops the pieces of her nose back into place and spits crimson. She sees her dead friends lying there with her.

She walks back to her room to rest and heal. This is not over. She will finish the job. Daemos. Tar. All of them. The storm. What has happened? She underestimated Daemos. How could he have gotten through all of them, not to mention all the other rumors? How did he not die?

It matters not. She will make it happen. She will find him again. She will conquer him again. It doesn't matter what Huemic attempts.

"Messengers. One to every village, every town, every kingdom with a worthy fighting force. We will assemble an army. We will march to Viscrucia, and we will burn it to the ground with Daemos in the middle of it," Huemic says to the lord. "It's time. Rise above all other Kingdoms. Lead and rule upon destruction. No noble will ever dare challenge your word after."

"Yes. I like that," says Lord Villous.

"It will take time. Time. Travel. Emissaries. Offerings. But we will do it. In a few seasons time; maybe more, maybe less but soon, the siege can begin."

"Do it. Make it happen, Huemic."

"Yes, my lord."

The lord ponders. The two talk alone in a council room. "I was right, Huemic. I still right! This is it. *Purpose*. Path. Faelin…was supposed to fail." Huemic listens closer. "This is not a setback. Faelin's failure got us here. We gather the lands. You burn. We kill. I rule them all.

"This will bring Daemos his death. No more running."

Mr. Brown trots along the narrow stream among the stone, leading the group. "The walk is peaceful isn't it, Mr. Brown," Silmeir says, breaking the silence. "Strange, I can't think of the last time I used that word. Been a long time since I said that." Mr. Brown neighs. "That's right."

A light mist has gathered upon the ground. Dark clouds move ahead as the air cools. Daemos's skinned flesh tightens because of it.

"Do you walk much, Vel-Syn?" Silmeir asks.

"Yes," she answers eventually.

"How else do you travel?"

"Other ways."

"Oh."

The three continue their journey. The mist grows.

Daemos notices a faint smell. Vel-Syn senses it too. She thinks about their trek. How long have they been walking? It's difficult to tell. Time is not what it usually is within the Halls of Stone. Silmeir and Mr. Brown lead them down one hall, then another, and then another. Right when it seems that they might reach a dead end, more halls appear. The mist is thick now. They all trudge along.

"Faster, Daemos," Vel-Syn demands. "Walking won't kill you, but I will if you don't speed up." She breathes heavier than normal.

"I'm right behind you, demon," he says.

"You're only behind me because I'm slowing down for you."

"You hear that, Mr. Brown," Daemos says, breathing deeply. "Do you think I'm moving slowly?"

"You have slowed down a bit, Daemos," Silmeir answers.

"No one asked you, Sil," Daemos says. Silmeir's mind is past sarcasm it seems.

Daemos looks down through the fog. He can barely see his feet. The Halls of Stone look the same but seem to move slower. Are the halls moving slower? Is he moving slower? Strange. Silmeir whistles a tune. It bounces back and forth between the hall. The movement of the sound is somewhat disorienting.

"Silmeir. How much further?" Vel-Syn asks.

"Further? We are nearly out. Can't you tell? They don't see it, Mr. Brown, but we know the way."

"He doesn't know kes! Daemos, he's taking us in

circles. This shell has no mind and no idea where we're going. He's wasting our time."

Daemos reaches out to the stone to help hold himself up as he walks. His body feels heavy. He looks at his other hand and sees tracers of its movement as he waves the intoxicating mist in front of him. He doesn't think much about it. He doesn't think much of anything. He just tries to keep moving. Keep moving. Keep following. Keep walk...

Vel-Syn slaps Daemos hard across the face. The blow knocks his head into the stone. Her mane of flame burns bright. Its changing colors undulate within the mist.

"Wake up, skinless! I never should've listened to you. Now I'm going to rip Silmeir limb from limb and eat Mr. Brown alive!" She swings again at Daemos. He manages to catch her hand, turn, and use her momentum to throw her to the ground.

So, the demoness wants to play...

Vel-Syn gets to her feet. Rain sprinkles down into the mist. Silmeir and Mr. Brown stop and turn their heads to see the commotion.

"Looks like they're fighting, Mr. Brown." Mr. Brown neighs in response. "Yes, let's keep moving. They could hurt us." They continue moving into their next widening passage.

Daemos advances. Now he's ready for her. "Careful, demon, or I'll scar that perfect skin of yours."

Fire erupts from Vel-Syn's eyes. "How dare you insult me that way! You have no conception of my true form; my original skin down in the Suffering, you insolent skin bag! It had eons of experience, eons of pain, and twisting torment! The passage through the Pain to this realm gave me this new body. You suggest my skin knows no pain! Then I'll rip you from yours!"

The two square off. Daemos smiles. He faces another demon in combat. To think that the day started out so dull. Vel-Syn swings through the mist. Daemos ducks and moves. He swings, and she dodges. She throws him against the wall. The *thud* rings down the hall. She swings with her outstretched nails. He blocks her attack. She swings with her other hand. He ducks just in time as her talons cut through the rock. He pushes her against the other wall. She snaps her flaming hair through the fog, but Daemos dives out of the way. The assaulting flame plunges forth again. He rolls away and gets to his feet.

The clouds darken, and the rain increases. Daemos takes advantage.

Yes. Use the dark.

Daemos quietly moves back. He sees her hair slowly dim as he gains more and more distance. It ceases. He crouches down in a corner, ready to strike. Daemos listens. Rain hits him and his surroundings. No sound from his foe. He sees the mist next to him. He waits. Did she go the other way, he wonders? He looks above him and around him. Still no sign. Maybe it's his turn to hunt.

Fire spirals through the gloom. Its origin is much closer than Daemos imagined. Vel-Syn can conceal her flame. Daemos didn't think this was the case. This makes the demoness even more dangerous. The fire searches for its target, burning in different directions. The blaze disappears and the black returns. Daemos pounces. He punches through the shroud to her most recent location. Just as he's about to connect, Vel-Syn catches his punch. Her hair ignites, revealing her at his side, not where he expected her to be.

She slaps him hard with her other hand, and then backhands him back to the wall. They both move forward. Reaching for each other, both hands clench the others. Mere inches apart, they peer into the other's eyes. Daemos tries to headbutt her in the face, but she evades the attack. They wrestle to the ground, rolling back and forth. Vel-Syn gets on top of Daemos. She pins his hand against the ground. Her hair swarms around his head, inching closer. Daemos feels the heat. Sweat runs down his skin.

Mr. Brown neighs.

"Are you done?" Silmeir asks. "We are."

Vel-Syn looks up. Silmeir's right. They've done it. They are outside the Halls of Stone. She looks behind and sees the narrow entrance. Rain cuts through the dissipating mist. She turns back. Mr. Brown neighs again. Vel-Syn looks down at Daemos.

"Like Mr. Brown said," Daemos says. "We're out."

Chapter 37

The odd bunch took shelter far away from the Halls of Stone that night.

"Yesilmi is where we need to go," Daemos says, sitting around their campfire. Vel-Syn's robust fiery-red hair adds illumination. The light cast by the two fires dance between orange and red hues amid the night sky.

"Okay," Silmeir says. "But why?"

"Yes. Why?" Vel-Syn questions from across the fire. "The Pain is our destination. Our Pain is in Viscrucia."

"Why do you want to go there, Vel-Syn?" Silmeir asks.

Vel-Syn ignores his question.

"Yes. Viscrucia is our final destination, but not yet. We need food. We need clothes. Better rest. Yesilmi is a good place for that. It's close. It's our best chance."

"You mean *your* best chance?"

"Yes. It's *my* best chance," Daemos acknowledges, unafraid to face her accusations. "The reason you're here. You may find some things you like there."

"Like?" Vel-Syn questions.

"Not everything in this land is trying to kill us. There is good food, people, and drink."

"What good drink?"

"A fine goblin ale. Best for many days' ride."

"She has never had goblin ale before, Daemos. She is open to trying it," Silmeir says.

Vel-Syn's hair flickers as she narrows her eyes toward Silmeir.

"Is that your best drink?" he sputters.

Daemos smiles. "No. No, Silmeir, the best is sweet. It's bold from life. You taste death. The salt of your enemy's suffering. Blood tear wine. There is nothing like it."

"Interesting."

"There is nothing sweeter."

Vel-Syn smiles.

That night proves rough for Daemos. He doesn't sleep well. Pain and hunger wake him up numerous times. He did not lie when he said Yesilmi is the best place for them to go. He still needs to recover, if he can.

The three continue their journey. They only come across one other group, traveling on foot. They trade a blade for a little food. If they had been riding a beast or a horse, Vel-Syn would have killed them immediately and not have bothered with the trade. The negotiations did not last long once they saw with whom they were trading.

The group continues. Daemos understands. Silmeir understands in his own unique way. Vel-Syn feels killing them would've been much simpler.

The three reach the edge of the Yesilmi. Word spreads fast of their arrival. This is not Viscrucia. There are decent people here. The sight of zombies and some unknown fiend do not make for a welcome visit. Doors and windows close as they walk through town. Animals and goblins scurry away. Daemos did not anticipate this, although he should have. His last memory of this place was very fond, even though Faelin later turned out to bring his body's destruction.

As the travelers reach the Goblins' Gully, a mob of goblins, fairies, and humans greet them outside its walls. Other townspeople carry torches and surround them.

"Leave! You are not welcome here!" a man shouts.

"Not welcome?" Silmeir questions. "Why not? We have done nothing wrong."

"Nor will you!" shouts a wood nymph. "We don't want trouble."

"Where are the Goblin Three?" Daemos asks. "Do they feel this way? Tell them Daemos has returned. I have caused no trouble here. We only come for food, drink, and sleep."

Gree, Lorsch, and Mackle each flip onto a different person's shoulder. "Aye, we the Three, Goblins be," says Gree.

"Are you Daemos?" Mackle questions.

"Daemos, don't look he, to be, thinks the Three," Lorsch chimes in.

"*Dead* does he look to be! And his friend! Don't know what to think of *she*." Gree says.

"And if *dead*, no food, drink, nor sleep do ye need!" Mackle says. The crowd agrees. Vel-Syn remains calm.

"Aye, Goblin Three," Daemos says. "We are not dead, we... Well, I'm not sure what we are, but we won't harm anyone. Like I said—"

"Look around! She'll burn the place down!" Lorsch says, motioning to Vel-Syn's hair.

"Wood and trees do not mix with fire and leaves!" Gree reminds.

"I could kill you all and burn your entire town to the ground," Vel-Sy says. "Then no more trees, leaves, or little Goblin Three."

The crowd raises their weapons and shouts, ready for the fight.

"Then no food, drink, nor place to sleep!" Mackle says.

Daemos knows this. He needs real food, sleep, and water. He can't just eat their cooked remains, yet Vel-Syn is eager to kill.

"Creatures and people of Yesilmi. You are right," he says, "we could accidentally cause harm to the Goblins' Gully. Might there be another place we may eat and stay? Someplace without your wood and trees?"

"No!" shouts a brazen man among the crowd. He carries a pitchfork and nudges his way through to the front of the crowd to engage the unwelcome guests. He lowers his weapon to an attacking position when he's suddenly stopped in his tracks. "What is this? I can't move!" He pushes his hands down on his pitchfork with all his might, but it won't budge. His hands shake.

The crowd looks to the odd bunch. They see Daemos's eyes locked with his attacker's. His bandaged hands mimic the man's who hold the weapon. Daemos slowly turns his hands toward the man. The man sweats as he turns his pitchfork against himself.

The mob sees that Daemos is the force of resistance. The prongs reach the man's neck. He closes his eyes in fear, unable to move from the wicked trance that befalls him. Tears shed. The mob steps back in fear. Daemos steps forward and wipes away tears running down the man's cheek with his bare finger. The man cringes.

Daemos steps back and presents the salty liquid to the demoness at his side. She licks the tears from his finger without hesitation. She smiles, relishing the taste of the man's dread.

Daemos pulls back his hand, thus removing the pitchfork from the man's throat. He extends his other hand, forcing him back into the crowd. The mob backs up further and gasps.

"What type of witchcraft can this be?" someone shouts from the crowd.

Daemos takes a deep breath. "Like I said. We don't want to harm you. We seek food, drink, and sleep. Is there somewhere else we can stay?"

The three goblins grumble to each other. The bulk of the crowd is silent, caught off guard by the uncanny display of power and unexpected reasoning. The goblins drop down from their pedestal hosts and flip onto each other, creating their goblin totem.

"No burn, no pain, death, nor maim, supposed Daemos promises thee?" the goblins demand in unison.

"Yes, we agree."

"Yes," Silmeir says as he pets Mr. Brown.

Two flying fairies look at each other with confused disgust from the sight of Silmeir.

"And she!" a woman in the crowd demands.

The crowd looks to Vel-Syn. She lets the moment and their trepidation linger. "Yes."

The mob slowly simmers with ease. Most of the crowd cautiously make their way back into the Goblins' Gully or their homes.

Lorsch backflips onto a large man's shoulder and whispers into his ear. His two goblin brothers quickly roll inside the Gully between their patron's feet. The large man motions to four of his friends and an exceptionally fast fairy.

"This way," Lorsch says, pointing around back. The disfigured group moves as directed. The remains of the mob follow behind.

They reach an old stone building, simple in structure, four walls, a few window openings, and part of a roof. Vines consume much of the exterior of the shanty. The stone is bare inside. The men set two torches inside niches within the walls. Silmeir descends from Mr. Brown, and the travelers settle awkwardly inside.

"Stay here," one of the men orders. Vel-Syn looks back at him, unconcerned by his demand.

"Thank you, fair people of Yesilmi," Silmeir says. Lorsch looks back to the group but says nothing. The hosts leave. Silmeir and Daemos get situated each in their own space against the walls of the dilapidated structure.

Vel-Syn ignites a fire in the fire pit at the center of the room. She watches Daemos. She had never seen such unique power within a man. He controlled his opponent's *flesh*. He took him from his most aggressive, enraged state, and within seconds, reduced him to a tearful blubbering babe on the brink of death. The death, which he did not grant. Why? They could have easily cut them down within seconds, burned the town in minutes, easily a hundred dead if they so choose...but he did not. Such a dark power he possesses, flesh over the man.

In time, people bring them food and water. The influence continues, she notes. The four weary companions eat and drink in relative silence until Silmeir ruins it.

"I used to love steak," he says upon finishing a bite of his. "It was my favorite thing to make and eat. Now, it doesn't taste the same. I can barely taste it."

"What is love?" Vel-Syn asks.

Here we go again, Daemos thinks.

"What in Suffering is Silmeir babbling about now?" his dark voice adds.

"That's how I think I ended up here," Silmeir comments.

"What are you talking about, fool?" Vel-Syn prods, losing patience.

"I would cook the animal for the village. Nothing compared to its taste. Nothing, except her. There was a girl, I can't, I…can't remember her name now, but a girl who would eat with me. She loved me. I loved her. One day, the soldiers were going to punish her to make an example to the rest of the village. I begged them not to. Huemic…Huemic gave me a choice. He said I had to go to Viscrucia on a mission. This meant death to us common villagers, but I agreed. That was long ago. I saved her then. When I came back, we had time together, but they forced me to keep going back. Each time I did it, I did it for her." Silmeir's eyes wander. His thoughts drift.

"Where's the girl now?" Daemos asks.

"Huemic killed her. I…can't exactly remember when or why. My memory…" Silmeir squints, twitching his head.

Daemos sees Silmeir struggling. It pains him. He is not the man he once was. Lord Villous and Huemic have mutilated and damned them both - destroyed their bodies and fractured their souls.

"I faced anything for her: death, Viscrucia, I didn't care. She was the only thing that mattered to me then. That is love. Nothing stands in the way."

The notion becomes a little clearer to Daemos, but still sounds ridiculous. It might make sense in Silmeir's warped mind. Daemos has more prescient matters that concern him. He doesn't care to think about love.

"It means you will kill for them," Vel-Syn states.

"That's what I said," Daemos concurs.

"Yes. Killing."

Silmeir's head bobbles toward his companions. He sees the personification of evil. They flicker in the fiery light of the flames piercing the night. "I see that between you. That similarity. In your way…yes."

Vel-Syn and Daemos share a look. Love, they get it. Simple understanding. Kill for someone. Protection. Keep someone alive. Like a mother to a child. No wonder Daemos never learned its meaning. His parents kept him alive. He must have felt it then. But now they're dead, and he feels it no more.

"How many times have you killed, Daemos?" Silmeir asks.

Daemos laughs. Vel-Syn smiles. "I can't count that high, Sil," Daemos replies. "You don't keep track when you've done it your whole life."

"How many times have you killed to save someone?"

Daemos's laughter fades to contemplation.

"A few times, maybe."

"Have you ever killed a friend?"

Daemos stares into the fire. "I don't have friends."

"Oh." Silmeir looks at the fire. His face is blank.

"Did your slaying ever not serve your own purpose?"

Daemos just looks into the fire.

"Would you ever die for someone?"

The banter ceases. Only the crackling of the fire whispers between them. Daemos looks to Vel-Syn. Her expression is void of feeling. He looks to Silmeir.

Silmeir's dead eyes stare right through him. Daemos has nothing to say. He knows the answer. Silmeir knows it. They all know it.

"That's what I did…making that first trip to Viscrucia… and every one after it. I accepted death so that she may live."

Silmeir's words stab Daemos in the heart. Maybe it, this *love*, wasn't so simple. He could kill. He has. He always will. But he now realizes he's never done what Silmeir has. Perhaps, he still doesn't understand it.

"Sacrifice," Silmeir adds. "That, to me, is love."

Daemos turns his head away from the fire. The side of his face still bearing skin smiles in the moonlight. He looks at his hand, opening and closing it. Remembering. Stopping the mob with a simple wave. He thinks about his newfound power. He had forgotten it for a short time while trapped within the Halls of Stone. That place plays tricks on you. He opens his hand up, remembering the tears he took from the brash man intent on killing him. *Tears*, the most precious commodity of his home, Viscrucia. He looks across the room to Vel-Syn. She licks her lips.

Chapter 38

The lord's emissaries travel great distances. They seek noblemen, royalty, and anyone with a sizable fighting force. Most scoff when they hear whom the heralds represent. The generous offerings delivered with the message, however, pique interest.

One is Queen Premous. She listens to the message in its entirety without interruption.

"I agree to Lord Villous's terms. Let him know in haste," the queen answers promptly.

The Kilsan messengers look at each other surprised. "Yes...Queen Premous. Absolutely, we shall. Do you need to hear more?"

"I've given my answer, messengers! Do not question. I know all that I need. Leave your lord's offerings and make haste, I said! Guards, see them out."

"Yes, Queen Premous!" the messengers respond. They turn and leave immediately. Guards escort them down a great hall.

Queen Premous sits atop an illustrious throne. Thin layers of polished metal decorate the throne room, giving off imperfect reflections. Fen, the general of her army, stands next to the queen. He is a formidable warrior and intelligent general. He has slain over a hundred men throughout his lifetime in combat.

"An aggressive strategy, my queen. As always, it will pay off," Fen says.

"Of course, it will, Fen. Clearly, a sign of weakness from the vile Lord Villous, and a plea for help."

"What do you have in mind?"

"Lead half of our men into battle alongside Lord Villous. Destroy the Viscrucians. The other half of our army will take Kilsan. It will be defenseless. When the opportunity is right, kill Lord Villous! Then send word to our remaining forces, and we'll take the lord's castle and land before anyone knows what's happened."

"It shall be done, my queen."

Ssagaecian clan leader, Gell, ruler of every mox on the south side of the Ssagaecian Mountains, laughs boisterously with five of his most loyal mox leaders when hearing the emissaries' invitation. They are a ferocious, yet light-hearted people. They clash their tankards and guzzle their mead. The Ssagaecian clans enjoy battle. Gell can use the extra booty the lord promises upon burning Viscrucia.

Gell is a proud conqueror. There are no better city and people to conquer than Viscrucia in his mind. It's the ultimate test for him and his clan; the ultimate battle. Perhaps he will take over that land and create a new city, an additional home for his clan and its mox leaders. For those that fall, this will grant them passage to the eternal dominion of their believed afterlife, Sera, in service to their battle god, Ssagaecia.

Nobleman Kerth takes the message to heart. His realm is to the far northeast of Viscrucia and Lord Villous's land. It is extremely vast and beautiful. Prairies, woods, meadows, and lakes make up his land.

Kerth is a short, strong, proud, and good-looking man. He has a thick, black beard and long wavy hair. His looks and persona set him apart in any crowd. Kerth despises Lord Villous, but he despises Viscrucia more. He has heard the tales, and he has seen its people. Eradicating the Viscrucians is the noblest thing he can do for his legacy and people.

His eldest son, Rayn, agrees wholeheartedly. He is a young and naive knight in his early twenties. They rarely run into Viscrucians. However, the few times have left lasting impressions. Kerth's family is good, noble, and pious.

Others like King Sarn, Sir Gurlinseff, Lord Rasence, and Queen Lin, do not care for the lord's offer. The thought of uniting with Lord Villous disgusts them. The thought of Viscrucia disgusts them. Let them all kill each other. Viscrucia is not knocking on their gates. Why knock on Viscrucia's and invite death to their people?

Opinions vary greatly. They always do when it comes to Viscrucia.

The emissaries Tanson and Mir reach their destination. They do not know much about King Olykon or his castle. They are youthful emissaries and have seen little of the outside world. Working for Lord Villous, they are not the smartest, nor does expanding their knowledge intrigue them. This works well for the lord. Huemic gave them only the necessary information on their destination and even less on the king they set out to bribe.

Tanson and Mir look upon two great waterfalls. The water plummets one hundred meters from the rivers above. The two waters eventually calm and merge together another one hundred meters from the base of the falls. A tranquil prairie of lush grass divides the water before they converge. Above the grass, a towering wall of onyx rock separates the two falls. Hidden away in the center of the onyx lies the entrance to the castle. One must seek this dominion out or stumble upon it by fate.

Tanson and Mir enter the black cave entrance. Luckily for them, the fire of a few torches illuminate the stone walls. The floor looks like black ice.

"This…is different. Tanson, where is everyone?" Mir asks. "I thought we'd be greeted by someone."

"Usually, there's a gate to a castle if that's going to happen," Tanson says.

"You call this a castle?"

"I don't know what to call it. I can barely see." The hallway curves back and forth. Shadows conceal the ceiling.

"I don't know, Tanson. There's no one here. Let's go back. Huemic didn't tell us much about this place, either. It's probably been abandoned for years."

"Are you blind? The torches are lit, stupid! That means there's someone here!"

"Indeed," a muffled voice calls behind them.

Tanson and Mir gasp while turning around, nearly dropping their small chest of booty. A cloaked figure moves forward from the shadows. They practically camouflage him. His hood hides his face.

"Kes! Man, you scared us," Mir says. The figure remains still. It looks like he holds his hands out together just in front of his chest, but they remain unseen beneath what appears to be unusually long and wide sleeves. "Greetings. We are emissaries from Kilsan. We traveled on Lord Villous's request. We are here to speak to your King Olykon. We bring gifts and good tidings."

The hidden figure remains still.

"May we speak to him?" Tanson asks. "We bring favorable news."

He stands still another few seconds and then bows slightly. "Kilsan. Lord Villous. Long journey," he says. His voice is deep and oddly muddled. "Forgive the darkness. Follow me. I will take you to him but watch your walk. Do *not* step on my cloak." He swiftly moves past them and leads the way down the curvy hallway. His cloak trails him on the floor by three meters. Tanson and Mir keep their distance as best they can. They pass many hallways with no doors. Their leader moves very fluidly as they try to keep pace.

The guide leads them into a large, circular room. Only a few torches burn from the obsidian walls. The vast darkness of the room prevails over the flame.

Tanson and Mir walk quickly. Their guide is about to

disappear amid the shadows when, suddenly, he turns around and stands just two meters in front of them. The two men stumble back. Their nameless guide moves toward them slowly. His cloak still conceals his face. The messengers stand their ground, unsure of what to do. The guide continues moving forward and passes between the two men without saying a word. They feel his long cloak brush against their boots in waves.

Mir looks behind them to ask a question, but the man is gone. He turns back around and sets the chest of jewels down. "Great. Now, we're more lost than we were before. What do we do?" His voice echoes around the room.

"Calm down," Tanson says.

"Yes," a mysterious voice replies.

Mir and Tanson look around. They cannot tell where the voice is.

"Calm yourself, young man," the voice continues. "Fear tightens your muscles. Don't want that."

"Who are you?" Mir asks. The two look around. They feel naked without a torch.

"King Olykon."

Tanson hits Mir in the arm and they kneel. "King Olykon. We are honored. Thank you for seeing us. My... How did you know we were here? I ask."

"How?" King Olykon asks and follows with laughter. The laughter echoes around. The two still cannot see him. "I hear you. Your footsteps. You talk down the hall. You announced your entrance without delay." The emissaries look at each other with idiotic confusion. "Not everyone lives according to the light like you do. I heard your every step and word." Mir tries to muster something intelligent to say but fails as usual. "Rise, travelers."

"Thank you, King Olykon," Tanson says. They rise.

"What brings you to my Castle of Shadows?"

"We bring a gift from Lord Villous himself. His lordship…"

"Jewels and precious stones?" the king interrupts.

"Uh, yes, King Olykon."

"A generous gift. What does he demand in return?"

"Nothing, great king!" Tanson says, laying his diplomacy on quite thick. His intention is true, but his inexperience is apparent. "Our lord demands nothing. Rather, he asks you to consider a great victory." A low, rumbling laughter resonates around the room. "Lord Villous is gathering great armies across many lands. United, Lord Villous will lead them to a great battle. They will rid this world of the scum and villainy that sullies the land by marching into Viscrucia, the city of all that is unholy, wipe out their wretched, murderous kind, and burn the city to the ground. Our lord asks you and your men to join us. You will enjoy the spoils of war. Much more reward is there for the taking."

"What does Lord Villous know of my people? My army?" King Olykon asks. He is suddenly visible and only two meters from the emissaries. The surprise shakes them with fear, yet again. He looks exactly like the man that brought them into that room of shadows except much bigger.

The king is cloaked and hold his hands in front of himself in the same manner. He stands nearly a meter taller than the guide that brought them here. Tanson notices that his trailing cloak is expansive. It is many meters wide and is even greater in length. Thick and heavy, it sits several inches above the ground.

"I…" Tanson stammers.

"What does he know?" King Olykon's voice rumbles. It oddly does not sound as if it comes from beneath his hood.

"I cannot say, King Olykon. We are but messengers."

"Yes," Mir says. "He told us nothing. Our Captain of the Guard only told us where to go and the message to deliver. That's all."

"'Tis unwise of your lord to send uniformed emissaries to the king of shadows. Ignorance insults royalty, my people. Unprepared, you do not know our customs, do not know the magnitude of the favor you ask. Do you know what we do with gems? What we use jewels for here in my kingdom?!"

Tanson and Mir look at each other, confused and unable to answer.

"Of course, you don't. You don't even know the history of this room. Don't know if you are alone with me or if there are a thousand other eyes upon you." Mir and Tanson's hearts race as the giant king of shadows descends upon them. "You pathetic errand boys know nothing. Therefore, your mindless lord knows nothing. Nothing of this dominion, the Shadow race, nor what we do with cretinous message boys!"

King Olykon's arms shoot out from his cloak sleeves and grab the messengers by their necks. The dark slimy skin masks its strength. He lifts them off the ground and pulls them toward him. Tanson and Mir fight as best they can but are no match for the king's grip. "Perhaps, we should bring our own war to him. Teach him the ways of our people."

Tanson reaches for his knife tucked behind him underneath into his belt but cannot find it. How can this be? Did the cloaked man who brought them into the room take it from him as he left? How could he know about it? If so, how could he have taken it without him noticing?

King Olykon leans his head back. His hood falls to his shoulders. Horror strikes the emissaries' faces; a sight Olykon knows too well. His head is three times the size of a normal man's. Fifty protruding eyes encompass it. Each eye has three layers of eyelids that open. The second layer is semi-transparent, and the bottom layer is sheer. The jet-black eyes peer at their dangling prey. No mouth or nose is seen on the king's head, just dozens of eyes, separated by dark blue skin.

As the men struggle, the large sleeves fall back on Olykon. The men discover another set of arms. They are shorter and much thinner than the king's arms that hold them. They bare no hands, just a single claw extending a foot in diameter. One slashes vertically through Tanson's belly. He loses all fight and goes limp. His stomach distends. The claw swipes horizontally, disgorging Tansen's entrails. King

Olykon moves forward. Tanson's intestines disappear beneath the king. Mir looks down but cannot see Olykon's legs, nor hear footsteps. Instead, he hears an odd chopping sound.

King Olykon tosses Tanson's body off to the side of the room. He circles around, still holding Mir by the neck. His claws shred Mir's clothes. His other hand rips them off and discards them to the side. Reaching the other side of the room, the king turns around again. Naked, Mir looks back. Tanson's entrails have disappeared. Olykon tightens his grip, demanding his prey's attention as he takes him to the center of the circular room.

"What is your name?"

Mir tries to spit his name out when the king's claws whip through both of Mir's knees. He gurgles in pain against Olykon's grip as his lower legs fall to the floor. The king releases Mir. The hard floor meets his open wounds without compromise. The sound of Mir's screams and his pain echo around the room and resonate down the dark corridors, bringing chants of "Olykon! Olykon! Olykon!" from the race of Shadows.

"Insolent fool! Your name means nothing to me! It has no value, nor does the request you bring, or your pitiful trinkets! *You* are the only thing that bears any semblance of value, and *now*, you will learn about the race of shadows and the history of this feeding room."

Mir lies helpless on the ground. King Olykon grows in height before him. The cloak lifts off the ground, but the king's body continues beneath it. He bears no legs.

It is no cloak, but the king's body. It moves like a serpent but is wide and flat, like some amorphous creature from the ocean depths. The king continues to rise. There's a long slit over a meter in length within the center of his belly. The crevice opens, bearing hundreds of tiny, razor-sharp teeth. It is the king's mouth.

King Olykon speaks unrestricted for the first time. His voice booms through the feeding room and into the tunnels. Its magnitude knocks Mir onto his back. "Dinner is served."

Mir screams as Olykon slides over and devours him alive. Chants of the king's name resume from the race of Shadows. "Olykon! Olykon! Olykon!"

Chapter 39

"Many emissaries have not returned from their travels my lord," Huemic informs.

Lord Villous spits out a piece of bone as he chews his meal. The wet morsel sticks to the floor.

"Em'saries, don't care. They're not soldiers. Need marching death!"

"Yes, my lord. They must prove their worth. Men face trials. Some pass, some fail. Numbers are what you need. Results. Not diplomacy," Huemic replies and nods.

The corners of Villous's mouth raise as he chews with his mouth open.

"Good."

Huemic walks to the door and reaches for the handle. Moaning stops him. He glances to the corner of the room from whence the sound came. Chains rattle. Huemic closes his eyes and exits through the door.

The sun shines through the woods bordering Kilsan. Huemic reaches a small clearing among the trees. He comes here as often as he can. It is a peaceful place and affords him privacy. He stands in the center and brandishes his swords. He takes a deep breath and clears his mind. Here he practices his combat skills and hones his martial arts. He swings, parries, defends, and attacks. He prepares for the war to come. He prepares to defend his lord. He prepares to exterminate the horde of Viscrucian vermin. Swords, knives, club, and hand-to-hand combat, he practices all that he can. His skill with two swords is second-to-none.

On his way back to the castle, he notices someone following him. He stops and lets his pursuer approach. It is a beautiful young woman wearing simple tan clothing. A tan braided headband with a single white stone in the center holds back her long, brunette hair. She wears matching braided wristbands on each wrist. She is not a princess, Huemic thinks.

"Sir Huemic?" the woman asks.

"Yes, I am Huemic."

"I am Talene. I am a priestess with the Sublime Order."

"You're a Sublime, huh?"

"Yes."

"Yeah, I've heard of you. Heard you were...devote."

"Yes. Good. We have heard of your intentions toward Viscrucia and...we would like to help."

"Intentions? What intentions?" Huemic asks, avoiding eye contact.

"Your intentions of bringing about the downfall of the city of sin. Of erasing that den of evil and cleansing the sinners, once and for all."

"That's an entertaining story, Talene, but I don't know what you're talking about."

"Huemic, the Sublime are not bards. We are quiet and controlled. We follow the Sublime's will." The Sublime followers keep their religion simple. Their word *Sublime* encompasses everything: religion, their God's name, their people, etc. "We have our missionaries, similar to your own. We are here to help you. Sublime know how to hold their tongue, among other things."

Huemic looks at Talene, intrigued. She is no threat to him. Now, he weighs what truth she tells. Can she actually be of value? "Help? That thought is amusing considering the people you speak of helping against."

"You still do not trust me. I guess...I understand. I wonder, do you know of all the forces you contend with? There is more out there now, than just cannibals with blades and vile appetites. The storm of blood brought more than just death. It brought something wicked."

Huemic continues his pretense. Talene puts her hand on his arm and stops him. "Huemic, you are up against great odds. The Sublime can help you. You can trust me. We are here to help your cause. Come with me to our sanctuary. Hear us out. Let us help you cleanse the evil from this land."

Huemic and the lord threw their own emissaries to the wind. This is Huemic's plan, after all. Strength in numbers. He figures there is little that priestesses can do against true evil. Against a horde of maniacs wielding axes and weapons fashioned from their victims? Even less. Still, maybe there is something he hasn't thought of. Perhaps, the Sublime have something to offer.

"How long is the journey?" Huemic asks.

Talene and Huemic travel over a week by horseback before reaching her sanctuary. Every night and morning, Talene freely gives her succulent body to Huemic, pleasuring him with sex and more. Huemic learns firsthand just how generous the Sublime are. Talene is by far the best, most giving woman he has ever touched. She makes him question much in life.

The Sublime sanctuary lies in the lush, picturesque land of Emereth. Towering redwoods grow across magnificent bluffs. Animals roam freely. Food and water are in abundance. The rivers and streams flow peacefully. Huemic takes in a deep breath of fresh air at the base of the Bressen mountains. It soothes his body and mind. He is happy that he made the trip. Emereth is a far cry from the dreariness of Kilsan. Working under his lord's service for so long, Huemic knows little else. He almost forgot that lands, and women, like this exist. The sight and sounds of pain and despair have eroded the innocence of his youth, so long ago. He was once gentle, but that time passed.

Talene leads them to a redwood tree at the base of a grassy bluff. They get down from their horses and feed them. Talene walks over and reaches into a niche within the tree. Part of the robust bark opens, revealing the entrance. Huemic follows her lead. The bark closes behind them.

"Watch your step," Talene says. They walk down a few wooden steps carved from the great tree. A faint light shines in the distance below. Reaching the bottom, they walk down a hallway. The walls change from roots to dirt. Soon torches are numerous and readily light their path. They reach an open room with many doors. Two priests, a male, and a female, stand in the center. They are both dressed the same as Talene, drab, tan clothes, with braided bracelets and headbands with a white stone in the center.

"Welcome back, Talene," the priest says.

"Thank you," Talene replies.

"How was your journey?" the priestess asks.

"Fruitful," Talene says, motioning to Huemic.

"Excellent."

"This is Huemic. He is captain of the Kilsan guard."

"Welcome, Huemic."

Huemic nods in return.

"We are here to see Abrus," Talene says. The priests nod.

"I will inform him." The priestess exits through one of the doors.

Huemic observes their subterranean sanctuary. It is simple, yet surprisingly clean and well-lit for an underground chamber. The ceiling is low. The air is not stale, nor rancid like the dungeon air in the bowels of his Kilsan castle. Instead, the air has an aroma of the refreshing forest.

After a few minutes, the priestess returns. "Abrus, will see you now," she says. Talene and Huemic follow her through an ascending tunnel. They reach a stairwell and make their way up. The climb is notably long. The top of the stairwell leads to a dome-shaped room. The ceiling is comprised of soil and rock. It stands a little over three meters in height. The width is much wider, nearly thirty meters. Huemic estimates that they stand just inside the top of the bluff behind the redwood they entered.

The priestess leads them to the center of the temple. "Wait here," she says, and then leaves the way she came. Ten pockets of light shine in through ten dense windows above, forming a halo around them on the floor.

"I see you've brought a guest, Talene," a priestess says as she walks into the room. She walks to one of the circles of light shining on the floor and takes her position.

"Yes, Sublime Priestess. This is Huemic."

"Welcome, Huemic. So nice of you to join us," another priest says as he walks into the room, finding another pocket of light to stand on. "We appreciate you making the long journey."

Huemic nods.

"Were your travels safe?" another priestess asks, walking in and following the same suit.

"Yes, they were. Thank you," Talene says.

Huemic notices how courteous the Sublime are. He cannot even get a word out before he is greeted with another pleasantry.

"But, of course," a new priest says as he enters. "If

anyone can ensure your safety, it is a guard captain."

Huemic feels awkward. He's being surrounded by a religious cult. They enter from five different passages. "It was no trouble. Th-thank you," Huemic replies, trying to blend in.

One by one, more priests and priestesses, enter the room and stand underneath a beam of light, creating a circle around Huemic and Talene.

"Talene," a deep, male voice calls out from one of the dimly lit passages, "job well done." Everyone turns and looks to the voice. The final two priests enter together.

"Huemic, this is Abrus and his wife Sharelon, the high priest and priestess of the Sublime Order," Talene says.

"We had no doubt you would succeed in your labor, Talene," Sharelon says. She is tall, beautiful, and has thick, lustrous flowing brunette hair. Her eyes are emerald green. Abrus is her equal. He has a thick, full beard, and curly brown hair. They are young, early thirties at most. All the priests are surprisingly young. They have the look of royalty and are esteemed as such by their counterparts. They stand on the remaining two patches of light next to each other. Ten priests in total form their circle; five men and five women.

"It will be just like this, Huemic," Abrus says with an unwavering smile. "The time foretold. The place sullied by darkness and evil, illuminated once more, and piously cleansed." Abrus and Sharelon reach out and take each other's hand. All priests do the same, adjoining hands, connecting the circle. Huemic tightens his jaw to prevent himself from chuckling out loud.

"This cleansing, Huemic," Sharelon says, "will mark the descension."

"The descension," the other priests repeat.

Huemic looks around, not knowing what the hell anyone of these nutbags are talking about. "That's... great. The cleansing...descension. With respect, how can you possibly help? Why did you send Talene to find me?"

"Your doubt is understandable, Huemic," Sharelon says. "The Sublime are peaceful. We love nature and its blessed creatures. But there are many that are not blessed."

"Surely, you have heard of the new evils that have befallen the land?" Abrus questions.

"Rumors and superstitions. Foolish tales and drunken song," Huemic replies.

"I wish they were, good sir, but the Sublime believe. I venture out across the lands to observe firsthand. Our missionaries spread love and peace, even in times of darkness. I have met and seen evil. It has been foretold. Now, it is here."

"What is?"

"A demon. It has entered our realm. Death and devastation follow its every unholy footstep. Your soldiers, and even all those that you gather, will be no match for it."

"When I lead all gathered forces to Viscrucia, no man, no creature, no matter their size, nor bite, nor numbers, will stand in our way," Huemic says.

"This…is no man," Sharelon says. "Straight out of the depths of the Suffering itself. This…is a *demon*. Your forces of violence, your weapons of anger, they cannot harm this dark being."

"And you can?" Huemic asks.

"Sublime are the *only* ones who can stop it," Abrus says. "Evil invites evil. Thrives in chaos and pain. If you were to destroy every Viscrucian in your path, this demon will still lay waste to any combatant that opposes it. Evil cannot vanquish evil. *Sublime* are holy. Sublime are innocent. Sublime are pure. This fiend cannot harm us. It cannot hurt the innocent. We are the only ones who can cleanse this evil from the land and send it back to the Suffering."

"How do you intend to do that?"

"The ten priests before you, minus Talene, will accompany you to Viscrucia. You have the difficult part. It will be your job to fight the Viscrucians. Make your way to demon. She won't be hard to find."

"She? The demon's a she?"

"Yes," Sharelon says. "Sublime will need protection. Assign several guards to us. When found, send a signal, and we will move in and take her away, to a safe place away from the battle where we can perform the descension."

"You think that will actually work?"

"Yes, Huemic," Talene says. "Sublime know it will work. You clear the path. Sublime will cleanse the evil."

Huemic ponders their absurd proposal. This is more ludicrous than he imagined. This demon; if there even is one, will rip their innocence to shreds. Even if they make their way to it and somehow manage to get it out of there, what are they going to do, compliment it to death or sing some stupid hymn and lullaby it to sleep? Innocent fools. They have no weapons. They are walking into the lion's den blindfolded, bound, and with fresh meat dangling from their necks.

"What say, thee, Huemic?" Abrus asks. "Can we count on you and your lord? Will you help vanquish this demon and bring an end to the sin of Viscrucia?"

Talene takes Huemic's hand in hers and melts him with her affectionate eyes.

"Yes," Huemic says. "Kilsan and the Sublime are allies. We will aid each other."

It's impossible for Huemic to say anything else with Talene by his side. Her tenderness washes him with euphoria. Plus, by some miracle, they may be able to help. And if not, their defenseless slaughter will give Huemic something to laugh about before he dies that day. If he survives, his first stop is in the bosom of Talene.

Chapter 40

Messages and rumors continue to spread. Not all, however, come from Lord Villous. Stories of blood, demons, and immortals spread out from the skeletal streets. Their impact does not wane. They are horror stories around the campfire. They are words of warning to travelers. They are intriguing…to others.

Fantastic tales reserved for myths and legends live today. Insane news pulses from these badlands. The spectacle of a gladiatorial arena draws not just warriors, but crowds of bloodthirsty peasants, merchants, and nobles, alike.

The group rests many days to regain their strength. Daemos introduces Vel-Syn to the goblin ale he promised her. She is pleased with this new drink. This world holds many new experiences for Vel-Syn, experiences other than the usual torment whence she came.

The townspeople of Yesilmi loosen their guard. Their unwelcome guests do as they promised by not murdering anyone, nor burning the village to the ground. Daemos even provides service as bouncer a few times when patrons get out of hand at the Goblins'

Gully. Upon entering the Gully, the once unruly guests immediately pacify. The goblins and fellow patrons raise their mugs to him.

Mr. Brown and his malignant companions sit around the fire. The full moon glows amidst the night sky. Thousands of stars accompany it. Daemos senses something. He doesn't know what it is.

"Daemos," the wraith calls to him.

"I feel it," Daemos answers. He walks away from the fire.

"Daemos, where are you going?" Silmeir asks.

"Sil asks too many questions."

"To look through the dark, Sil," Daemos says. He walks out of their hovel. He sees nothing out of the ordinary but still *feels* something.

"Further."

Daemos walks down to the main road near the Gully. A few torches light the dark road heading into Yesilmi. The path out reveals nothing. Off to the left, on the outskirts of the town, stand more dilapidated remains, much like the one he stays in now. Dark, cold, desolate, yet there is something out there, something… of *flesh*.

Daemos ventures through the border. The home and shops were once nice; some above ground, others beneath it. Time has been the primary destructor. Plants and weeds have overcome them. Why they were abandoned is unknown. It matters not.

"Pain," the dark voice within calls to him. *"Feel… find…the pain. Don't look for it, feel it."* Daemos heeds his

advice. He stops and closes his eyes. He doesn't attempt his blood vision. He must hone his new senses and sharpen all his abilities. The evil voice is his teacher.

Daemos breathes deeply. He listens. He feels. His abdomen twitches. It pulsates. Strange. The sensation enhances into carving, into pain. They are cuts from a knife. They are deliberate, they are personal, they are...*self-inflicted*. Daemos opens his eyes. He knows this all too well. This is the cutting of a Viscrucian. This is home, yet so far away. Daemos moves. The pain guides him. He finds the side of a small hill. Stones and foliage cloak it beneath the darkness. There is nothing here, but the pain beckons him.

Daemos steps between the rocks. The shadows conceal all. Suddenly, Daemos feels the pain sharply. He looks to the side of the hill and still sees nothing. He reaches out and puts his hand through the vines. He feels...skin; oiled and treated. Daemos grips it and pulls it back. It gives freely. He holds it up in the night sky to gaze upon it under the moonlight. It is a common Viscrucian flesh curtain. Daemos has found his entrance.

He enters the shadows of the unknown and soon finds himself descending a spiraling stone staircase. The sounds of cutting and heavy breathing match his sensations. Voices follow. It sounds almost like rhythmic chanting. "...of pain. That which we seek. Blood reveal..." the voices call.

A light grows ahead. Daemos steps into a small,

subterranean basement. He stands hunched over beneath the low ceiling. A small fire crackles in the center. Its smoke exhausts into an opening above. Two men sit with their backs toward the only exit, each on one side of the fire. Their chanting stops. They rise and turn to face their visitor. Each holds a bloody knife. Their torsos bleed. Daemos feels their pain.

He recognizes the men. They are Viscrucians alright, Kane and Isan. Kane is a short, lean, and garrulous man from Daemos's recount. Somewhat handsome, his jawline and nose are sharp. His black wavy hair hangs to medium length.

Isan is the opposite; a tall, large, strong man, somewhat close Daemos's size. His hands are like an ape's. Unlike Kane, however, Isan speaks very little. His violence speaks for him. Isan's face is round and brutish. Both men are young; early twenties, and newer to the streets of Viscrucia, but they fit right in. They can be a deadly pair. They keep coming back for more, and yet, now they are here.

The men look to each other, and then back to Daemos. "We have sought you out," Kane says. "The name of pain."

"The face of pain," Isan adds.

"We were at the Death Pits that day," Kane continues. "We saw your spectacle of pain. Rumors have spread. You said you have returned from the Suffering. Is this true? What is your name?"

The men do not recognize Daemos. Have his features and face changed that much? Is it only Silmeir, in his altered state, and Vel-Syn, a demon from the Suffering, that can recognize him? Is his former life truly lost to man? Is he no longer a man now but something else?

"We followed what clues we could. It led us to Yesilmi, but there was no more sign to behold, no more path to follow. Then, we realized the way, *your* way. Your path...is pain. So, we had to follow the same. It worked. It brought you to us."

These men are devoted, no doubt about it, yet they still clutch their blades.

"We believe it is you, Lord."

"But we have to be certain," Isan states. He thrusts his knife forward at Daemos's face.

Daemos dodges just in time. He shoves Kane over the fire and into Isan. The men separate and resume their attack. Kane swings low at Daemos's leg. Daemos shifts out of the way, narrowly missing the knife and backhands Kane in the face, sending him to the wall.

Isan slashes wildly. Daemos brandishes a blade and parries the attacks. He swings hard, striking Isan's knife. Both blades slam into the hard wall and stick. Isan reaches out and grabs Daemos's throat with both hands. Kane rushes in and lunges in with his knife toward Daemos's stomach.

Daemos torques his body just enough to miss most of the attack before it plunges into the wall behind him. Daemos's side is cut, but the knife is stuck the same as the others. Daemos pulls back his hand to strike, but Kane reaches out and grabs it. Daemos is pinned. The attackers reach for their next weapon.

"Here comes the pain," Kane goads.

The obvious finally hits Daemos. He clenches his fist and feels the sensation of his assailants' pain once again. He uses it. Kane and Isan grimace and look down at their fresh wounds. Their grips loosen as they cringe. Daemos breaks free of their grip and pushes his fists downward. The men are flung back to the ground, each landing on a different side of the fire. Daemos clenches his fists tighter. Kane and Isan feel their wounds intensify at Daemos's command.

"Is this what you seek?" Daemos asks.

"Yes, Lord…it is. We had to be sure it was you. We wish…to serve you," Kane answers.

"How can you serve me?"

"Many ways, my lord! Many ways. Teach us! Teach us this power and let us serve you with it."

"Yes. Teach them the pain."

Daemos thinks, *I've rarely traveled with companions and fought the same fight. But now, I travel with two, and Villous will surely send more. I'm still not myself. I haven't fully healed. I'm still…vulnerable.*

"You need warriors. Men who will die for you."

These men could serve us, Daemos continues talking to the wraith. *We may even need more.*

"We are warriors," Kane says. "Tell us who to kill and it shall be done!"

Daemos releases them from his supernatural grip. The men catch their breath and sit up. Daemos looks upon them.

"Thank you, my lord. I am Kane, and this is Isan."

"This power, I may not be able to give you. But learn you shall. Follow without question. Do you wish to serve?"

"Yes, Lord," Kane and Isan reply together.

"You wish to learn?"

"Yes, Lord. We are Viscrucians. Pain, nor death frighten us. We are ready."

"Show me," Daemos commands.

Kane and Isan look to each other and notice the fire between them. They turn their gaze toward Daemos. They each make a fist with their hand closest to the fire and extend it over the flames. The burning heat washes over their skin. Daemos feels their pain but sees the determination among them.

"You have much to learn," Daemos warns them. "But if you succeed. If you survive, my priests...my Priests of Pain, you shall become."

Kane and Isan smile through their suffering. A brutal future awaits. The burning of their flesh is a small precursor of the affliction to come.

Chapter 41

For two weeks, as Daemos continues to heal, Kane and Isan undergo their training. They become understudies to the living embodiment of pain himself, and a demon who has known the Suffering for eons. It is brutal. It is grotesque. Vel-Syn enjoys it.

Silmeir's unique perspective provides intriguing insight. Mr. Brown stays far away. He does not appreciate the screams. Much of their training is spent in that very cellar where they first met Daemos. This helps deaden the cries. Otherwise, the townspeople would have surely asked them to leave long before.

Daemos knows it is time to return to Viscrucia. His body is mending. His mind, however, is still a little shaken. The pain he went through, his death, and the Suffering ahead of him have taken their toll. Still mentally stronger than most men, yet he has not quite recovered to his former self. He learns this as he heals in Yesilmi. His mind is finally given some time to rest and think, not just react. He learns he has his own demons of which to contend. This brings Kane and Isan's first assignment. After giving them a little time to heal, Daemos calls them.

"Isan, Kane."

The two men get up as fast as they can. "Yes, Bringer of Pain." Their determination has not faded in the slightest. Daemos knew from the beginning he liked them.

"I have your first mission, your first test. It's time to return home." The two men look at each other and smile. Their pain disappears at a chance to prove themselves on an actual assignment, not just surviving torture.

"Yes, name it," Isan says.

"Home? You mean Viscrucia?" Kane asks.

"Yes, Kane."

Kane and Isan look at each other.

"Apologies, Lord, for the question, but where were you born?" Kane continues. "Most that dare visit the…" Isan nudges Kane to shut him up.

"Look at me," Daemos says, moving closer.

Kane looks at Daemos's mouth. Half of his lips are gone. Teeth embedded in gums are no longer protected by surrounding flesh.

"I am no visitor. I was born there. I died there. Viscrucia is my home."

Kane gulps. "Yes…yes, my lord. Apologies."

"Tomorrow morning, you two will ride there. Hidden within one of my hideouts is my *face* and armor."

Puzzled, Kane and Isan look at each other.

"Your *face*?" Kane questions.

"Yes. It's what I call my mask. It is black and red with a silk underlining. You will know it when you see it. The rest of us will ride out one day after you. You are to meet us on the outskirts of Viscrucia on the east end. Once in Viscrucia, you will have a day to find them and escape. Take anything else you wish from my hideout. If the mask and armor are not where I tell you, find it."

"Yes!"

"There are only two outcomes. You will find it and bring it to me, or you will die. Do you understand?"

"Yes!"

"We will not fail you, Bringer of Pain," Kane adds. "We will survive. You will have your Face and armor again."

Daemos nods and turns away.

Kane and Isan head out the next morning. They ride as fast as they can. The journey is not easy on their injuries.

"You think his face is still there?" Isan asks.

"I think so, big man," Kane answers. "His hideout didn't sound easy to find. Pretty out of the way. If not, we hunt down the raiders who took it. If they're wearing it, it shouldn't be too hard to spot. We've been hunting a long time. Remember the deer near the Ssagaecian mountains when you were eleven?"

"Yes."

"I know you do! Now that was a good hunt. We'll get it. Another journey, big man. What do you think of this new group?"

"The people torturing us?"

Reminded of the pain, Kane looks over his bandaged wounds. "Good point. It will be over soon. Just takes time. We'll be stronger because of it. Did you ever think he, or the others would look like that?"

"No. I don't ever want to look like that."

"Vel-Syn, though! She looks pleasing!"

"Her head is on fire."

Kane laughs.

"Stay away. If you touch her, she will kill you. I have no doubt."

"Good advice," Kane replies with a smile.

Isan accepts Kane's optimism. One of them has to provide it. Isan likes to keep to himself. Kane, having traveled with him since they were children, however, generally knew what he was thinking.

"Do you believe it?" Isan asks.

"What's that?"

"That he was really born there. Born in Viscrucia."

"Weeks ago, I would've said, no way, just rumors and fairy tales. No one could be born there and survive. Impossible. But after what we've seen, been through, bled through, and...and his face..." Kane pauses. He looks away like he might get sick. "Yes. How else could anyone survive that?"

They make it to the bone streets of Viscrucia and follow their new master's instructions to the hideout. It is well hidden from the common citizen, yet inside, four Viscrucians have discovered the lair before them. They ransack the room, plundering anything they can find. The man in the far back holds the mask. The two parties square off.

"Well, this day gets better and better," the man in the back says.

"You're right," Kane replies. "We were afraid we would find that mask you're holding with no one to kill for it. My friend here has only killed two today. He was getting bored."

"Lot of talk for a little boy," a large man in front says, making fun of Kane's diminutive size. "I'm surprised you still have your tongue. I'll change that. I think I'll take your jaw, too."

Kane smiles. Even with scores of quippy comebacks he could spew, he doesn't hesitate. He is too excited to kill in his master's name. Isan and Kane act simultaneously. Kane leaps forward while pulling out a long thin knife and slams it into the side of the insulting man's face. Isan does the same to the Viscrucian in front of him with his long reach alone. Their blows slam their opponents' heads into each other. Each cranial piercing blade penetrates the other's head, nailing them to one another.

Kane's weight propels the two victims backward toward the remaining enemies. The man holding the mask drops it to grab a weapon. His partner beside him raises a longsword, but it gets caught in his friend's back falling toward him. The weight of the dead men knocks the sword from his hand. Seeing it fall, and he quickly looks up just in time to see Isan slam a heavy, edged mace into his face. The thunderous blow kills him instantly.

Kane leaps again from the body he rode to the ground, but the remaining Viscrucian gets a small knife out just in time. It cuts across Kane's side as Kane lands on him, but the damage is not enough. Kane instantly sinks his teeth into the man's throat and rips away. Kane's actions take another man to the ground. He rises, holding the murder mask. His face, shirt, and hands are awash with blood. He looks down and sees the gash in his side.

"That was fun," Kane says, smiling from ear to ear. Isan nods. They simultaneously raise one of their weapons and clang them together with identical movements.

"Let's take care of that," Isan says, referring to Kane's wound. "The Painful One will have supplies here to mend you."

"I agree, my Viscrucian brother. But first, look at this." Kane raises the mask he holds in his bloody hand. The men study its design. They hold something dear to their master: his *face*.

"It's a work of art."

After cleaning Kane's wound, Isan stiches him up with the supplies they find. They search Daemos's hideout for anything else they can use and then rummage through their victims. Finally, they cleave for currency.

The next day, Kane and Isan greet Daemos, Vel-Syn, Silmeir, and Mr. Brown outside of Viscrucia precisely as they said they would.

"Bringer of Pain, here is your Face and armor, rightfully returned to its owner, as requested," Kane says. Kane and Isan bow before Isan hands Daemos his mask. Daemos's party looks at the mask. Daemos studies it and notices the blood on it.

"I like it," Silmeir says. Mr. Brown neighs and shakes his head. "Mr. Brown does not."

Daemos wipes blood from the mask with his finger. "Is this your blood?" he asks.

Kane sits up straighter on his horse, like a soldier being called to attention. "No, Lord of Pain. We found four scavengers in your hideout, trying to take it for themselves. The blood is theirs, my lord."

Vel-Syn looks at the two disciples, Daemos's priests in training, and then to Daemos. "Seems they are committed."

"Gratitude, Vel-Syn," Kane says smiling.

She turns back to the priests. "Will this continue or falter?"

"It will continue until our death," Isan replies.

"We shall see."

"Well done," says Daemos. "You have succeeded in accomplishing your first task. More will follow."

"We look forward to each one, my lord," Kane says. "As a token of our gratitude, we have offerings to present you."

Isan hands out white bracelets to Daemos, Vel-Syn, and Silmeir. "They are fingerbone bracelets cut from the thieves trying to take your mask. They are finely polished."

"We made a bone necklace for Mr. Brown, too," Kane adds.

"Interesting," Silmeir says. He accepts the necklace and puts it around Mr. Brown's neck. Mr. Brown whinnies. "He likes the necklace. Thank you."

"And last, we give each of you a skull from our kill. If you desire, we will continue to add to the collection," Kane says.

"We do," Vel-Syn replies.

"Well done, my disciples. If you survive, my priests of pain you will become."

"We can think of no higher honor, my lord," Kane and Isan answer simultaneously.

Daemos puts on his face. His disciples smile. Mr. Brown neighs and shakes his head. Vel-Syn takes in the new look.

"I like this," the dark voice calls within. *"Let's put it to good use."*

"Kane, I am no expert in cleaning the dead and creating jewelry," Silmeir comments, "but all this must have taken a long time."

"It did, Silmeir," Kane answers. "We are not experts, either. That's why we got help. In the Carving Ground. A man named Petrid helped us in exchange for much of their remains. It was a hefty fee."

"Who is Petrid? Do I know him?" Silmeir asks.

"He's a carver, Silmeir, and a killer," Daemos answers from behind his mask. His voice sounds slightly different now beneath it. "Kane, ride on the outside next to me. Isan, ride on the outside next to Silmeir. If anything happens to Silmeir, you will experience pain you never thought possible."

"All will die if they are foolish enough to attack, Bringer of Pain," Isan says. Kane and Isan move their horses into position.

"And you'll protect Vel-Syn?" Kane asks.

"Vel-Syn needs no protection. Now, I'm protecting you from her," Daemos says. Vel-Syn peers over at

Kane. Kane's eyes widen, realizing how foolish his question was. He looks away and shakes his head, grumbling to himself.

"Let's go."

The group enters Viscrucia together for the first time. Mr. Brown neighs and shakes his head, not liking this place. It's his first time.

"Easy, Mr. Brown," Silmeir says as he pats his ride. "Don't worry, we're safe. Isan will kill anyone who comes near." Isan holds his horse's reins in one hand and a curved dagger in the other, ready to act.

The last time Silmeir was here he found Daemos. That fateful day led him directly to this moment. If he had not immediately fled to inform Lord Villous, he may still be whole. He may not be a husk of his former self. Fragments of these thoughts fire within, but his mind is too fractured to pursue them further.

The return to Viscrucia means nothing to Vel-Syn. Like Daemos, she was born of this world here. However, her time has not been overly eventful. Pitiful fools tried to attack her, and she made them suffer for it. Nothing new.

The last time Daemos was here, he died. Then reborn. Then he escaped thanks to his newfound abilities. The memories are difficult for Daemos to contend. The visions of his mutilation torture him every night. The payback he delivered to Tar and his men are what gets him through it. His life is pain. His death was pain. It fits that he returns home, to the city of pain.

Like the last time the odd bunch entered a town

together, the group grabs people's attention immediately. Some people recognize various members of their party. Even if they don't, it doesn't matter. Their entrance makes waves throughout Viscrucia. In a short time, everyone hears about them. It also doesn't take long before the city does what it does best.

Isan sees a cloaked individual limping toward Silmeir from the side. "Fellow tourist, might I..." the man says.

Isan yells out, "Mox!" He raises his dagger and hurls it into the man's chest. He falls to the ground, revealing the axes he carries in each hand beneath his cloak. Just before, Isan noticed the Ssagaecian's two companions dressed similarly in front and behind them. Ssagaecians often attack like wolves, flanking their prey from all directions. Silmeir is the weakest and most natural target to attack first.

The second man runs up behind them. Vel-Syn snaps her head back, unleashing a fireball from her illustrious mane. The man's shirt catches fire. As he tries to put out the flames, Vel-Syn has her horse kick the man in the chest. He flies back through the air. The flames take care of the rest.

The final Ssagaecian runs at them from the front. Kane jumps on his saddle and leaps off his horse like the world's largest frog. Daemos raises his hand and stops the Ssagaecian's flesh in his tracks. Kane then splits his head in two with his ax. Blood explodes from the damage. Kane brandishes a dagger in each hand as he regains his footing on the ground and moves in front of his group to take on the next assailant. None follow. Isan scans the streets, ever-vigilant. He sees no further threats.

"My gratitude, Isan," Silmeir says.

Kane grabs the weapons from the fallen and hands most of them to Isan. With his ax, Kane lops off the men's heads. He places them in a bloody saddle bag and hops back on his horse. Daemos looks at his disciple. Kane's face is covered in blood again. Daemos laughs.

"Yes, my lord?" Kane asks.

Daemos motions his head, mimicking Kane's jump. "I've never seen that before."

"Yeah, well, it's just something I do when the kill calls for it."

"Who taught you that?"

"No one."

Before arriving in the Carving Ground, they face two more attackers who remembered what Vel-Syn did to their friends. Their deaths are brutal, to say the least.

Hearing the news, Lesigom the bard scales the walls and bounds rooftop to rooftop. He finds a comfortable perch with a suitable vantage. He has been waiting for this day. Lesigom knew it would come. He quickly looks around to take in every sight and sound. He pulls out his blood jar and quill. Opening his trusty flesh pad, he begins.

> Viscrucia has seen many sights,
> But never before a Demon with Knight,
> Two Viscrucians by their side,

And a man half dead,
More than just along for the ride,
What does this mean?
What will it bring?
As always,
Death, pain, and suffering.
This marks a day of days,
Will Viscrucia swallow them up,
Or will more join the woman ablaze?

Reaching the Carving Ground, Daemos and party step down from the horses. They walk to Petrid's shop and enter. Ten men stand before Petrid. He towers above them all. Petrid recognizes the mask, the man's stature, tattoos, and a few scars, but the rest is different: reddish skin tone, new scars, healing body parts previously skinned, and the companions surrounding him. Petrid's old acquaintance never arrived wearing his mask either. The two groups stand in silence.

Petrid walks out in front of his men rubbing his hands together. Isan moves forward in front of his group, standing as the first line of defense.

"Step back, boy. I just helped you and your tiny friend here make the killing trophies you wear now, and you dare insult me by stepping to me in my own shop, in *my* Carving Ground?" Petrid warns, not even looking at Isan. His eyes remain fixed on Daemos. "No one intimidates me. Not even a demon and a ghost."

Isan tightens his fists. Seeing this, Petrid moves. Isan throws a left hook. Petrid blocks it with his forearm and jabs. His hand smears across Isan's face and mouth. Petrid's fingers grip the underside of Isan's jaw and dig their nails into his neck. He grips tightly, spins Isan around, and pulls back him away from his group while turning Isan's head to the side.

Kane rushes to his friend's aid. Petrid juts his right hand out with blinding speed. His unusually long reach and extended talons reach Kane's neck. Kane stops and backs up. He checks his neck while drawing a blade with his other hand. It's merely a flesh wound. Only a few drops of blood show. Kane breathes heavy. He smiles at Petrid as Petrid stares right back. His men draw their weapons but stand firm, seeing he has control of the situation. Daemos, Vel-Syn, and Silmeir watch the confrontation unfold.

Isan coughs. His breathing is difficult with Petrid's talons penetrating his throat, freeing his blood to run.

"You only have one free hand now," Kane goads. "You think that's enough to kill me?"

"Boy, if I wanted you dead, you already would be."

Kane's eyes flutter, and his balance falters. He regains his focus and spins the blade in his hand. Isan groans, and his knees buckle. Suddenly, both Kane and Isan drop to the floor, unconscious. Petrid pushes Isan off his foot with his leg.

"Good killers, but they have much to learn," Petrid says.

"Like the sleeping effects of the revissen poison," Daemos adds.

Petrid flicks the blood off his fingernails. He pulls

out a rag, wipes his hands on it, and then tosses it onto
Isan's body.

Petrid turns his head back to his men. "Leave us.
And take these young men with you."

"Petrid," Vel-Syn calls out. "Do you plan to kill this
one?"

"Not yet. Things change, though."

"If you do, I will burn this entire place down, along
with everyone in it, and I will personally take your
skinned corpse to the Suffering. He is mine." Fire
suddenly burns from her eyes. Her hair grows in
volume and emits a generous amount of heat. Petrid
says nothing. "Silmeir."

"Yes, Demoness?"

"Let's see if there's anything out here that interests
me."

"Yes, Vel-Syn."

"If not, we can kill someone."

"Okay."

Everyone leaves except Daemos and Petrid. The two
men look at each other, on guard as always. Daemos
shows Petrid the Viscrucian symbol for respect. Petrid
hesitates, and then reciprocates.

"I recognize that mask," Petrid says. "I carved it for
a Viscrucian a long time ago from the blood and bones
of his kills. A trophy among trophies. Constructed of
the corpses of feared, deadly citizens. Men no others
dared face."

"I remember."

"Do you? I think not. That Viscrucian walked alone."

"He did. Times have changed. You inlaid the mask with silk, a delicate substance I did not know of at the time. Melloc. Den. Lamaris. I turned their weapons against them."

"It can't be."

"It's me, Daemos. What's left of me."

"Take off the mask."

Daemos thinks about the request, and then removes his mask. A look of horror strikes Petrid's face. Even for him, the master of mixing art and death, the sight is shocking. He did not expect this, nor the feeling that is suddenly upon him. He feels…sadness.

"Unholy Suffering. What happened?"

"A lot."

The sadness continues. Petrid bites the inside of his lip to resist the emotion, but it's too late. A tear runs down his cheek.

"Careful, Petrid," Daemos says. "That's worth more than gold here."

Petrid can't help it. Another tear streams. He pulls out a blade. The sound rings through his shop. Daemos slowly draws out his own. Petrid marches forward and swings his blade up toward Daemos. Daemos greets the blade with his, stopping it in front of his face. The metal clangs.

"It's good to see you, brother," Petrid says. "Welcome home."

Chapter 42

Faelin coils her whip and secures it around her leg. Her long coat conceals her weapons, although it fools no one. Her piercing eyes, broken nose, the way she walks; everything about her, gives her intentions away. She wants blood.

Her mission: the same mission she nearly accomplished over a month ago, proves more difficult than before. Finding men up for a new manhunt of their lord's enemy had never been this way.

Tar, Jommutin, Nays Sim; all men were feared warriors of Lord Villous. Their loss affected the morale of the guard. Their egos were wounded. Her father's public shaming of her only exasperated the situation. Faelin's friends, Ness and Ensa, were killed for her failure. Death by association.

Faelin is like a walking plague. Soldiers and villagers stay clear of her as best they can. This is new territory for her. She always had power. Now, she has shame. No matter, her will won't be broken. Her resolve doesn't wane. She doesn't need her father's help, nor his soldiers'. If she must do it on her own or seek assistance outside of Kilsan, so be it.

Her quest for death begins. She travels straight to Viscrucia. Foolish it may be, but she cares not. The men she left Daemos with were savages. If Daemos somehow survived, he had to be at least wounded, if not near death itself. She's determined. This is all the advantage she would need.

Faelin stops far from the city. Clouds of multiple shades hover above it. Thunder rumbles. She didn't believe the rumors. How could she? But her eyes do not lie. Most of the clouds are various hues of blue and gray. Some are dark, others the opposite. However, some clouds are unlike any she has ever seen. Pink clouds and a few others with various shades of red capture her gaze. The remnants from the storm persist. Blood is somehow still trapped within.

She can barely believe her eyes, but the soil proves it. Most is normal, but a few dark patches still reveal the crimson rain and the rising of the dead. Pockets and holes puncture the ground. Skeletal handprints remain where one of the dead escaped his previous resting place. Some bones remain after the vultures and coyotes had their fill.

Faelin walks the streets of Viscrucia. The city is different. It's calmer, in an odd way. The dirt and bone streets are more red than usual. The biggest difference, however, is the people. More people than ever before stalk the streets. The killings continue, but they are not as frenzied or frequent. The killers converse more. People are calmer. This is truly odd in Faelin's mind.

Faelin stays vigilant and keeps guard. She finds the

last place she saw Daemos alive.

Esim's shop and house of torture is burnt to the ground. Nothing remains but a pile of muddy walls and broken stone collapsed upon itself. The horror Huemic and her father had accused her of is now a reality. She had failed. Her men are dead. Daemos, has most likely survived.

Faelin finds a hidden corner in a back alley. She tries to compose herself. The rush of emotions has overtaken her. She checks her surroundings. Alone and safe, he wipes her tears. She'd be dead if anyone found her like this. The shock of reckoning the truth proves difficult. After a minute or so, she composes herself and moves.

Faelin scours Viscrucia. She only kills one woman and manages to avoid other conflicts. She asks around, but the ones who know Daemos have not seen him. Petrid is one of them. When Faelin questions him, his suspicion is apparent. He keeps his answers brief and divulges no information. Faelin senses the distrust. Given his stature and recognition within the city, she leaves without questioning further. This is her greatest chance of survival.

Next, she travels to Yesilmi; one of the last places she saw Daemos alive. She thinks about that night from time to time. It did not go as she planned. She tried to poison him, but Daemos was on guard that night. She wanted to kill him in his room, but he disarmed her, and she had no chance of killing him by hand.

It was then that she gave in to her desires. She found him attractive, scars and all. He wanted her. That want, that lust, felt good, even if he was her father's enemy. Deep down, knowing it would enrage her father felt good, too. She could still have a little fun and get the job done.

Nothing. No word. No sign. No Daemos. She enters the Goblins' Gully, and that giant bastard hadn't been there probably since the last time they were there together. She leaves. She figures he won't go someplace where he'll be easy to find.

From village to town to city, and everywhere in between, Faelin searches for her prey. Months pass. She asks nearly everyone she can find, but still found no sign of him. He vanished. Perhaps he died from his wounds. Possible, sure, but Faelin doubts it. She must know beyond a doubt. She hears songs and bards' tales of varying degrees. Some stories are wild and beyond belief, while others sound possible. More killers gather near Viscrucia. Many are quite young.

Other kingdoms and villages far from the cursed city are the same as always, totally unaffected by the sins of another. Peace, quiet, and natural beauty live in endless bounty. It's readily attainable. Faelin ventures to these cities the same. Perhaps Daemos escaped as far away as he could to heal and leave his painful past behind. Faelin doesn't know, but she's still determined to find out.

Seasons pass. Through her travels, Faelin acquires four mercenaries to accompany her on her search. She pays well. Although her father is a chauvinistic asshole, being his daughter still has its perks. All her new companions have visited Viscrucia before, and they had the scars to prove it. This experience is a requirement Faelin demands.

Kin and Elken are large, burly twin brothers. They have short brown hair and long thick beards. Each stands a little over two meters in height. They looked good once, but broken noses and scars mar their faces. Both men wield large claymores.

Wom is a dirty, unkempt, heavy, bald man that smells awful. Morensa, is his opposite. She's a tall, fierce warrior with long blonde hair. Wom carries a heavy battle ax, while Morensa slays her enemies with a thin and maneuverable longsword.

Growing weary of failure, Faelin travels back home to Kilsan. They were only a week's ride away, and she needs the rest. While back, Faelin stays out of sight. She doesn't want to see her father, nor Huemic. She only speaks with a few friends.

They inform her about the emissaries traveling across the lands. She learns about the army her father amasses to lay waste to Viscrucia once and for all. This news gives Faelin renewed determination to seek out Daemos and kill him before her father's new army does. She thanks her friends and informs her traveling companions.

Next, they travel to Yesilmi. Maybe enough time had passed. She's running out of ideas on where Daemos can be. That's when she finds her first clue.

Daemos had been there, and he was not alone. Faelin hears it all. She hears about his new companions, the demoness and the walking dead, their confrontational entrance, their friendly departure, and his new abilities. The few who speak to Faelin that night at the Gully speak fondly of him. She can't believe her ears. She conceals the rage that burns inside her as best she can. She wants to kill everyone there. The last time she was there, no one had heard of him. Now, that ugly, scarred fuck is somehow popular? What in Suffering is this world coming to?

The next morning, Faelin and her crew ride for Viscrucia. It's the first time she starts to hate the city. She can't think of it without thinking of him. The positive remarks about Daemos roll over and over in her head. She wants to puke. The man is a psychotic murderer! He doesn't kill anyone for a few days; that they know of, and now he's the tavern saint? Absolute kes!

Days later, Faelin and her men make it to their destination. Her anger subsides, and calmer thoughts prevail. She prepares her mercenaries. They split into two groups to cover more ground. Kin and Wom take the south side, while Elken and Morensa guard Faelin as they searched the north side. They plan to meet in the center of the city, in Slaughterer's Row, but much to Faelin's surprise, the city has changed, again.

Chapter 43

Viscrucia grows even more. More people than ever now walk and limp through the bone streets. Young, old, tourists, and citizens; there are simply more.

Elken leads the way through the sea of killers. Faelin follows, trailed by Morensa, who guards her back. They move carefully. Faelin walks with a large skinning knife in one hand while her other hand rests on the handle of her whip. She sends a clear message for people to keep their distance. She will not be fooled and is immediately ready to kill if provoked.

Most of the time, this tactic works…most of the time. A thin dark cloth wraps around her face and head. Only her dark, lavender eyes peer through. She doesn't want to be seen. Daemos cannot know she's here. Knowledge of her presence would spell certain doom.

The city's stench is unmistakable. It's a hot day, and the air is ripe with currency. Faelin sees it trading hands. Killers buy weapons, jewelry, slaves, and information, among other things. Some payments are freshly cut, some cured, while others are polished bones with a fine shine. Faelin feels it's best to pay and not ask for information; not after the last time she spoke to Petrid. Rumors can quickly spread to her target. She must tread delicately and conceal her intentions.

Walking through the wounded, Faelin knows Daemos is here. The whispers match the rumors she heard in Yesilmi, talks of wounded followers, of an impossible, fire-haired woman, and that of an unusually large, horrifically scarred man, that now many are somehow following. This is troubling.

Could Daemos be gaining followers? What happened to the Viscrucia of old? Why are citizens not lining up to challenge him? How has he not been killed yet? One thing missing, however, is his face. Not once has anyone mentioned what he looks like or how badly he's scarred. Faelin expects to turn a corner and run into him at any second, but it doesn't happen.

After hours of search, Faelin, Elken, and Morensa find Wom and Kin near the center of the city.

"Wom, Kin. Good to see you. Glad you still live," Faelin says.

"The same," Elken answers.

"We haven't found kes. We've heard talk and rumors, but nothing more. This place has changed. It's different. More walking scarred than I've ever seen before. What about you? Any sign of him?"

"Yes," Elken answers. "If what the people of Yesilmi say is true, then we've found him."

"You found him? You saw his face?" Faelin asks.

"No," Wom interjects. "We did not see his face."

"Then how do you know it's him?"

"The man we saw wears a mask. It was black and

red. It's him. We're sure of it."

"How? How can you be sure?"

"Because of the demon standing by his side," Elken answers. "I've never seen anything like her before. Her hair was of flame, of actual flame…and she was big."

"Yes," Wom concurs.

"Big? How big? As tall as Daemos?"

"I don't know," Wom continues. "The masked one was sitting down. She stood near. But she was tall and strong. Something about her. But very tall for a female. And that hair…"

"Fire, hair of flame," Elken says. He and Wom look at each other. They speak almost as if they're in a trance. Faelin turns her head and squints her eyes at Elken.

"Where? Where is he?" Faelin asks.

"At the center of the city, beneath the hall," Elken says.

"Hall? What are you talking about? What hall?"

"We'll show you."

Elken and Wom lead the way. In the heart of Viscrucia, Faelin sees the hall. It is large and rudimentary, but massive for Viscrucia. The hall is open with no walls. Tall wood beams support the roof. The roof keeps out the sun and the rain. That is it. Benches fill the area within. It seems this is merely a place of gathering to eat and…*talk*, unique for Viscrucia. Numerous killers gather within. They do not attack.

"Hey. Stay on guard," Faelin warns her team. "Everyone's still a second away from death if we're not careful."

The mercenaries adjust accordingly. Two of them turn around to cover their backs. Faelin slowly walks up to a citizen to let her presence be known. A scarred killer sits at a nearby bench talking to another. He sees Faelin approaching. Faelin greets him the Viscrucian way. He returns the greeting but turns toward her, revealing the firmly gripped blade in his other hand, signaling he is ready to fight.

"It has been a couple seasons since I was last in the killing city," Faelin says to the man. "What is this hall? Why is it here?"

The man looks over Faelin for a couple of seconds, unsure of her intentions. "Why should I tell you, woman?"

Faelin thinks quickly. She is too impatient to leave and ask someone else, nor does she want to draw attention by fighting this man for the information. She reveals a small gem she holds in her hand. "For your trouble."

The man looks at the other man he was talking to, and then back to Faelin. She slowly pulls out a bone necklace and offers that as additional payment, signaling she has, in fact, frequented Viscrucia before.

"Okay, then."

Faelin slowly places the gem and necklace on the table, and then pulls her hand back quickly. "The hall."

"It was just built. Gives people a place to talk. Not many killings in here, yet. Killers want to see them. They have questions. Some want to learn and join. Others find them an abomination. They haven't gone out of their way to kill other citizens."

"And where are they?"

"Down at the other side of the hall," the man says firmly, ready to end the conversation. Faelin nods and leaves.

"Other side of the hall," she says to her mercs. "Let's walk by. Cover me. I'll stay hidden between all of you. Don't do anything! Just walk past. Let's go."

The group surrounds Faelin. The crows fly and caw. Weapons clash and screams erupt in the distance. Faelin sees the party she seeks. They sit at the last and largest table at the end of the hall. There are many men. At least seven sit at the table. The men in front and behind must be acting as bodyguards. There is a line of people over fifteen people in length, all waiting to speak to the group at the table. Off to the sides, more are cutting one another and themselves. It's not combat, however. It's something else. They're doing it willingly.

As they get closer, Faelin peers through the men surrounding the table. She sees some Viscrucians at the end, and then Petrid. He's involved in this now? She doesn't recognize the others. Next is some grotesque ghoul. This asshole really knows how to pick his friends. Then Faelin sees the flame.

The woman is powerful, indeed, but breathtakingly beautiful. Faelin did not expect this. Her mouth gapes a little out of shock. The beautiful demoness turns her head toward Faelin, almost as if she knows Faelin is watching. Faelin turns her head and hides behind Kin and Elken. Before they pass out of view, Faelin crouches and sneaks another look. There! She sees him. Daemos. He sits next to the demoness beauty. A battle mask conceals his face, but that's him! She can tell by his size alone. The demoness stands and peers over at Faelin's group.

"Move!" Faelin whispers. Her party exits onto a departing street. In seconds, they disappear.

Faelin leads her group hastily. They zig zag in and out of streets for a good fifteen minutes, making sure they have distanced themselves. They find a secluded area and finally rest. The group sits while Faelin paces frantically. The group looks to one another regarding their leader.

"Who is that demon woman?" she erupts in tirade. "Why is she here? Is she helping him? How long has he been back in Viscrucia? He must've been here a while if he has that many people with him! And were those bodyguards? How does he have bodyguards?" She continues pacing.

"Those are all good questions, Faelin, but it doesn't really matter, does it?" Morensa says.

"What do you mean?"

"It doesn't change our objective. We found him. Now, we need to kill him, right? Nothing has changed."

Faelin paces more. "You're right. Nothing's changed. Now we just need to kill him."

"Right, so let's get a plan and do it already," Wom says. "We've been searching for this guy for seasons. The sooner we act, the better. Before he gathers more people to his aid."

"We need a plan."

Chapter 44

"We need more time! We can't go to the Suffering! There is more to do. More to kill!"

Daemos listens to his conscience, his guidance, his demon within. He stands alone inside one of his hideouts. New disciples of his stand guard outside.

"We are not done, Daemos. Look around! We're creating a legacy here. A legacy…of pain. Never forget the pain that brought us together. Your death! The pain that has not been returned! The vengeance that is still to come!"

Daemos hears his dark voice. He clenches his fists, and his knuckles crack. The wraith reminds him of the torment he suffered. He thinks about Lord Villous, about Tar and his crew, and that evil bitch, Faelin, too. He thinks about vengeance. Surprisingly, he hadn't really thought about it until now. This afterlife he now lives has been an interesting journey.

"That's right. We still have people to kill. Vengeance to satisfy."

"What about Vel-Syn?" Daemos asks within.

"We can handle Vel-Syn! I am not going back to the Suffering! I won't allow it!"

Daemos realizes he has more to contend with than

he imagined. He thought he was ready to die. Perhaps not. And his question about Vel-Syn? Why? Does he…does he *feel* for Vel-Syn, this demon sent from the depths only to drag his soul to the oblivion of the Suffering?

"Lord of Pain!" a voice calls from outside. The man can be heard running toward Daemos's hideout.

"Enter," Daemos says, recognizing the voice. One of his new disciples enters.

"The hall, my lord! It's on fire."

"See. More must suffer. More must die by our hands. Pain is due."

Daemos walks to the heart of Viscrucia, still wearing his murder mask. He sees the great hall consumed in flame beneath the night's sky. Rain falls, but it is not enough to extinguish the blaze. Vel-Syn walks over to him. She smiles, looking upon the inferno. Daemos understands; it reminds her of home. She enjoys the spectacle and the searing heat.

"This is an attack on you, bringer of pain, and the demoness!" Kane says. "A personal insult. Find them!" Kane motions to the latest disciples. "They will pay for their desecration in the same way! We will throw them to the hall and burn them alive!"

"Sounds like this night is only getting better," Vel-Syn says.

Daemos looks around. Something is not right. "Where is Silmeir?"

"He was under Ronir's watch," Kane answers. "I'll take you to him."

They find Ronir lying on the ground outside of Silmeir's quarters unconscious with blood trailing down the back of his head. Ronir is a newer disciple.

Kane kneels and slaps him awake. "Ronir! What happened? This was your first task!"

Ronir comes to. "Uh...Silmeir!" He looks around, and then up to Daemos. "They took him. Some men and a woman."

"A woman," Daemos and the dark voice say together.

"They said you must come alone, or they'll tear him to pieces. I'm sorry. I didn't see them coming. Forgive me, Bringer of Pain."

Daemos clenches his fist and turns it. Ronir's neck muscles spasm and crank violently, breaking his neck from Daemos's supernatural command. "No. You failed your test."

"Isan! Disciples! Your lord needs you!" Kane says.

Daemos finds Mr. Brown. Brown neighs, kicks his front hooves, and rears his head away from Daemos.

"Easy, Mr. Brown. Easy," Daemos says, raising his hands. "Silmeir is gone. Bad people have taken him. Help me find him."

Mr. Brown neighs and kicks, but soon stops.

"That's it, Mr. Brown. Help me. Help me find Silmeir. He needs your help." Daemos puts his hand on his broad crest. Mr. Brown stands still. "That's it. Help me save Silmeir."

Mr. Brown nods his head. Daemos nods in return and jumps on top of him. He grabs the reins, and the two take off before Kane, or anyone else can stop them.

Mr. Brown bolts through the rain after his master. He knows his unique, undead-like scent better than anyone. He knocks tourists aside as they flee the city. The burning of the hall is personal, yes, but it's even more effective as a distraction. Faelin is a cunning little minx, indeed.

Silmeir's kidnappers made it far. Past the desert plains, Daemos arrives at the hills. He senses them. He knows they are close.

He steps down from Mr. Brown and continues on foot. He wants to keep Mr. Brown out of harm's way if he can. Silmeir would never forgive him should anything happen to the horse.

Daemos walks between the hills. He is familiar with this area. The rain obscures their tracks, but he can still read them.

"Daemos," a voice calls in the distance.

Daemos treads softly, but they know he's here. He walks into a small clearing amidst the hills. Silmeir is tied to a lonely Carrion Lotus tree. It is a white, deathly looking tree, that still lives somehow; much like Silmeir. The tree is a little wider than Silmeir. Its sparse leaves are red, that turn to black in the fall. Daemos checks his surroundings. No one else is in sight.

A whip flashes out from behind the tree. It coils around Silmeir's legs and the tree. Faelin emerges from behind holding the whip.

"Stop!" Faelin demands. "In one move, I'll rend his legs into pieces."

Daemos stands still. Faelin's team of mercenaries

appear above on the rocks surrounding Daemos's position. Each has bow and arrows drawn and aimed at Daemos.

"You come alone?" Faelin asks.

"You see anyone else, bitch?"

Faelin draws a blade and slashes Silmeir's forearm.

"If anyone else shows, Silmeir dies, and I'll personally finish your torture."

"You didn't have the stomach for it then. Do you now?"

Faelin slashes Silmeir's arm again.

"I think of nothing else. Tar was my man. What did you do to him?"

"Do you think it was worse than what he and his men did to me?"

Faelin smiles. "Take off your mask. Let me see what he did, or we put four arrows in you now and more later."

Daemos reaches up and takes off his mask. He reveals Tar's carnage. The mercenaries grimace from the sight. A couple of them lower their bows.

"This is the scheme we've aided? Faelin said it was she that was wronged," one of the mercenaries mumbles.

Little spots of red start to glow from the White Carrion Lotus Tree. The light grows in volume. It comes from bioluminescent insects emerging from the tree. A hundred or so take off and fly around the clearing. They flutter around the archers like fireflies. Morensa, Wom, Kin, and Elken look around, unsure of what is happening.

"The bloodflies are out."

Faelin laughs, not caring in the least about some stupid insects. "You are one ugly fuck! I've never seen anyone close to as ugly as you are now!"

Daemos's remaining portion of his lips curl up as he smiles in return. "I have."

Faelin's laughter pauses a moment.

"Did you forget about Tar, already? My face, his handiwork, has that effect on people. That's why I put him through much worse than what he did to me. I tore his face clean off."

Faelin's lips tremble.

"Don't you recognize my eyes, Faelin?" Daemos blinks, and Tar's piercing blue eyes return. "They're his. I took them from him after he tore mine out."

Faelin looks closely. The bloodflies illuminate Daemos's face through the darkness. "No. That's impossible."

"Yes. Know well before I kill you that after I cut his genitals off, I made Tar the ugliest piece of kes ever to walk this land before sending him to the fiery depths of the Suffering."

"No! Kill him!"

Daemos opens his left hand, causing Faelin's hand to open and drop her whip. Daemos grabs a dagger from his side and throws it into Faelin's shoulder, knocking her to the ground.

Petrid, Boils, Lesigom, and Isan emerge from behind the mercenaries above and disarm them.

Daemos walks up and removes the whip from

around Silmeir's legs and unties him.

"Thank you," says Silmeir.

Faelin lays bleeding on the ground. The bloodflies descend upon her. She squeals with new pain. The bloodflies glow brighter red.

"I tried to tell you," Daemos says.

Faelin's eyes squint as the clearing near her grows brighter. Vel-Syn walks next to Daemos. Her fire illuminates her path.

"The bloodflies are parasites. They feed off blood. They knew when to leave their nests within the tree. They'll turn your blood into seeds. In time, this area will be lush with carrion lotus trees thanks to you and your men. You should be happy."

Isan ties Faelin's arms and legs around and behind the tree. Her mercenaries, bound and gagged, sit a few meters before her. The bloodflies pulsate red light as they feed on their wounds.

"Vel-Syn saw you at the hall," Daemos says. "I figured you would go after Silmeir. He is the easiest target. You got past my disciple. He failed his first test. I was not surprised, which is why I had him watched from a distance just in case. I tried, but I couldn't wait. Vengeance beckoned me.""

"You think you scare me?" Faelin contends. "The only chance you have to survive is by sparing me. My father is gathering the largest army the world has ever seen! All the Ssagaecian clans, Queen Premous's army, Noble Kerth's men, and so much more! If you don't return me unharmed, he will march upon Viscrucia and stomp you and that fucking city out of existence! You think you're scary?! You don't even compare to Lord Villous! My father is the evilest man to ever walk this land. If you don't return me, you will see. He's stacked piles of corpses from men like you and burned them all to the Suffering!"

Daemos nods to Isan.

"Yes, Lord of Pain," Isan says, holding an ax.

Isan walks to Faelin, raises his weapon, and chops off her left arm. Faelin screams. Her body sinks a little to the right without the support of her left arm being tied behind the tree anymore. He raises the ax again and lops off her other arm. She falls face down to the ground. She cries horribly. Her mercenaries scream behind their gags. Blood pours down her shoulders and neck into her mouth. After a few seconds of screaming, Isan grabs her by her neck and thrusts her back up to the tree. The bloodflies flock to her wounds.

"Vengeance."

"Pl-please!" Faelin tries to speak.

"Don't worry. Next, Isan will chop your legs off. That's what you intended to do with me, right?"

"What about me?" Boils asks.

Daemos turns and looks at Boils, a little surprised. "Yeah...go for it. Chop away, Boils! Everyone gets a turn!"

"I like him."

"We'll burn your wounds closed to stop the bleeding and deliver you back to Daddy."

"No!" Faelin pleads. "Please! Kill me now! If

you…if…if you don't, he'll keep me…alive. Please. Kill me!"

Lesigom sits off to the side and takes a swig from his flask. He writes in his flesh pad beneath his coat to block out the rain.

"I beg you!"

Isan and the others look to Daemos to see what verdict he'll grant: mercy or more pain.

Chapter 45

Daemos, his traveling party, and their prisoners return to Viscrucia. The flames that consumed the hall have since died. Piles of burnt wood and ashes remain. The clouds have passed, and the rain has stopped.

"The lord of pain returns!" Kane yells out, announcing it to all within hearing distance.

The killers of Viscrucia gather around the heart of the city once more, curious as to what new spectacle tonight will bring. The disciples of pain nail the prisoners to the remains of the hall. The wood is still too hot to bind them with rope. It would burn through if they tried.

Wearing his mask, Daemos gets down from his horse and addresses the crowd. "Viscrucians. Long have I called this place my home. But Lord Villous of Kilsan...calls this place kes!"

The crowd yells and boos.

"He could not kill here, not like us. Now, he has gathered an army! The largest the world has ever known. With it, he plans to march here, destroy me, my disciples of pain, all of you, and burn Viscrucia to the ground!"

The crowd roars with hostility.

"Our city! Your city! For years, he has tried to kill me. These men here tried again tonight. His men tortured me, took half of my life, and half my face!" Daemos removes his mask. "But he can't kill me or Viscrucia!"

The crowd cheers.

"We are killers! That's why we come here. But this time it's different. It won't be every man for themselves. For Viscrucia to withstand this assault, we must fight together. The killers must unite! Who will stand beside me and my disciples of pain to kill the largest force this world has ever seen?"

The crowd explodes with excitement. Thousands of Viscrucians raise their weapons in the air and clash them together.

"Show them who we are! Show them what Viscrucians do!"

Later that night, Vel-Syn enters Daemos's room. Daemos sits in a chair, unmasked.

"Lord Villous sounds interesting," she says. "Is he the evilest there is, as she said?"

"No. I am," Daemos answers.

"I guess we will see. I am curious to see you on the battlefield now that you've healed. I will delay our departure for the Suffering. I want to meet this Lord Villous. I want to see the genocide of thousands as you promise."

Daemos stands up and walks over to Vel-Syn. "You

shall have it, your demoness. Consider it my gift to you."

Daemos and Vel-Syn look into each other's eyes. They say nothing. The demoness conceals her thoughts well. She leaves.

"Disciples," Daemos calls to his guards outside of his door. "Send me Kane and Isan."

"Yes, my lord."

Kane and Isan arrive. "Yes, Bringer of Pain."

"I have one final task for you as disciples."

Kane can't help but smile. "Anything, my lord," he says.

"You are to deliver a gift, and a message."

A few nights later, Huemic and Lord Villous discuss the latest results from the emissaries returning from their missions.

"That makes another battalion," Huemic says.

"Any word from the Shadow Kingdom?" Lord Villous asks.

"No. It matters little. We have more than enough armies, plus the additional help I mentioned."

"Good."

Knocking bangs from the throne doors, echoing across the grand room.

"Enter fools!" the lord says.

The large entry doors open and a guard runs through carrying a large bag in one hand. His other hand has been chopped off. Bloody bandages wrap around the stump. "My lord!" he exclaims. The man breathes heavily. Three more guards follow him. The sentries outside close the doors behind them. The guards take a knee once in front of their lord.

"Get up!"

The men stand. "Daemos, he attacked us."

"What? He was here."

"Yes, well, no. He wasn't, but two of his men, they attacked. They killed two other guards outside of the castle. I barely survived. They gave me a message to deliver."

"Daemos wasn't here! Errand boys killed my men!" the lord yells.

"Apologies, Lord Villous. They surprised us. Came from nowhere."

"Silence!" Huemic demands. "What's in the bag?"

The guard breathes heavily. Sweat and blood trickle down his face.

"Bring it me!" Lord Villous demands.

The guard walks up the steps to the throne. Huemic walks down, passing him, and stands next to the other three accompanying guards.

"Open it."

"My lord, forgive me, I…"

"Open it!"

The guard cringes and slowly opens the bag with his remaining hand. He reaches in and pulls out a spinal cord. Attached at the end is Faelin's head. The vertebrae have been cleaned of all blood and tissue. Faelin's face and hair remain intact, however. Her once beautiful face is now disgusting. The look of horror at her death remains. The stench is unavoidable.

Lord Villous takes the remains of his daughter. He looks down at her. "Faelin."

The fearful guard looks around at the others and then back to his lord. "The two men gave me a warning. They said, Daemos showed mercy by ending her life. He…he did this. He personally ripped her head from her body. He took her final breath away. They said, if you attack Viscrucia, there will be no mercy. Daemos, the Lord of Pain, will show you what true suffering is. Since you kept the trophy of the wraith, he wanted to add to your collection."

Lord Villous reaches out with his golden dagger and pierces the blubbering guard's neck. He has heard enough. The guard chokes on blade and blood.

"Mercy?" the lord says, standing up. He grabs the end of his daughter's spinal cord. "Mercy!" He swings it around and smashes his daughter's head into the guard's, knocking him down. "Mercy!" He continues pounding the guard's face to a pulp with his daughter's. "Guards! Were you there?"

The three other guards step back, shaking their heads.

"Huemic!"

Huemic draws his sword and spins toward the guards, slashing their throats in one swing. They drop to the ground gurgling as Lord Villous continues bashing his messenger.

"My lord," Huemic says. The lord yells with anger as he swings. "Lord Villous!"

The lord stops. He gasps for air from the exertion. He looks down at the heads. Neither remain, only a pool of gore. "Send message to all armies. Time has come. Upon their arrival, we move and strike!"

"It shall be done."

"Daemos! You'll burn! Viscrucia will burn! I'll have your head! We're coming for you!"

The lord's screams carry throughout the castle, through the village, and outside the castle walls. Isan and Kane sit atop their horses outside the walls in darkness.

Kane smiles. "Looks like he got the message."

"War is coming," Isan says.

"Let's deliver the good news."

Chapter 46

Isan and Kane return to Viscrucia.

"This is new," Kane says.

"Don't worry. It won't last," Isan says. "Soon, there will be more death here than ever before."

No fighting. No killing. There is an odd tranquility about the streets. Viscrucians eat and sharpen their weapons. They heal their wounds, preparing for battle. It is the rest before the war. They ready their poisons. Buildings are fortified. They set traps outside the city. They prepare every way that they can. Thousands of arrows are crafted. Armor, gauntlets, and helmets are made. The killers keep them light and maneuverable. They plan on most of the combat being up close and personal, the way the city intended.

Dozens more have joined Daemos's ranks to become disciples of pain. His cult continues to grow. It's infectious among the like-minded maniacs. They've seen the destruction of his flesh, and they've seen what he does to those who have wronged him. He commands power. His abilities are unlike any other. Is he immortal? They believe the demoness at his side to be. She aids in the education of the disciples. There's so much to be learned from them, the disciples believe. Many were searching to find themselves. For many within this chaos, he is the master they seek.

"We have two more skulls for the collection, Bringer of Pain. And a hand of the guard that delivered your message," Kane says.

"Well done," Daemos says.

"War is coming," Isan says.

"You've made me proud, Kane, Isan. It is time that we honor you. You've completed your last task as disciples. Are you ready for the final step? Are you ready to receive my mark?"

"Yes, Bringer of Pain," the men say together.

"Petrid, Lesigom," Daemos calls out to them. "Gather all of the disciples and anyone who wishes to join. Lead them to the place I told you about: the building in ash. I will meet you there. There, the ceremony will begin."

Petrid, Lesigom, and Boils Bogilocus lead Isan, Kane, the disciples, and well over a thousand Viscrucians to the site of Daemos's death. After her emergence from the Pain, the fire Vel-Syn set that day took on a life of its own. It burned the building down along with many others around it. The wildfire cleared the way for where the congregation stands now. Remnants of charred wood and burnt stone remain among the destruction.

Vel-Syn directs Kane and Isan to walk to the center. As they do, Vel-Syn's hair strikes some of the remaining wood. A small flame grows and burns what it can, forming a circle around what was roughly the diameter of the old building. The mass of killers gathers around the circle of flame.

The crowd parts. Daemos walks through his followers and enters the ring of fire. Kane and Isan kneel.

"Viscrucians and disciples, this is a place of death and rebirth. I was born in Viscrucia. It is here where I died. It is here where I was reborn. When I leave this world, it is here that I will journey to the Suffering. But this is not my time."

Vel-Syn looks at Daemos.

"Damn right!"

"This is Kane and Isan's time! This is their rebirth!"

The crowd cheers. More killers flock to see the spectacle.

Daemos looks to Kane and Isan. The roar of the crowd dies down. "You have never questioned me. You have never failed me. You sacrifice for me. I sacrifice for you." Daemos slits his right wrist with his left index fingernail. He holds his right hand out and open for everyone to see the blood running down into his hand.

"You bleed for me," he continues. He slashes his left wrist in the same fashion. "I bleed for you. Born as men, Viscrucians they became, disciples they chose. They are reborn now…" He places a bloody hand over one side of each of their faces, covering them with his blood. He digs his nails in and mauls down. "As priests of pain." Five long gashes now mar their faces.

Kane and Isan do not move, nor make a sound. This is child's play at this point compared to the other atrocities they've suffered in their unwavering faith to their master. Their blood and the dark blood of Daemos runs down their faces. This is his mark, an unmistakable wound that resembles their lord's. Their devotion is absolute. They are priests of pain.

The crowd cheers. They brandish their weapons and clash them together. Kane and Isan look to one another with their new faces. They look different. They feel different. They look back to Daemos and bow. He bows in return.

"Rise my Priests."

Kane and Isan stand. They look around to the thousands that cheer and celebrate them. The crowd slowly quiets once more.

"You have honored us, Bringer of Pain," Isan says. "Your blood is an honor. Your pain is an honor. You said this is a place of death and rebirth. As your priests of pain, we will do our part and add to this tradition. We will build a temple here to honor you. A new Church of Pain!"

"And after we win this war," Kane adds, "we'll build it from their dead fucking bodies!"

The mob erupts into a wild frenzy. Weapons clash. The sun sets. It's time for war.

Chapter 47

"All messengers have returned, Lord Villous. The Sublime, Queen Premous's army, Gell and the Ssagaecian clans, Nobleman Kerth with his son, Sir Rayn, and all others that agreed to fight are traveling now to meet at the gathering point. It is time that we embark, as well."

"Good, Huemic," Lord Villous says. "Tell our men. Inform village. Let other armies camped know. Have servants ready my armor. We go to Viscrucia. Death will come."

"Yes, my lord."

The disciples gathered as many military scouts and wandering soldiers they could for Daemos before the war. Naked, Kane and Isan organize their clothing and weapons. Vel-Syn walks up to them.

"Why do you let him do this to you? Why do you follow him?" she asks. "I did not care before, but now I am curious. This will be my last chance to ask if you die."

Kane thinks a moment. He shares a look with Isan. "When we were children, soldiers came and destroyed our village," he replies. "I was twelve, and Isan was ten. We were out playing in the woods when it happened.

We escaped. Our families didn't. Since then, we've had no home. No people, no family, just each other. I guess we don't trust people. We've seen a lot of things since then. We've faced many enemies. We survived. When we found Viscrucia, it was a place like no other. We fit in for some reason. Strange. But this place, it became like…a new home."

"What we saw in the pit that day, it wasn't human, like the blood storm," Isan adds. "He survived. Impossible how, but he survived."

"We saw something in him. Something different, like us, in a way. But something beyond. We were drawn to it. I don't know why, but we had to find him."

"And now?" Vel-Syn asks.

"Now, we're home, and he will save it," Kane says.

Vel-Syn smiles and leaves. Kane takes a deep breath. "I thought she might kill me."

"Me too."

"Shut up. Are you ready for this?" Kane asks Isan.

"Yeah, just not sure what to expect."

"Something different, brother. Something else."

Kane looks at the claw marks running down Isan's face - his new mark of priesthood.

"You look good, by the way. His mark looks good on you."

Isan turns to Kane, both stand naked. He says nothing. Kane looks away, figuring he said enough.

They lead the disciples to an open area behind Aemeggur's butcher shop. The men walk naked, carrying a knife and their battle gear in hand. Wooden beams stand five meters high. The captives, bound and gagged, dangle from them upside down by their feet.

"Pick one," Daemos calls out.

Isan, Kane, and the disciples each select one and all set their armor down.

Daemos stands naked underneath a hanging prisoner. For the first time, the men see his ravaged body.

"It's time, men. War is here."

Daemos slashes the throat above him and stands underneath. The man convulses as his life bleeds out, pouring onto Daemos. His disciples have never seen a battle ritual like this.

"Blood and death are ahead. Their blood! Their death! Kill away."

The men follow their leader's command. Intrigued, Vel-Syn watches from afar.

Neck after neck opens. The bodies writhe.

"Feel your victim's blood. It will improve your sense of feel. Your grip will get stickier. Your enemies will see their blood upon you! Show them what's to come!"

The men rub the blood over their bodies.

"Dress. This may be the last time. Carry your deadliest weapons. Wear your best clothes and killing gear. This is the most important day of your lives! Kill or be killed." The men dress for combat and arm themselves.

Daemos wears the black painted armament he wore when he faced the wraith, now his inner guide. Thick leather boots and flexible animal skin clothing are his body's first line of defense. Lightweight bone- and metal-fashioned guards add further protection.

He arms himself, blade after blade. He tightens his hands. His grip is sticky.

Finally, Daemos picks up his Face and fastens it to his blood-soaked head. He turns around and looks upon his warriors. Crimson flesh contrasts with the whites of their eyes. Their blades are clean. Their minds and skin are not. Corpses sway above in the wind. The men are ready.

"Perfect."

"Pure evil. Let's show our unwelcome guests some Viscrucian hospitality."

The invading armies have amassed outside of Viscrucia. Tens of thousands of soldiers, warriors, and armed slaves stand ready to battle to the death at their masters' bidding. Lord Villous and the Sublime are unseen. Huemic leads the march. His horde surrounds the entire city within arrow range.

Clouds fill the sky. Not a single ray of light escapes its dark shroud.

The Viscrucians are spread thin across the city's perimeter; the invaders grossly outnumber them. Viscrucia is no fortress, either. There is no exterior wall to scale, no gate for a single point of entry to defend, no moat keeping marauders at bay. It is not set up for defense. There are no exterior doors. All are welcome to enter should they dare choose.

"Light the arrows!" Huemic shouts. A giant ring of fire surrounds Viscrucia as thousands of arrow tips light. Huemic's horse trots forward, breaking from his army's ranks. "You're surrounded Daemos! Give yourself up. Walk out alone and unarmed, and we won't burn your wretched city to the ground!"

Daemos emerges from his brethren, laughing. "Huemic! I should've known his royal kes-ness wouldn't have the balls to hobble forward and face me himself! So, he sent you, his pathetic errand boy." The Viscrucians laugh. "I have a better idea. Why don't you all come forward and face me one at a time, like real warriors? Maybe that way you'll have a chance after I've grown tired from killing a thousand of you fools!"

The laughter continues.

"Luce!" Huemic yells.

Flaming arrows soar through the sky, trailing smoke. Daemos casually walks back under cover of a building. Fellow Viscrucians follow his lead. The arrows hit across the city. Before their flame can spread, the fire disappears. The soldiers are confused.

"Light and fire! Do not stop!" Huemic orders. Arrows and flame soar through the air by the thousands. A haze of smoke builds around the city. Soon after each arrow hits the city, its accompanying fire extinguishes. Arrow after arrow, the barrage continues for over a minute to no avail. The outlying army remains bewildered.

Insolent laughter breaks out once again. A single flame appears at the city's threshold. It is Vel-Syn. Daemos walks up to her side. "Huemic! You don't have a demon in your army to help you, do you?" The laughter continues.

Vel-Syn raises her hands. Her eyes ignite with flame. "Rise."

The ground shakes, and then cracks. The earth beneath the soldiers' feet opens up. The army looks about worried. A dead hand bursts from the soil and grabs the closest soldier. He screams as it pulls him beneath. A skeletal hand erupts from the ground and digs into another soldier's ankle.

"It returns," says Petrid.

Screams break out among the ranks. The demons return, and the dead rise again. Hundreds of hell spawn belch forth from the barren landscape. Huemic sees one coming for him. It snarls and leaps toward him. He cuts it in half with one swing of his sword. He looks around. It's pandemonium. The winged demons fly through the air taking men into the clouds like before. The screams of thunder return. The clouds swell with red.

"Here it comes," Boils says.

The blood rain returns. The army is horrified. Waves of screams bellow across the land. The Viscrucians cheer upon the sight of the holy deluge. The death toll outside the city begins. The cracks in the ground soak up the carnage.

Daemos blinks his eyes, turning them black. His blood vision illuminates. A sea of crimson swells before him. It is everywhere.

"*Absolute pain,*" says his dark voice, referring to the beauty of the carnage.

Daemos's top killers are spread across the city. Petrid, Boils, Lesigom, Kane, Isan, and Daemos command the men. "Arrows!" The men draw their bows and fire. More of the invading horde goes down. They keep firing.

Huemic raises his shield for protection. He scans the battlefield. This is not how the siege is supposed to go. The city should be burning by now with them mopping up their foes out in the open terrain. Their strength in numbers should make for a quick battle. But this isn't happening. He's losing men by the hundreds. Demons and arrow pick them apart. He must take the fight to them. They still have the advantage in numbers.

"Sound the horn!" Huemic yells. "Attack! To Viscrucia!"

A soldier blows his horn, signaling the army. The men unleash their battle cry in response and charge the city, ready to engage in real combat. The flying demons follow. Picking off soldiers one by one, they carry them to the clouds and have their fiendish way with them.

Kane smiles. "Time for the fun to begin!" The Viscrucians fall back. He and Vel-Syn retreat to the heart of the Viscrucia.

The soldiers charge into the city. Their massive numbers squeeze in between shops. They flood the alleys and streets like the tunnels of an ant colony. Spears and swords thrust through windows and flesh curtain entrances, delivering killing blows the soldiers never see coming. Rocks and daggers are thrown unseen from the tops of buildings. The entry is deadly. Many soldiers, slaves, and warriors fall by Viscrucian blades.

The fighting is savage. People are stabbed, chopped, cut, sliced, and cleaved. When unarmed, the

Viscrucians bite, gouge, and claw with equal efficiency. The soldiers parry the Viscrucian attack with their shields and then strike with their swords. Their armor protects them from numerous blows but slows their movement. The Viscrucians, however, are swift and deadly.

The death toll rises. Blood flies everywhere, painting the city red. It rains from the bloated clouds. It flies from every ax strike, every opening of flesh. It pours from the dead bodies covering the dirt and bone streets. It splashes up from the ground as the warriors plod through, killing each other. Daemos sees all through his blood vision.

Huemic slashes through victims from atop his steed. Nobleman Kerth fights from his horse as well. Regal armor covers him head to toe. He cuts through demons, lops off heads, and slashes men down with his steel blade. His son, Sir Rayn, fights proudly from his horse. The Ssagaecian clans are formidable and well-versed in combat. They fight together in tight-knit groups. Gell, their ruler, swings his spiked ball and chain like a wild man. He yells with excitement. He and his men have the time of their lives. He licks the blood from his red stained lips. If the disciples and citizens get too close, he bashes and bludgeons them with his mace.

Lesigom throws blades from the rooftops. He moves and strikes quickly. His long hair is soaked in crimson. When he runs out of blades to fling, he jumps down onto an unsuspecting invader, takes him out, and quickly gathers more weapons from his kills. Boils Bogilocus breaks his opponent's bones with his femur-pieced bone club in one hand and lops off appendages with the jeweled machete he earned from Daemos in the other. Many opponents flee his presence from his ghastly features alone. Petrid's height is magnified on the battlefield by his weapons. He slashes victims with a whip in each hand. Dozens of small blades attached make each strike a killing blow.

Kane and Isan find each other amid the war. Isan swings ferociously, cutting down many men with his brute strength. Kane yells with bloodlust as he bounds, rolls, and swiftly stabs his attackers. They work together, and their kills mount.

Isan gets punched in the face, leaving a strange feeling. He spits blood and punches back. Suddenly, he feels his opponent's pain. Isan then kicks him to the ground and stabs him in the chest. He puts his hand on the dying man. He feels a connection to the man's pain within himself.

Isan looks over to Kane and sees him choke a man with his bare hands. The man's body goes limp.

"I can feel his flesh…" Kane says.

"And pain," Isan adds.

"The Bringer of Pain, it is his gift to us!"

A slave charges Kane. Isan reaches out with his hand. The slave slows down but doesn't know why. Kane reaches out. Now, the man can't move. His wounds bleed more, and he winces. Kane and Isan walk up to him and slit his throat. The slave falls to his death.

"We are his priests of pain. Let us spread his word," Isan says.

Vel-Syn melts her adversaries. As their clothes catch fire, they often stumble into others, taking more down like a spreading wildfire. Her skin remains flawless. No foe manages to harm her. If she allows them to get close enough, her incinerating touch is the last thing they feel. Others stop dead in their tracks upon catching sight of her. Her beauty and fire transfix them. Then she bursts their bodies into a deadly blaze.

Daemos slaughters dozens of men. He cleaves them with blades and separates their flesh from bone with his dark powers. This is what he was bred to do.

The day is perfect until he hears *his* voice.

"Daemos. Something is wrong."

"What?"

"Silmeir. Find him. Before it's too late."

Daemos looks around. The landscape has changed so much it takes him a moment to recognize where he stands. He thinks of where Silmeir is supposed to stay until the killing stops and he can ride Mr. Brown to safety.

"Vel-Syn!" Daemos calls out. She looks at him. "Follow me. We have to find Silmeir."

Fires rise within the city. Corpses burn on the ground and the walls on which they're impaled. Small fires burn doors and flesh curtains, while other shops and buildings look like funeral pyres.

Carnage is rampant. The armies hack each other to pieces. The fighting is everywhere; the streets, shops, rooftops, kitchens, death pits, and outside the city as soldiers flee, and then are swooped into the sky or pulled down into the mud. Viscrucia is death this day.

Petrid's arms grow weary. He surveys the bloodshed. More and more soldiers swarm the city. Invading SSagaecian moxes gang up on citizens. Soldiers continue to defend attacks with their shields and heavy armor, and then strike through their enemies. Slaves of the invading horde fire arrows like cowards. Viscrucian numbers dwindle.

Boils challenges the Noble Kerth. Kerth swings his sword from atop his steed. The men battle back and forth. Lesigom sees the fight across the blood-soaked street. Kerth swings for Boil's head. Boils ducks and somersaults underneath the horse. He slashes upward with his machete, slicing open the horse's barrel in between its protecting armor. The horse instinctively tries to jump from the pain, but immediately collapses onto the ground. Bogilocus smiles and steps onto the horse. He looks down upon Kerth as he tries to escape from beneath the weight of his horse.

"This is not a city for nobles. So long," Boils says. He grips his jewel-encrusted machete with both hands, preparing to deliver his death strike. Lesigom smiles. Kerth reaches for his fallen sword, inches away.

A ball and chain swings through the air. Bogilocus's head explodes on contact.

"No! Boils!" Lesigom screams.

The headless body of Boils collapses to the ground. Gell, the Ssagaecian leader, swings the gore-soaked ball and chain in his hands. "Ssagaecia!" he yells in triumph. Clan members nearby yell in kind.

Lesigom charges at Gell with a dagger in each hand. The two swing and evade. Their fight takes them down another street.

Kerth squirms out from his dead horse. He grabs his sword and runs.

Fen, Queen Premous's general, stabs a disciple through the heart with one of his swords. He's on the hunt. "Where is Lord Villous?" This is his primary task, per his queen's order. Scouring for the lord, he sees Kane and Isan dispatch two of his soldiers. Fen pauses his search. He can kill Villous later.

"Hey!" Fen shouts, calling out the two priests.

Isan and Kane turn and look. The men find each other from across the slaughter. The blood rain continues, blanketing all. Fen holds a sword in each hand. Isan holds a skinning knife. Kane carries an ax.

"This will be fun," Kane says.

Fen's countenance is stone. He wants retribution. The men engage. Fen swings with his left. Loving his newfound power, Kane raises his hand and slows Fen's attack. Fen swings with his right. Isan counters in the same manner. Fen's hands stop in the air.

Kane laughs. "Didn't expect that, did ya?"

Fen kicks Kane in the stomach, knocking him back a

couple of steps. He then moves in and headbutts Isan in the nose, breaking it. Fen shakes his arms free of their hold. He swings his right sword at Isan's body. Isan hops back, but not in time. The sword slices his side. Fen swings again, and cuts Kane's right thigh, dropping him to one knee.

"Nice trick, boys, but it's not enough," Fen says. "Here comes the pain you Viscrucian kes deserve!"

Kane lunges forward and grabs Fen's wrists with each hand. Seeing the little man try and hold his wrists, Fen laughs.

"Isan and I are full of pain, and we have much more to give," Kane says. Kane digs his fingernails in between Fen's armor and into his skin. Fen cries out. Kane closes his eyes. The contact with Fen's flesh and the additional pain is what he needs to harness his powers. He connects more closely with it now as his hold grows stronger. Fen can't move; his hands are pinned down by his waist. He looks up. Isan trudges forward and swings his ax. Fen's head flies, and his body falls.

Isan drops to his knees next to Kane. They look at each other, bleeding and in pain.

"So, who gets the head?" Kane asks.

Isan laughs. "I do. I cut it off."

"So, I pinned his arms down. I saved you!"

"Shut up, little man."

The priests of pain take a moment to rest from the war and bleed together.

Chapter 48

Huemic rides his horse through the war-torn city of Viscrucia. Fires burn. Putrid gore soaks everything. Carrying two swords, Huemic slashes down every nearby Viscrucian he can. As he stops to catch his breath, he hears a familiar voice.

"Easy, Mr. Brown. We'll escape once the killing dies down."

"I know that voice," Huemic says to himself. He steps down from his horse. He walks over to a blood-splattered shop entrance curtain and cuts it down. Startled, Mr. Brown neighs inside and shakes his head.

Silmeir sees his uninvited guest. "Huemic."

"Silmeir," Huemic says.

He returns one of his swords to its sheath. He then grabs Silmeir with his free hand and yanks him out of the store and into the open. Silmeir falls into a puddle of blood. He attempts to get to his feet, but Huemic immediately kicks him back down. Mr. Brown neighs and starts to move toward Huemic, but Huemic swiftly raises his sword in Mr. Brown's direction, keeping him from charging further.

Silmeir gets to his feet and pulls out a dagger. Huemic

sees the result of the infliction he, Tar, and Lord Villous damned upon him. The cursed berries, the poisoned water; he became one of the forgotten yet, somehow, still lives. Huemic sees the gaping hole in the remains of Silmeir's old face. The blood cascading down his pale flesh makes him look even further from human.

"Kes, Silmeir!" Huemic mocks. "Look at you! Can you even see me?"

"I see you, Huemic."

"Are you alive? It doesn't look like it."

"I live."

"Why are you here?"

Silmeir says nothing. He stares at Huemic, slowly circling him.

"Wait, did you join Daemos?"

"Yes."

Huemic laughs. "Why?"

"I did not know at the time."

Silmeir continues circling. Huemic shifts his positioning to follow. His sword no longer faces Mr. Brown.

"Silmeir, you simple fool. I never did like you."

Not liking that, Mr. Brown bolts forward and knocks Huemic on his ass. His sword falls from his hand. Mr. Brown tramples Huemic with his front hooves. Silmeir moves around Mr. Brown, looking for an opportunity to strike.

Huemic searches for his sword. He reaches into a puddle of blood. The sword emerges in his hand and he thrusts up, stabbing Mr. Brown. Mr. Brown unleashes a terrible cry as he falls on his side.

"Mr. Brown!" Silmeir screams. He drops to his knees next to his dear friend.

Huemic rolls away. He slowly gets to his feet and pulls out his other sword.

"This time, you die for good. You and your stupid horse. Just like your woman, Essa," Huemic says.

Silmeir turns and glares at Huemic. Wrath seethes.

"Huemic!" Daemos yells.

Huemic turns around. "Daemos."

Vel-Syn fends off multiple enemies, allowing Daemos the space to fight Huemic.

The two men square off five meters from each other. Fires, screams, blood, and bodies paint the background. Huemic wears extravagant armor, while Daemos wears skins and bones.

Silmeir pets Mr. Brown as he lies helpless on the ground.

"Could it be?" Huemic questions. "Is it really you behind that mask?"

"You'll have to kill me to find out," Daemos says. "Think you can do that, Huemic? It didn't work out for you so well last time."

"No, it didn't. It's working much better this time around. Like what I've done to your beloved city?"

"It's never looked better. Where's your owner?"

"He's around. Are you worried you won't get to see him before you die?"

"This is the city of death, Huemic. Everybody dies here. You've visited before, but now it's time we get you a place to stay." Daemos points over to the ground.

"Underneath that pool of blood looks just right."

Daemos picks up a sword from the ground. He holds one in each hand, as does Huemic. Crimson rain wets their faces. They move forward and start swinging.

Swords clash. Swing and parry. Block and thrust. Huemic moves with precision. Daemos strikes with force. They wade through the blood covering much ground. The violence mounts. Their blades open each other up little by little.

Vel-Syn takes on the soldiers swarming her from all sides. She remains unharmed. A gleam catches her eye. She turns. A golden dagger shines through the shadows of an alley covered by a wooden roof. The golden dagger leg appears next, then the rest of him.

"Lord Villous."

"The demon."

Vel-Syn kills her last attacker. Lord Villous disappears back into the shadow of the alley. Vel-Syn walks forward. Finally, the man she's been looking for reveals himself. He's the architect of this war, the one who marched tens of thousands to their deaths. They will meet at last.

A tan shroud leaps from the shadows and covers Vel-Syn. Her hair extinguishes underneath, and its weight drops her to the ground. She can't move, and her strength escapes her. Six Sublime emerge from the alley. They wrap Vel-Syn in their holy sheet and suppress her hellish power.

Silmeir sees it. The rain sullies their tan cloaks. A priestess notices Silmeir, as well. She runs her finger across her braided headband representing the Sublime. She bows and then helps carry Vel-Syn into the darkness. Silmeir's strange mind recalls the gesture and clothing. The Sublime.

Huemic spins and hits Daemos square in his mask with the hilt of his sword. The mask cracks further down the center, and the blow dazes him. Huemic spins back the other way and slashes Daemos across his back. Daemos stumbles to the ground.

"This is it," Huemic says with a smile. "The killing stroke of Daemos is a moment away."

He twirls his sword in hand, flowing with confidence. Daemos grimaces from the unexpected blow. The cut limits his movement even further.

"Daemos!" Vel-Syn cries.

Weary, Daemos looks for her. His vision is hazy. "Silmeir. Where is Vel-Syn?"

"Priests of the Sublime order have taken her," Silmeir answers. "They must be without sin to do so. She is defenseless against them."

"That's right, Daemos. They've taken her beneath to the hidden temple of the ancient church. There, they'll extinguish her life and send that demon bitch straight back to the Suffering where that bloodsucking whore belongs! No more demoness to protect you."

Daemos's vision comes into focus.

Huemic moves in. "But don't worry, I'll kill you first so you can greet her headless corpse as it comes through on the other side!"

Huemic stabs down with both swords. Daemos blocks each sword off to the side with his own and punches Huemic in his balls. He gets to his feet and swings hard. The blow nearly knocks both swords from Huemic's hands. Huemic backs up to compose himself.

"Oh my," Silmeir says.

Huemic hesitates. "What?"

"I've never seen Daemos mad before. This will be interesting."

Daemos's eyes are wide as they peer through his mask.

He feels the pain from the cut he delivered on the inside of Huemic's right arm. Daemos clenches his left fist and pulls back. Huemic's arm rips open. Huemic screams and drops the sword. He doesn't understand what just happened. Daemos stands. Huemic swings with his other arm. Daemos catches his wrist. He wraps his arm around Huemic's wounded one and wrenches up, snapping it in half. Daemos takes Huemic's remaining sword from him and returns the favor with the hilt. Huemic falls on his back into the pool of blood.

Daemos steps on Huemic's unbroken arm, preventing any chance of attack.

"This is also the land of pain, Huemic. Are you ready for more?"

A jeweled knife is pulled from Huemic's scabbard. It moves over Huemic's eyes. Silmeir's face follows, blocking out the rain.

"I now know why I am here, Huemic. I am here to kill you. That is my purpose." He slowly drags the knife across Huemic's neck and face, opening Huemic up like the creature did to him. Huemic screams as tears purge. "I see your tears. I understand now. Daemos delivers pain. I deliver your death, as a gift to the Suffering."

Silmeir submerges Huemic's head beneath the blood pool. Daemos steps on Huemic's other arm to fully pin him down. The struggle is useless as Huemic chokes. His eyes bulge in terror at his killer. Fingers plunge through and scrape Huemic's wounded flesh, loosening it into a sea of anguish. Hands cup underneath and raise it above. Silmeir guzzles his tormentor's blood, flesh, and tears.

Silmeir smiles and looks at Daemos. "You are right. There is nothing like it."

Silmeir pushes his knife down through the crimson. Huemic struggles no more. His eyes stare through the crimson.

"Welcome, my Viscrucian *friend*."

"My friend."

Daemos reaches down, pulls the blade from Huemic's face, and places it into Silmeir's bloody hands.

"This is your Viscrucian blade, Silmeir. The blade you took from Huemic and killed him with. It's sacred now. Let it bring you the killing memory of this moment when you sent him to the Suffering where he belongs."

Silmeir nods.

Daemos grabs a few other knives lying around and runs to the alley.

"Kill them, Daemos. Kill them all."

Chapter 49

Daemos runs down the enclosed alley only to reach a dead end. Footprints lead to the wall next to him. Daemos screams and kicks through the wall, breaking open the hidden door.

He descends an extensive stairwell lit by torches. Reaching the bottom, he runs through a hallway. It opens into a large room. Torches light barer, stone walls. Footprints show the way along the dirt floor. Mice and other rodents scurry along the base of the walls.

The room ends in a semicircle with five exits. The footsteps lead into the center exit. Light and chanting follow.

The hallway is short and narrow. Daemos can barely duck through it. He sees fire at the end of the tunnel. Vel-Syn sits in the distance.

Squeezing out of the hallway, a hammer bashes Daemos in his mask. He instinctively raises his hands and the blades he holds for protection. A gold dagger stabs Daemos in the arm. He falls to his hands and knees inside the chamber.

The murder mask is cracked vertically in half. It hangs loosely from Daemos's head as blood falls from it.

"Daemos," Lord Villous says. He spins the heavy

hammer in his hand. His dagger arm glistens in the torchlight. "I waited so long for this. Years. But now, finally, I'll have your death."

Daemos looks up from the ground. Vel-Syn sits just a few meters away wrapped in the tan shroud. A tan cloth is tied around her mouth. Her incendiary hair does no harm. They're in a large circular room. Ten pillars form another circle within. They reach high above to a rounded ceiling. Old skylights have been filled in by the ground overhead.

Torches placed high up on each of the pillars now light the room. Sublime priests stand just in front of the pillars. Each of their shadows stretch out to the center of the room, pointing to Vel-Syn. They keep their arms crossed in front of them. Their sleeves conceal their hands. The six priests that grabbed Vel-Syn above are painted in rain.

"Let see what Tar did you." Lord Villous places his golden blade underneath the loose fasteners. He removes Daemos's Face.

The Sublime cringe.

"What sight. Shame. My hand should've cut your flesh. No others."

"I sent Tar and his worms to the Suffering for it. You'll see them soon."

Daemos rises off his hands. Two of Lord Villous's soldiers move behind Daemos and draw their swords. Daemos drops the knives from his hands and stays put.

Lord Villous walks away from Daemos and Vel-Syn so he can get a good view of them both. Two other soldiers stand by his side.

"What is this place? Why are we here?"

"This is a temple, Daemos. A holy place from a long time ago. Do you remember me? I am Abrus, the Sublime high priest. We met once a long time ago outside of Yesilmi."

Daemos spits blood at his feet. "I knew I should've killed you. You're telling me this is a holy place? Here in Viscrucia?"

"Yes, Daemos. I am Sharelon, Sublime high priestess," Sharelon adds. "Don't you know the history of your city?" she asks.

"History doesn't survive long here. Shouldn't you know that?"

"This used to be the holy city of the Sublime, our order. They lived here in peace, above and below the soil in harmony with the land. Many of the old tunnels and rooms still exist under the city. That's how we got here."

"This is the great temple in the center of the old city," Abrus says. "They prayed here. It was a paradise."

"Now it's our paradise."

"Yes. One day it came to an end. Legends say it started here in this temple. The Unclean murdered the high priests and their people. Soon bloodshed swept through the streets, much like today."

"An ancestor."

"A few of our people escaped," Sharelon says. "The Sublime survived. Legends foretold of a cleansing. The sinners of this land would be wiped clean. The Sublime would return. It would happen through descension."

"I thought that day had come," Abrus adds. "I saw it with my own eyes, outside of Yesilmi. A storm unlike any other swept over this city. I thought the storm would finally wash the evil away…but then the clouds ran red with blood. Screams echoed across the desert. The Sublime did return. It was their screams crying out."

Members of the Sublime look upon their leader, grimacing.

"In our ancient language they wailed. They were looking for someone, someone of unspeakable evil, someone to drag down to the depths of the Suffering."

Daemos glares at Abrus.

"I was wrong. Today marks the day of descension. The day the Sublime return to our rightful home.

"Descension?"

"Yes. The cleansing of a demon," Sharelon says. "We will send her back to the Suffering from which she came."

The priests pull out knives from their sleeves. The handles are wrapped in tan cloth. The blades are carved from white stone.

"We Sublime are without sin. This demon cannot hurt us. It can only hurt the sinful. We will commit our first sin to save this land, to rid the world of this demon, and to bring back peace. It is a sacrifice worth committing. The demon will die, and the Sublime will return to our rightful home."

"Then I'll kill you, Daemos," Lord Villous says.

"It is time," Abrus says. "Let us bring *light* back to this land. Cleanse the *darkness*."

The Sublime raise their knives together.

Vel-Syn looks to Daemos. Her eyes see the end is here.

Daemos sees it, too. Their death is imminent. Pain

followed by the silence. Sheer silence. Nothing. The soundless void outside of time. He knows it better than most. Images and feelings eventually follow, burning through the void. Killing on the streets. Facing the black death of the Abyss. His inner demon. Facing the creatures. His torture, his agony, followed by his death. Waking to the taste of blood, floating in a pool of pain. Opening new eyes upon a scene of absolute carnage, a scene of death, mutilation, and revenge. Reborn with new vision, power, and pain. Finding allies for the first time and opening himself up to help from others. Sending Faelin to the Suffering that she deserves. Reverence and worship from those who have never given it before. A religion born...only to be smothered in its infancy.

Daemos closes his eyes. In the darkness, his path illuminates.

"No light."

"Vel-Syn," Daemos calls, "kill the flames."

"Only darkness..."

Vel-Syn closes her eyes. The red fire from her hair burns out. The torches lose their blaze. The temple becomes shadow.

"And blood!"

Panic takes over.

Everyone is blind, except Daemos.

Blood vision illuminates the temple. He now sees more clearly than ever, in front and behind him. Every vein, every artery shines through the black. Victims framed in bright, beating red. He sees blood and nothing else, red quickening across a sea of darkness.

It pumps from the hearts of the bulky soldiers. Crimson swims through the healthy bodies of the Sublime. The lord's clogged arteries belch it slowly through. And at the center is the most beautiful blood he's ever seen. Onyx plasma shines amid the obsidian void. Her pulse shapes her body. Vel-Syn's dark soul finds Daemos again.

Daemos grabs the knives he dropped and stabs the confused soldiers guarding him. One by one he slaughters the priests and remaining soldiers. He throws his blades through the air. The pious blood pulsating through the priests now paints the pillars and stains the floor. Daemos's view illuminates with more and more arterial detail. Confusion and fear are answered with screams and carnage.

Daemos turns their holy blades upon themselves. With a Sublime knife in each hand, he slashes Abrus and Sharelon's throats last.

"The legends were wrong," he says. The Sublime stay sinless.

"Damn you, Daemos!" Lord Villous screams in the darkness.

Daemos steps through the gore to his final victim. He chops off the lord's golden arm with one holy blade and his hand carrying the hammer with the other. Next is his golden leg. Before Villous can fall to the ground, Daemos drops both blades and grabs him by the throat with one hand.

He lifts Lord Villous high in the air and grabs the last weapon he carries, the Black Fangs.

"I have changed. You killed the old Daemos. You showed me unimaginable pain. But, you will not find death today. Look into my new eyes. What you see is pain. That's all you will now know, for I..." Daemos puts the Black Fangs to use and rips out the lord's genitals, "I am the god of pain."

Daemos throws Lord Villous aside.

"Welcome to Viscrucia, kes bag."

Daemos slashes through the shroud with his claws, removes Vel-Syn's gag, and raises her to her feet.

Daemos takes her neck and pulls her in, kissing her intensely. Vel-Syn returns the passion, and her hair bursts back into red flame, illuminating the holy massacre. They taste each other's lips for the first time.

They depart and gaze upon one another.

"I will do anything for you. I will face the horrors of the Suffering as long as you're by my side, Vel-Syn. I kill for you. I will die for you, in this world or any dominion. Nothing stands in my way"

"I will destroy anything that tries to harm you," Vel-Syn returns. "I'm not taking you back to the Suffering. We have our own here. I will kill for you, forever. I will die for you. Nothing will stand in *our* way, God of Pain. We will be eternal."

They exchange their violent vows, born here in the birthplace of Viscrucia, another holy massacre. In a church filled with pain, they consecrate their love in a wedding of blood. The god of pain and the demoness dive back into each other's lips. Their embrace is unbreakable.

Chapter 50

"Rayn!" Nobleman Kerth shouts, calling out for his son. He walks down one alley, and then another, until he reaches a dead end. "Kes! How the hell do you get out of this cursed city?"

"You don't."

Kerth turns around. Petrid stands at the other side of the alley, blocking the exit.

"So, another one of you scarred ghouls wants to fall by my sword."

"You don't belong here, noble born. You shouldn't be here. Now, you're going to die here."

"This city doesn't belong here! It's an unholy abomination. If I don't do it today, mark my words, my family will rid this sin from the land!"

"Viscrucia is an island. Our ways are our own. You brought your fight to us."

"That's right. And now I bring it to you!" Kerth yells. He charges forward.

Petrid lashes out with his whip.

Rayn runs down the corridor, following his father's voice. He gets to his destination, but it's too late. He sees Petrid swing away. His father is slashed to ribbons.

"Father!"

Petrid turns. "Another noble brat." He swings. The whip strikes the edge of the alley wall just after the boy escapes. "Run! Run far away. Don't ever come back here, boy!"

Petrid looks down at his kill. "Fine armor."

Petrid makes his way back to the heart of the city. Remaining soldiers, clans, and invaders flee. Only a few screeching demons still soar.

The crimson rain reduces to a sprinkle. A few Viscrucians walk and limp about. Bodies are everywhere. Slowly, more and more Viscrucians converge.

Daemos and Vel-Syn step out of the shadowed corridor. They look upon the war-torn city. Fires burn. The citizens are bloodied and cleaved. Everyone is in pain. It registers on all their faces.

Lesigom walks among the wounded. His head hangs low.

"Lesigom, what happened?" Petrid asks. "Did you kill Gell? Is the Ssagaecian leader dead?"

"No. I killed his mox. I slew many, but so did he. Gell escaped."

"Another time then, Les. Another day, another kill. Until then, you have much to write about. Many songs to sing."

"That I do," he says.

Silmeir sits next to Mr. Brown, still petting his loyal friend.

"Mr. Brown?" Daemos asks.

"He is gone."

"He was a good friend. We will honor him. You made him proud. You delivered just vengeance."

"Yes, for both of us. For both of us."

The mood is somber. How many of these men will survive their wounds? Perhaps the price was too high.

"Bringer of Pain!" a voice calls out, breaking the silence. The sparse crowd looks to the call.

Kane and Isan hobble together.

"My lord," Kane says, clutching his wounds. "Your faithful prevailed. Viscrucia lives! Your enemies died!"

Kane raises a blood-caked blade high for all to see. The mob responds and cheers. Kane's incessant mouth turns the tides yet again.

Vel-Syn and Daemos heal their faithful as best they can. Slowly, Viscrucia rebuilds. The rivers of blood stain the bone streets permanently red, providing some much-needed color to the city. The disciples build the Church of Pain Isan and Kane promised Daemos.

The subterranean city is explored. A vast number of rooms, buildings, and old households are discovered. The survivors make new hideouts and even homes among the ruins. Advanced locks are quickly developed. The holy city is converted to a new religion devoted to pain. Disciples grow in numbers, and more are given the mark of priest.

Petrid and the surviving artisans craft new carvings. Murals, statues, and monuments depict Viscrucia's recent history. Blood, bone, flame, and flesh are just some of the materials used to create the gorgeous atrocities. Lesigom and other bards write new tales and play new songs. Daemos's legacy is preserved at last. A monument over six meters high portrays Daemos holding the wraith high above a mountain of corpses.

Daemos looks at his broken *face*. His bloody reflection glistens on the polished black and red surface of the painted bone. He repositions the dangling clamps to the top and bottom. He raises the mask to his face and puts it on. His hands run over his mask to visualize. The corner of his mouth rises on the uncovered side of his face. He pulls his hands back.

The murder mask only covers half of his face now. His skinless side stands out. The mask covers his remaining flesh. The sight of Daemos's past life is dead to the outside world. The shroud of mystery and omnipotence feeds his increasing, ever revering disciples.

Daemos sits atop a throne of cured corpses. He drinks blood tear wine from a chalice made of human hands. Vel-Syn, his fire-haired demoness, sits by his side drinking with him.

Displayed on the wall nearest Daemos is the spine of the wraith. It is finally home with its *owners*.

On the opposite wall nearest Vel-Syn hangs Petrid's most magnificent work of art ever designed. Stretched across a large circular frame of bone is Lord Villous. Skin and sinew are stretched and tied around the frame. Each appendage and section of fat vary in their aesthetic construction. He is now living art and part of the god of pain's collection. A trough below collects his fluids.

"Please…God…" Villous pleads, drooling on himself.

Vel-Syn, the demoness from beyond, and Daemos, the god of pain, cheers their chalices. They drink the finest wine of their hanging suffering. Over one hundred disciples kneel before them in the great Church of Pain.

Villous weeps. Tears stream down his cheek.

"This is just the beginning."

THE END

Acknowledgements

First and foremost, I want to thank my parents, David and Penelope Weber, for their never-ending support. This book would not be possible without you. Thank you to my sisters, Whitney for great advice, and Laura for watching horror movies with me, and to my extended family. Thank you, Katie and Eric Weber, for the best help in raising Feyd.

Thank you: Tim Marquitz, my editor, for his guidance and hard work. Mark Wilson, for great writing advice since college. Marc Hufnagl and Jackie Byers, for reading and writing help from the early years. Catie Dinsmoor, for believing in me, without you I would not have finished. The Faust family, thank you for the support, knowledge, skills, and encouragement along the way. The great Chaz Kuper and the amazing author Tonya Kuper. To author Gary Bush for great resources. Mike Saniuk for humor and support. Billy Kroupa and family for everything.

Thank you: Andrew Torkelson for his expert photography and editing skills. Scott Smith for brilliant design skills creating the mask. MoorBooks Design for great execution and design work.

Thank you Feyd, for being the best son I can imagine.

And thank you to all of you for reading! I am profoundly grateful.

Robert Weber has worked in front of and behind the camera for decades in film, television, commercials, and sports, and is a former NCAA Division I Tennis Coach. His love for horror began as a child, watching the Crypt Keeper read Tales from the Crypt. Robert and his son Feyd live in Omaha, Nebraska.